WAIT IN DARKNESS

Bette stood in her bedroom, surrounded by her stuffed animals and other toys. Sometimes the animals would come to life and speak to her. At night, she let them prowl in the darkness of the town. They killed yowling cats and barking dogs. There were not many animals left in Butler. Peaceful town.

The room was dark. Bette looked at her face in the mirror. She smiled and her young teeth fanged. She liked doing that. She could make the fangs come and go at will. There were other children of her age in town . . . like her. Many of them.

They waited. They would wait for weeks, or months, perhaps even a few years. No one knew exactly how long. Except the Master. The Master assured them that evil can spread in secret and darkness. The Master told Bette what she must do: gather the young ones. Secretly. Spread the word of The Dark One—and wait.

TALES OF TERROR AND POSSESSION

MAMA (1247, $3.50)
by Ruby Jean Jensen
Once upon a time there lived a sweet little dolly, but her one beaded glass eye gleamed with mischief and evil. If Dorrie could have read her dolly's thoughts, she would have run for her life— for her dear little dolly only had killing on her mind.

JACK-IN-THE-BOX (1892, $3.95)
by William W. Johnstone
Any other little girl would have cringed in horror at the sight of the clown with the insane eyes. But as Nora's wide eyes mirrored the grotesque wooden face her pink lips were curving into the same malicious smile.

ROCKABYE BABY (1470, $3.50)
by Stephen Gresham
Mr. Macready—such a nice old man—knew all about the children of Granite Heights: their names, houses, even the nights their parents were away. And when he put on his white nurse's uniform and smeared his lips with blood-red lipstick, they were happy to let him through the door—although they always stared a bit at his clear plastic gloves.

TWICE BLESSED (1766, $3.75)
by Patricia Wallace
Side by side, isolated from human contact, Kerri and Galen thrived. Soon their innocent eyes became twin mirrors of evil. And their souls became one—in their dark powers of destruction and death . . .

HOME SWEET HOME (1571, $3.50)
by Ruby Jean Jensen
Two weeks in the mountains would be the perfect vacation for a little boy. But Timmy didn't think so. The other children stared at him with a terror all their own, until Timmy realized there was no escaping the deadly welcome of . . . *Home Sweet Home*.

Available wherever paperbacks are sold, or order direct from the Publisher. Send cover price plus 50¢ per copy for mailing and handling to Zebra Books, Dept. 2072, 475 Park Avenue South, New York, N.Y. 10016. Residents of New York, New Jersey and Pennsylvania must include sales tax. DO NOT SEND CASH.

THE NURSERY

BY WILLIAM W. JOHNSTONE

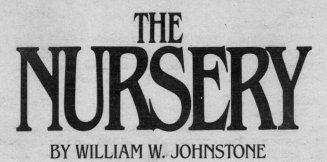

ZEBRA BOOKS
KENSINGTON PUBLISHING CORP.

ZEBRA BOOKS

are published by

KENSINGTON PUBLISHING CORP.
475 Park Avenue South
New York, N.Y. 10016

Third printing: May 1987

Printed in the United States of America

The boundaries which divide Life from Death are at best shadowy and vague. Who shall say where the one ends, and where the other begins?

Edgar Allan Poe

PROLOGUE

It was a strange sight, something out of a science fiction movie. Sixty-six thick glass vats, tear-shaped, each vat containing a fetus, all in the same stage of growth, suspended in a clear, heavy liquid. The umbilical cord was attached to sophisticated life-support systems. The fetuses rested in fetal position in the heavy liquid, eyes unopened, arms folded across the chest, feet crossed. The artificial uterus and the fetus were at term—head floating, the artificial cervix not yet dilated, the unruptured, man-made amnion intact.

The unborn waited for life. Their futures were planned for them, their master chosen. They were now, and always would be, here to serve the Prince of Darkness.

They had been taken from their human mothers by force, and they would live their long lives under the rule of dark savagery.

If all went according to plan . . .

ONE

He kept looking for that familiar sign that seemed, in his youth, at least, to thrust itself out of the horizon: ODEY'S DRIVE-IN.

You always knew you were home when you spotted that sign. And you just *had* to pull in and get yourself one of Old Man Odey's hamburgers, with lots of onions and pickles and mustard and maybe a big order of french fries. For sure a Coke.

Whether you were coming home from college, home from a game, or home for a visit, you knew you were only a half-mile from city limits—and it was a good feeling. Because you were coming back to Butler, Louisiana. Nice folks. Friendly folks. Small Town U.S.A.

Mike kept straining his eyes for that first glimpse of the sign. He longed for that warm feeling of Homecoming.

But the sign was gone.

Mike felt something was gone from his life, as well. His youth had passed by, gone forever. Where had it gone? What had it taken from him? And what had he gained—except adulthood—by its passing?

He pulled off the road and onto the once-bustling parking lot. Now it was all grown over with weeds. The building was in that last stage before total decay: windows broken, one side of the awning all caved in, menu sign a rusting memory of times that would surely never come again:

HAMBURGERS	.20¢
HOT DOGS	.15¢
COKES	.05¢

"Jesus Christ!" Mike said, as age suddenly fell on him with a heavy hand.

He looked again at the sign. He had only imagined those prices.

A JAX beer sign banged in the late May breeze.

Memories flooded him, a rush of laughter and melancholy, all intermingled with peppermint lipstick and the jukebox blaring Elvis and Buddy Holly and the Big Bopper and Cathy Carr and Carl Perkins. And there was old Creepy Brannon, the town's night marshal, tapping on the window of a '49 Ford, telling you, "Better get on home, now, kids—it's past midnight. Go on, now."

And you went, 'cause he was the law, and there was still some respect for the law back then.

Other days and other ways. Long ago and far away.

"Hey, gimmie a cherry Coke and a root beer float and a couple of burgers!"

"Man, have you heard The Coasters' new one? Groovy!"

Mike shook his head and got out of his car, standing for a long time amid the weeds of the parking lot. He was content to just look at the old building, letting memories wash him, bathe him in a glow that was no longer real. No longer relevant.

Meaningless.

He sighed heavily.

He was a man who stood six feet one inch, very solid, packing a hundred and eighty-five pounds on his frame. Trim waisted, huge barrel chest with lots of meat and muscle through the arms and shoulders. Big hands and wrists. His hair was cut short, military fashion, gray peppering the dark brown. His eyes were a pale, off-color green; flat, noncommittal, unemotional. They darkened considerably when he was angered.

He was forty-three years old. A soldier coming home.

He was graduated from high school in 1957, at seventeen, going directly into the Army, and for twenty-five years, the Army had been his home. He had worked hard and earned a college degree. Gone through OCS. Served five years in Southeast Asia. Been wounded four times. He had been one of the youngest men in modern times to earn the Silver Birds of a full colonel. And he was a Mustang, coming up through the ranks before going to OCS. But there had never been any chance of his making general. Mike was too blunt; no politician. He could not and would not play the bullshit game of ass-kissing.

He was a Medal of Honor winner.

At forty-three he had been asked—ordered—to retire.

"Fine," he had told the general. "Dandy. Take your lace-pants military and put it in your ear!"

The words returned to him. "Colonel Folsom, what do you think this is, the old brown boot Army? These aren't draftees; these are volunteers! The highest paid volunteers in the history of America. We had to *beg* some of these kids to join. Beg, cajole, bribe, and convince and promise their mummys and daddys we'd tuck their precious, little, spoiled pudding pies in bed every night. I don't like it either, Mike, but goddammit, that's the way it is."

"General," Mike had protested, "we've got people out there in uniform who can barely read and write. We're being forced to print some instruction booklets in comic book form so the stupid fuckers can understand them—hopefully. We—"

The general waved him silent. "I know, Mike. I know. High schools are graduating kids who can barely function at a literate level. No discipline—blame that on the courts and the press. Mike—I don't know why I'm arguing with you; there is nothing we can do about the public school system. We have to make do with what we get."

"You do, General," Mike had responded. "I sure as hell don't."

Why bring it back? Mike thought. It's over. Finished. Put it out of your mind and forget it.

"Hey, you!" the voice cut into his recall, wrenching him back to the present.

Mike turned. A cop stood by a patrol car. Mike had been so engrossed in retrospection, he had not heard him drive up.

"You got troubles or something?" the cop called over the weed-filled, rutted drive.

Mike shook his head. "No. Just looking at the place. Last time I was through here, the drive-in was still in operation. Old place brings back a lot of memories."

"Good ones?" It was a question spoken without a smile, and Mike thought that odd.

He shrugged. "Mostly, yes. Why the interest in a falling-down, old drive-in?"

"Been some vandalism out here. Young punks from out of town tearing up the place."

12

"Do I look like a vandal?" Mike smiled. Or a punk? Driving a Jag? he thought. Normally a frugal man, the Jag was his only extravagance. He had always liked fast cars, had built hot rods as a kid.

"What does a vandal look like, mister?"

Good question. "Sorry, officer." Mike made the first peace overture. "You're right."

The cop smiled, changing his entire appearance. "My turn to say I'm sorry, mister. Chief has been in a rotten mood lately."

Mike laughed. "I know the feeling, believe me. Who is the chief now?"

"Ford. Don Ford."

"Stinky Ford?" The question popped out of his mouth before Mike could bite off the words.

"Sir?"

"About my age? Kind of stocky, dark hair?"

"That's him. But instead of stocky, try fat, and his hair is thinning." He laughed aloud. "Stinky?"

"That's what we used to call him back in grade school. Name followed him clear to high school. I wouldn't suggest you call him that now, though."

The cop nodded. Mike got the impression he was being studied very closely, with more than a cop's natural suspicion. "My name's Bernard. Ted Bernard."

Mike did not recall the last name of Bernard. But he'd been living elsewhere for twenty-five years. He walked up to the cop. In his early to mid-thirties. He stuck out his hand. "I'm Mike Folsom."

Mike couldn't tell behind the dark glasses of the cop, but he got the impression the man knew his name. "Colonel Folsom?"

"Now retired."

"You're famous, sir. Everybody knows about you." Mike smiled ruefully.

"Well," the cop amended his statement. "Everybody here in Butler, that is. You're a hero." Something passed over the man's facial expression, only briefly, then was gone. "I don't mean to pry, Colonel, but are you going to stay around here long?"

"I plan to live here. Go into some kind of business. Certainly live in the old homeplace." He was curious as to the motive behind the question, but for the time being, kept his mouth shut.

"That old place is kind of run-down, sir."

"Yes, I expect it is. Ten years is a long time."

"That how long it's been since you've been back to Butler, sir?"

"Almost to the day."

"Yes," the cop agreed, almost absentmindedly. "Sir—ah—a word of warning. Things are—well—kind of different around here. You'll see, and those words didn't come from me, all right?"

Mike nodded, not knowing what in the hell the man was talking about or why he would warn Mike.

"And you be careful who you talk to in this town, all right?"

Again Mike nodded. "Look, officer, you want to tell me what's going on?"

The cop studied him. "I'll tell you what, Colonel, you take my advice—sell out and get out."

He turned, walking back to his patrol car. He drove off without looking back.

Mike shook his head in confusion. "Welcome home, soldier. What'd you expect, a brass band?"

Mike had been deep in the bush of Vietnam when the word finally reached him his parents had been killed in an accident. The news was two weeks old. By the time Mike returned to the States, cleared Fort Bragg, and made his way to Butler, his parents were cold in the

14

grave.

In a manner of speaking.

He had spent only one day in Butler, most of that time with a stuffy old attorney, taking care of business matters, settling the estate. That was not too difficult a task, Mike being the only child. His father had been a successful hardware store owner who liked to dabble in oil and stocks. Mike had always known his father was monetarily comfortable, but he had never known just how comfortable. After everything was deducted, Mike was left with just a bit over a half-million dollars. Free and clear. He was stunned at the news. Mike told the attorney to put the money to work, keep him informed, and went back to the Army, back to Vietnam. Killing Cong.

The attorney might have been stuffy, but he knew his business when it came to investments. In five years, Mike became a moderately wealthy man. He didn't know whether that impressed him or not.

It didn't impress his wife; she divorced him, taking a nice chunk of cash with her.

He drove the last half-mile into Butler, expecting to see a great many changes. He saw none that impressed him. The town had shrunk. Far fewer shops on Main Street.

Stinky Ford the chief of police? Stinky, who always looked kind of funny at the guys' peckers in the dressing room.

He laughed, then cautioned himself not to be so hasty in judgment, for he was remembering Stinky as a child, not as a man.

Mike had spent the night in Baton Rouge, pulling out early that morning, before dawn, for he was, by habit, an early riser. And the swamp and marsh country had gradually given way to slight rolling hills as he drove northwest. Chatom Parish was a large parish,

15

with only three towns and no industry except for small, individually-owned oil pumpers and a lumber mill located on the far side of the parish from Butler.

But where was the industry he had heard all those rumors about last time he'd been home? Big doin's comin' to Butler, he'd been told.

Obviously, those "big doin's" hadn't made it.

But why?

Mike drove to the attorney's office, which had been over a drugstore.

"No," the man behind the counter said. "The old man is dead. Harry, Jr. is running the show. Harry Wallace, Jr.," he explained. "Built him a brand new office building. Fancy. Just go down two blocks, turn left, and look to your right. Can't miss it."

The man giving the directions and the information looked familiar to Mike, and Mike must have looked familiar to him, for he peered at the ex-soldier closely, smiled, and said, "Don't I know you?"

"Mike Folsom."

"Well, I'll just be darned. Don't you remember me, Mike?"

Mike studied him, pushing his memory back through the years. A slow grin creased his lips. "Sure. Sure, I do! Jack Geraci." They shook hands. "Been a long time, Jack."

"Almost twenty-five years, boy. Damn—you lookin' good, son! Not an ounce of fat on you. You must have been one of those Green Berets?"

"No." Mike shook his head. "I never made that outfit. I was the Eighty-second Airborne for a time, though."

Jack grinned. "I seem to recall reading that you wasn't always with them, though."

"That's right. I commanded a Ranger Battalion for a time."

16

"And . . . ?" Jack prompted with a widening grin.

Mike knew what he wanted to hear, so he said it. "And I was with an antiterrorist unit for a little while."

"Damn right, you were. Never was one to toot your own horn, was you? You commanded the team that rescued our guys from those terrorists after they'd been kidnapped. Y'all killed them all, didn't you?" Without waiting for a reply, he said, " 'Bout a hundred of those terrorists, wasn't it?"

"Twenty-two, Jack. And we took several alive. And there were quite a few guys in my command."

"Should have killed every damn one of those filthy crud, I say. Wish they'd have sent your men into Iran."

God, I don't! Mike thought.

Jack let a worried expression slip onto his face. He tried to cover it unsuccessfully by bubbling, "Hey, boy! We got us our twenty-five-year class reunion comin' up this summer. Can you imagine that, Mike? Twenty-five years ago we graduated high school."

Something was really troubling the man. Mike picked up bad vibes through forced jocularity. "Yeah, time flies," Mike said inanely. "Look, Jack, I've got to tend to some business. Let's get together."

"You know it, boy! Lots of years to talk about. Hey—you married?"

"Was. Divorced."

"Oh. Sorry to hear it. Kids?"

"Three. Two boys and a girl. She has them. Lives up in Maine."

"Tough."

"Yeah. See you, Jack, soon, now."

The young attorney looked at him through reproachful eyes. "I wish you had seen fit to notify me of your

17

decision to return, Colonel Folsom. I would have then had time to air the house properly, have it cleaned, and some badly needed repair work attended to. As it is, the house is scarcely habitable. Why—"

Mike waved him silent. "Don't sweat it, Mr. Wallace. I'm looking forward to spending several months working on the house, doing it myself. All that I can, that is. Just give me the keys and I'll be on my way and you can get back to whatever you were doing."

The young attorney's manner changed abruptly. He smiled. Like a fish. "Please accept my apologies for my behavior, Colonel Folsom. I've been rude. Morning started off wrong. If you'll just tell me what you want for the house, I'll get it on the market as soon as some repairs are made."

"Mr. Wallace," Mike said patiently, "I have absolutely no intention of selling that house." But I damn sure would like to know why two strangers in less than an hour suggested selling out. "I plan to live and work right here in Butler."

The smile remained on the man's fish-mouth, but his eyes turned cold. "Of course, you do, Colonel. I wasn't thinking." He laid a ring of keys on the desk, pushing them toward Mike with the tip of a pencil. "Things—have changed somewhat since you lived here, Colonel. Dull. Can't imagine why you'd want to live here."

What in the hell was going on around here! "It's my home, Mr. Wallace."

"Certainly it is." His tone was conciliatory. "Mr. Rider at the bank will get in touch with you concerning your investments—which are considerable, I assure you. I have your portfolio here at the office, but you should have an identical copy."

"I do. Burke Rider?"

"Yes. I believe you two graduated from high school together, did you not?"

"That's correct. I'll look forward to seeing him. So—good day, Mr. Wallace."

The attorney rose dutifully and shook hands with Mike. It was like shaking hands with a dead codfish. "Good day, Colonel." His smile seemed to hold just a touch of maliciousness. "Do enjoy your first—night at home."

Mike met his gaze. The attorney had stressed "night." He wondered why? "I fully intend to do just that, sir."

The attorney's smile seemed pasted on. False. Mike wondered why he felt like he would enjoy punching the attorney right in the mouth?

He drove to the old two-story home, and once more, as he pulled into the driveway, memories flooded him. He could almost smell the aroma of his mother's baking pies and cakes and fresh bread, and the heady smell of freshly-ground coffee brewing—and his father's pipe, Prince Albert smoking tobacco.

He shook away the memories before they overwhelmed him, turning him maudlin, and got out of the car, taking a good, long look at the house where he was reared.

He had to smile. Frankly, on the outside, at least, it looked like hell.

Yard all overgrown, house needing repairs and painting, a broken step and railing. He began making a mental list of things to do, things to get. He finally dug into his hip pocket for a leather-bound notepad as the list grew too long for memory.

He walked around the house, soaking up memories as they filled his head like the bouquet from a fine wine after opening it and allowing it to breathe and spring to full blossom.

The house stood on high ground at the very edge of town. The two-story home was centered in the middle of five acres. In the rear, behind the back yard, were woods and a small creek running through the timber. The nearest neighbor was several vacant lots away, those empty lots also owned by the Folsom estate.

He walked around to the front and unlocked the door, stepping inside. There he stood in mute, unbelieving shock.

The house was sparkling clean.

Furniture was dusted, carpets vacuumed, drapes clean, sofa and chairs uncovered, the sheets washed and neatly folded by each piece of furniture. Not a cobweb to be seen. The pictures above the mantel over the fireplace were dusted and in order.

Had young Mr. Wallace been pulling his leg about cleaning up and airing the house. No. No, Mike didn't think that twerp would have that kind of sense of humor.

"Then—who?" he said aloud. "And why?"

His voice echoed hollowly in return, but the reverberation gave him no answer. It died away.

He walked through the first floor of the house; everything was in perfect order, clean. The calendar in the kitchen was the right year, but the page turned to June, and this was nearing the end of May. Someone had circled the first of June. Why? He had no idea. The kitchen floor was mopped and waxed, the tile shining. He opened cabinets. All the glasses and dishes were freshly washed. The refrigerator was running; so someone had notified the power company. He would call them, find out who had been so considerate. And why?

He walked to his father's liquor cabinet in the den: two quarts of Seagram's Seven Crown. Not the brand his father used to drink, but the brand Mike drank, and he had not been a drinker while in high school, picking up the habit only after he had been in the service for a few years. And he had settled on this brand of whiskey

20

only ten years ago. Almost to the day, he recalled. No one in Butler could have known that, because he hadn't been back in that time.

Then . . . ?

His silent question trailed off into nothing, as silent in its mystery as the thought had been in forming.

He walked slowly up the stairs to the second floor. The carpet here, as in the lower part, had been vacuumed, the rails freshly polished. In his bedroom, and only in his, the bed was newly made with clean, crisp sheets. Towels in the bathroom. A new bar of soap in the shower stall, unopened. His brand. Sitting in the medicine cabinet, a bottle of Old Spice after shave and cologne. He had started using that exactly ten years ago. Almost to the date.

What in the hell was going on around here?

He walked down the steps; the house was almost exactly as he remembered it. He checked the drawer where his mother used to keep flashlights and emergency candles. Everything was there. He opened the flashlights, checking them. New batteries in both of them.

Then he realized the house was cool. The air conditioner was on.

No one knew I was returning, he thought. No one. Not one living soul on the face of this earth.

"Jesus!" He momentarily panicked. "Have I got the right house?"

But he knew he was in the right house.

He walked outside, around to the back, to the small shed where his father kept the riding mower and other gardening and repairing equipment. It was a sturdy building, with a strong lock on the only door. The key slid effortlessly in the heavy lock, opening with a faint click. The smell of oil and gas struck him immediately. The gas can was full; the riding mower had been serviced. All the gardening tools had been cleaned of rust and oiled, all in their proper place, just as his father liked to keep them.

"Cute," Mike muttered. "Very cute."

Games, the thought leaped into his mind. Someone is playing games.

But who?

And why?

He drove into town, to a huge, new supermarket, and stocked up on food, fresh vegetables, bread, and milk. It was there that the heretofore unasked question that had nagged him all moring finally was put into silent voice in his mind, along with the answer: there was no noise in Butler. No honking of horns, no loud mufflers, no yelling of kids, no laughter of teenagers, no cars or trucks with radios blaring rock and roll or country western music.

Nothing. Not one unnecessary sound in the town.

Only the loudness of silence.

, and stocked up on food, fresh vegetables, bread, and milk. It was there that the heretofore unasked question that had nagged him all moring finally was put into silent voice in his mind, along with the answer: there was no noise in Butler. No honking of horns, no loud mufflers, no yelling of kids, no laughter of teenagers, no cars or trucks with radios blaring rock and roll or country western music.

Nothing. Not one unnecessary sound in the town.

Only the loudness of silence.

d their eyes from his open gaze. But he knew they recognized him; still they refused to speak.

Why?

Silence on oiled wheels.

Even the cash registers were the newest computer-types, making only a very soft "ping," or "bong" when they pinged or bonged at all.

"Miss?" he spoke to the cashier.

She looked up from her punching of buttons with a vacant look in her eyes, a dullness, devoid of any feeling. No, that wasn't correct. She looked at him with eyes that registered resentment. "Yes, sir?"

"This is a very quiet town you have here."

"Sure is." Punch. Ping.

"Don't see many towns this quiet."

Bong!

"Really?" Ping. "We like it." Pong. "People who don't like it don't stay here very long." Bong!

"Where do they go?"

She lifted her almost deathlike eyes to his. "I don't know. I guess they move away." Ping. "Who knows?" Ping. "Who cares?" Bong. "That'll be fifty-five dollars and twenty-two cents, please."

He paid her. "Thank you, dear. You've been a veritable fountain of information and the absolute epitome of gracious southern hospitality."

"Huh?"

The cash register went, "Bong!"

Driving back to his house, Mike muttered, "Curiouser and curiouser." He glanced up, the reflection of the flashing lights in his rear-view mirror. He pulled over to the curb, watching in his side mirror as the cop got out of his patrol car and walked up to the door.

"Driver's license, mister. Take if out of the wallet."

Mike handed him his license.

"You ran a stop sign back yonder, mister."

"No, I didn't," Mike said. "Not unless it's an invisible sign."

"If I tell you you did, then you did," the cop flared. "Get out of the car, put your hands on top of the roof, and spread your legs. And shut your smart mouth."

Mike looked up at him from the seat of the Jag. He knew he was about to get rousted by an ignorant redneck cop. He gripped the steering wheel with his big hands, feeling the old familiar anger begin to smolder deep within him; not a hot anger—that had been trained out of him years back—but an icy-burning anger. Mike hated rednecks probably more than anything in the world, hated them for their ignorance and their burning wish to remain ignorant, not caring enough to attempt any uplifting out of misinformation, unenlightenment, bias, prejudice, and just plain stupidity.

And Mike did not like to be rousted. Good cops do not roust people. Good cops, educated cops, know that there are men in the world capable of killing with their fingertips, a rolled-up newspaper, their bare hands.

Mike was one of those men.

As he got out of the car, he smiled, seeing in five seconds five times and five ways he could have killed the cop. He faced the cop, smiling, no fear in him.

"What are you grinning about, mister?"

"Nescience at its most extreme."

"Hah?"

"Forget it; you'd only strain yourself."

Mike watched the cop's face change as confusion altered and reddened his features. The cop was accustomed to instant obedience, and he wasn't really sure how to handle this situation.

"Back off, Lennie!" a voice sprang from behind the men. Ted Bernard. "That's Colonel Mike Folsom. He'll tear your head off and stuff it up your butt!"

Lennie stiffened, then glanced down at the driver's license for verification. He handed the license back to Mike. "He was about to give me trouble, Ted." His gaze did not waver from Mike's eyes.

"More than you could handle, Lennie. Why'd you stop the colonel?"

"He ran a stop sign."

Ted smiled. "No, he didn't. I been following you

24

both."

Lennie seemed to relax, a smile playing briefly across his pinched mouth. He had that look of people who are not only grossly ignorant, but who are also dangerously unpredictable. His eyes were mean. He said, "If you're waitin' for an apology, Colonel, you'll have a long wait."

Mike smiled at the small-town cop. "Lennie?"

"Yeah?"

"Fuck you!"

The blood drained out of Lennie's face. His eyes widened. He abruptly spun on his heel and stalked away, getting into his patrol car, roaring down the street. He left streaks of dark rubber on the concrete.

Ted walked to Mike's side. Something about the man was mildly disturbing to Mike, but he couldn't pinpoint the mental agitation.

"You like to live dangerously, don't you, Colonel?"

"I cannot abide a cop who likes to roust people. Somebody needs to take his gun and badge and shove them up his ass."

Ted laughed. "Lennie might enjoy that, Colonel."

Mike looked at him for further explanation but the cop only said, "Things look like they may get interesting around this place."

"Ted, would you please tell me what is going on in this town? What has happened around here?"

But the cop would only shrug noncommittally. "How did you find your house, Colonel?"

"What do you mean?"

"Just that. It looks pretty rough from the outside."

"It needs some work, that's for sure."

Ted nodded his head in agreement. "Don't push Lennie, Colonel. I mean, you could take him in any kind of fight, but he's got a screw loose." He tapped the side of his head.

"Then why is he a cop if he is mentally unbalanced?"

"Chief Ford likes him." Before Mike could question him further, Ted said, "See you around, Colonel."

Mike leaned against his car, watching the light traffic flow by. People glanced at him, at his Jag, but no one waved or offered any other sign of greeting.

And this used to be the friendliest town in all of west central Louisiana, Mike thought. Famous for its hospitality. And something else jogged into his mind. Butler used to be easy to reach by road. But Mike had had to backtrack twice on the way into the town; the parish roads he used to travel had all been closed, blocked, dead-ending into nothing. Odd. What's happened around here? To the town, to its people?

Something is all out of kilter.

A pickup truck rolled by. Mike heard the rear tires grabbing against the concrete as the driver slammed on the brakes. The truck backed up.

"Mike?" the female voice called. "Mike Folsom? I can't believe it."

Mike looked at the driver. He didn't know her, but he damn sure would like to get to know her. That thought was further enlarged as she bounced out of the pickup after parking by the curb in front of Mike's Jag.

She was one of those blue-eyed, blonde-haired southern country girls so much is written of and about. Five feet four or five, and built to last, everything in the right place and plenty of it. She wore no-nonsense men's Levis that if worn any tighter would have been indecent; they hugged her groin in an enviable embrace, and her breasts were high and full.

She stood before him, hands on lovely hips. She smiled, exposing teeth that were very white and perfectly formed.

She was gorgeous. Her skin was smooth and without

26

blemish. Lips full, no lipstick or gloss. Cheeks with just a touch of nature's own makeup.

Mike stood looking down at her, attempting to find some flaw in her. He could not.

"By God," he blurted. "You're beautiful!"

She laughed at him, and her laughter was that of pure silver bells, but it was not a forced type of laugh. It was open, honest, and friendly.

"You don't know me, do you?" she smiled the question, a hint of mischief in her eyes and voice.

"No, but I plan to." Damn, Mike railed silently. This is not at all like me.

"Darn you, Mike Folsom! I was in love with you all during school."

"You didn't go to school with me. I was a pretty dumb kid, but I wasn't blind. If you'd been in school with me, I'd have been sitting on your doorstep every night, just like a hound dog, baying at the moon."

She cocked her head and Mike thought it was the cutest gesture he'd seen in a long time. She said, "I think I'll just keep you guessing a while longer. I'll admit, though, that I was a few years behind you in school."

"A few! As young as you are, you couldn't have been born when I left Butler." For a fact, the woman didn't look to be over twenty-five.

"Ooh, you just made my whole year, Mike. I'm thirty three."

"I'm forty-three."

"I know exactly how old you are. I've still got all my scrapbooks. Mike, don't you remember the little girl who used to hang around your folks' house when you'd come back home from the Army?"

A slow smile changed Mike's appearance. "Well, I'll just be damned! Rana Carter."

"Now you've got it. But it's Drew now. I was so

27

crushed when you brought that woman home with you. I had dreams you'd someday come to your senses and sweep me off my feet and we'd run away someplace."

"I am certainly sorry I didn't, Rana."

She extended her hand and Mike took the softness in his big paw. He was very reluctant to release the small hand.

"Likewise, Mike. But it is so good to see you. I could use a friend at this time in the worst way."

Curious thing for her to say, he thought. "Well, I will certainly be your friend, Rana."

"Thank you."

They stood for a silent moment by the side of the road. Mike had not been joking when he had blurted that Rana was beautiful; she was.

"When did you get into town, Mike?"

"This morning." He gazed into the soft blue of her eyes. Deep eyes, the kind a man could get lost in. Easily. "Town's different, Rana. It's changed. And I don't like the change."

She laughed, but it was a forced laugh, unlike the first joyous, hearty laugh. "Didn't take you long to pick up on that, Mike. You're right; we'll talk about it."

"Soon, I hope," Mike said. Again, he looked into the blue eyes and felt them pull him into their deepness. "The years have touched you very gently, Rana."

"That's lovely, Mike. I always suspected you had the soul of a poet. Son," she said, using that expression that is peculiar to the South, "you're lookin' pretty damn good yourself; you *are* in shape, aren't you?"

"I try."

She smiled. Lovely. "No, you don't try, Mike—you do! How many miles a day do you run?"

"I try to do five."

"Push-ups?"

28

"A hundred. Other assorted calisthenics."

She glanced at her watch and Mike sensed she was about to leave. He did not want her to go. That feeling was very strong in him. He was attracted to her in a way he had not experienced in years, if ever.

"Oh, damn!" she said. "I have to go pick up my chick at the doctor's office."

"Anything serious?"

"Oh, no. I think she's a hypochondriac. Most kids have to be dragged to see a doctor. Lisa would go every day if I'd let her." She shook her head. "Hard for me to believe she's fifteen."

"Fifteen! But you're only—"

"Yeah," her rueful smile cut him off short. "You know us country girls, Mike; we marry young. Besides, I told you—I was crushed when you got married. I got married right out of high school. Mike—come out for supper. Please?"

Even without the note of almost desperate urgency in her voice, wild, rampaging Cape buffalo could not have prevented Mike from accepting the invitation to supper. Trained to be observant, Mike had noticed she wore no wedding band. But she said her name was Drew now, and she had a daughter. "Your husband might not understand."

"I'm divorced, Mike. Have been for some time."

"What's wrong with the men in this area? Letting you run around single. Someone should have snared you the instant you got free."

"You're giving me the big head, Mike. But maybe I've been waiting for you to show up? Your marriage?"

"Busted up years back. Sometimes the military can be rough on marriages. Takes a special type of woman to hang in there."

"Getting back to supper . . . ?"

"How do I get to your place?"

29

"Easy, if you remember the country roads in this parish. Those that haven't been closed, that is," she said dryly. "After Carl and I split the sheets, I went back to being a farm girl. I'm out at the old home-place."

"Your mom and dad?"

"Dead. Years ago. Mom followed dad in less than a year. Just couldn't live without him. They really loved each other, Mike."

"Something that is going out of style, I believe?" His tone held more sarcasm than intended.

"Oh? Mike Folsom, the cynic? I'll have to ply my amateur pyshciatry act on you; see what's made you so bitter."

"That should be interesting."

"Yes," her reply was soft, her voice grabbing Mike in the groin area in a velvet clutch.

Cars and pickups drove past them. They did not notice the flow of traffic. Had they, they would have noticed the same car passing them several times.

"You still like your steak chicken-fried, with gravy and mashed potatoes and fried okra and hot biscuits?"

"You bet! And don't forget the apple pie."

"Not a chance of that, boy. Come out early, Mike. Six would be fine. We'll have some drinks and yak."

"I'll be there on the dot."

"I'll be waiting," she responded.

He watched her leave, enjoying the swing of her hips encased in denim.

Sensational derriere, he thought. Great breasts, too. He grinned. Things were definitely looking up.

But his good mood was dampened a bit as he drove through the town, his eyes taking in the closed businesses and weathered homes—empty, the curtainless windows looking like never-blinking eyes gazing sightless at a past that existed no longer.

This was a growing town when I left, he thought. Even ten years ago it was on the move, so Mr. Wallace, Sr. told me. Big things planned.

But Butler looked like, in some respects, a town caving in.

So what happened?

"Oh, goddamn!" Lisa bit at her lips as climax approached her for the umpteenth time. "That feels so good!"

"Keep it down!" Dr. Max Luden hissed at the teenager. "Damn nurse will hear us."

His cock was pumping in and out of her wet tightness and his hands gripped the softness of her young ass.

"I can't help it, baby. You get me so sexed up I just can't stand it!"

"We've got to hurry," he urged the girl. "Rana will be here any minute."

"Fuck Rana," the girl bad-mouthed her mother.

A cross hung upside down in the examining room.

"Now, that's an idea," Max laughed softly. He ejaculated, his semen pouring out of the girl's vagina, wetting her soft, young thighs.

Lisa put her head back and curled her toes, jerking in climax. Her sleek tanned legs were spread wide, trembling as the good doctor pulled out of her and reached for a towel. He cleaned himself and tossed another towel to Lisa, pointing toward the small bathroom.

"Go wipe your pussy," he told her. "Get the smell of cum off you. And don't forget your birth control pills."

"Don't worry about that, baby," she assured the doctor. "The last thing I want right now is a kid."

Max sprayed a deodorant around his groin area and pulled up his trousers and adjusted his tie and white coat. He fixed a smile on his face, he opened the door, and walked into his office. He buzzed the receptionist.

"Yes, sir?"

"Has Mrs. Drew arrived yet?"

"Just walking in, Doctor."

"Send her in, please."

Rana sat down in front of the doctor's desk. "How is Lisa, Max?"

"Great," the M.D. smiled. "She just had a slight itching problem that needed lubricating, that's all."

"Max, you make her sound like an automobile," Rana smiled.

The doctor looked a little tired. "She can go, all right."

Mike drove back home and stowed his groceries. He walked out onto the back porch, the mystery of who and why cleaned up the house still bothering him. Deep in thought, mostly about Rana, he turned and was startled as he came face to face with a dark-skinned woman standing on the back steps.

He was about to tell her off, in very blunt language, when the woman smiled. Recognition wrapped her misty-memory arms around him and he returned the smile. "Bonnie?" he said. "Bonnie Roberts? Sure it is!" God, what a tan she had.

Her smile did not waver. "Hello, Mike." Her voice sounded—odd to him. Kind of a hollow, husky quality. But that wasn't it exactly. It had a deep sort of echo to it. He'd never heard anything quite like it.

He opened the screen door and motioned her inside. She stepped onto the porch, moving with a light, fluid movement. Very graceful. "I can't stay very long, Mike. I really shouldn't be here at all, you know? It's the light. The sunlight, I mean."

32

He did not have the foggiest notion what she was talking about. Was she drunk at ten o'clock in the morning? She didn't appear loaded. He nodded his head and smiled. He recalled that Bonnie had always been a little weird—as compared to the norm of that time.

"Do you have a cold, Bonnie?"

"Cold? Why—no, Mike, I'm not in the least cold. Actually, when you get used to it, it's really very pleasant, if you don't mind the restrictions."

Mike stared at her, confused. Now he was sure the lady was zonked at ten in the morning. Her tan appeared to be darker on her face than on her bare arms. "Oh? Well—sure, Bonnie. Hey, come on in. This is my lucky day. Two friendly faces in less than an hour."

She sat down in a kitchen chair and looked up at him. What a tan, Mike thought.

"Is my face still friendly, Mike?" she asked seriously. "I can't tell anymore. But Jimmy Grayson keeps pestering me about—well, you know."

No, Mike didn't know. This lady was really wiped out. "Bonnie," he smiled, "your face is very friendly. I don't recall you having an unkind bone in your body."

She smiled a mysterious smile. Her teeth were startlingly white against her face. "Yes, we did get to know each other's bodies quite well, didn't we? Well—I had to pay for that, Mike, believe me. But I was forgiven. I didn't apologize, either, I can tell you that for a fact. He says I am too strong-willed a woman for my own good."

He needs to get you off the booze, too, Mike thought. They had gone steady for a year in high school, almost wearing out the back seat of Mike's '49 Ford. Bonnie really liked to screw, and would holler like a banshee when she came. And when she was, as she put it, "in her time," would take Mike orally like his cock was made of peppermint candy. And not a whole lot of that went on in Butler in the fifties.

"Apologize, Bonnie? To whom?"

As her eyes met his, Mike could have sworn there was a light mist around her face. He blinked his eyes and the light mist was gone.

My imagination, he thought.

"I see," she said softly, her voice still containing that echo quality. "You don't know. Well, no matter, you will know soon enough. But you must be prepared."

He chuckled weakly. "I was a boy scout, Bonnie, remember?"

She did not laugh at the small joke. Her face was set as if made of stone.

"Bonnie, did you clean up this house?"

She smiled up at him.

"All right," he felt relief wash over him; the mystery was solved. "But—" The hell it was! "How did you know I was coming in? All those other things? The after shave, the whiskey?"

"I did it for you, Mike," she sidestepped the main question with a compliment. "But I knew a warrior like you would not drink to excess."

She's not zonked, Mike thought. My God, she's clobbered.

"I have to go now, Mike," she said, rising from the table. "I can't stay in one place very long; I'll be caught."

I can damn well understand that, he thought, you're probably kept in a rubber room when you are caught.

"We'll see each other again, perhaps. But I must warn you. Be careful. For now, that is all I can say. Be careful. And don't tell anyone you've seen me. That's for your own good."

Before he could reply, she was gone, the back door

slamming shut. "What in the hell!" he said, walking to the back porch. She was not in sight. The huge back yard, several acres of it, was empty. She had disappeared, as if the earth had opened up and swallowed her.

In the kitchen, he tried to recall what Bonnie had been wearing.

He could not, and Colonel Mike Folsom was and always had been a very observant man.

But he could not recall a single item of clothing Bonnie had on.

"Son of a bitch!" he cussed.

He dropped his hand to the back of the chair where she had sat. He jerked his hand away. The chair was ice-cold, and wet. He put his fingers to his nostrils and sniffed. A musty odor assailed his olfactory nerves, sending tremblings to his brain.

The odor of damp earth. But more than that.

It was the smell of a freshly opened grave.

TWO

Mike answered the knocking on the front door, stepping out onto the large porch. He was still puzzling over Bonnie's disappearing act and her warnings to be careful and not discuss his seeing her with anyone.

Chief of Police Ford stood on the porch, hat in hand, grinning hugely at Mike. "You old son of a gun, you!" he shouted the words. He stuck out his hand and Mike took the offer of friendship. Howdy & Shake. "How you been, old son?"

"I've been all right, Don. Fine. Dandy. Yourself?" It was almost too easy to slip back into the one-word vernacular of this region.

Chief Ford patted his ample paunch. "Eatin' regular, as you can see with your own eyes. Lord, boy, but don't you look in shape? I'm okay. Can't stay, Mike. Just wanted to tell you I jumped all over that Lennie Ellison right after Ted told me what went down 'tween you two. Lennie din have no right to get huffy with you. Hell," he winked hugely, conspiratorially, a two-men-of-the-world wink, " 'way I hear tell, you one of our richest folk, now. Can't be offendin' the wealthy now, can we?''

Mike laughed, a little embarrassed. ''Hell, Don, I'm just me. No different from the fellow you knew in high school.''

''Yeah, boy,'' the chief's face sobered, ''you some different, and you know it. Hell, we here in Butler think a trip up to Shreveport's a big deal. But you, old son, hell, you been all 'round the world, near 'bouts. Jumpin' out of airplanes, won all kinds of medals—got the Big One, too—in the war. Yeah, you some different, all right. Can't imagine why you'd wanna come back here to live in little ole hicksville Butler, Louisiana.''

''It's my home, Don. I was raised here. What's the saying—I've come back to my roots.''

The chief shook his head. ''I reckon, Mike. Not much goin' on here, now, though. Least not that a man like you would be much interested in.''

''Maybe I'm looking forward to the peace and quiet of a small town.'' Mike smiled.

''Well—then that's damn sure what you'll get here, boy. No night spots no more. Shut 'em all down. Just 'bout the time the no-honkin' rule went into effect. You be careful, now, Mike, don't go tootin' your car horn. Cost you five dollars if you get caught,'' he grinned.

''The town is smaller, Don.''

''Yep. Justa dryin' up anda dyin' on the vine, so to speak. Sure is.'' He plopped his cowboy hat on his head and turned to leave. He stopped, turning around. ''Gotta be movin', old son, but durned if it ain't good to see you.''

''Seems to me, Don, if the town was dwindling in population, you wouldn't need a no-noise ordinance. Whose idea was it?''

''Why—'' Don looked both confused and slightly irritated at the question. ''Town council, of course. Mr.

Becker was the one who suggested it, though."

"Becker? I'm not familiar with that name."

"You're not, huh? Well—he's a rich man. But kinda like that Las Vegas feller—Hughes. Was that his name? Real secretlike. Becker come in here 'bout ten years ago. Bought up a lot—and I mean a lot—of land. Near 'bout twenty thousand acres at one pop, and still buying it up. It's in several corporation names, but it all boils down to belongin' to one man."

"He really must be a wealthy man."

"Worth hundreds of millions, so I'm told. But he's such a good man. Done all kinds of nice things for the community. Keeps to hisself out there in the country. Bought the old Blake mansion; you 'member it. Never see him in town, though. Well—see you 'round, old son." He smiled. "Mike? It is good to see you. You know, we got us a class reunion comin' up this summer?"

"I plan to attend."

"Good, boy. Fine." He winked, but in this wink and the words that followed, the chief was telling the home-town-boy-returned that he knew everything that went on in his town. "Don't you be wearin' out our little Rana, now. Man, ain't that prime pussy? I'd lick her ass just to get to see the little puckered hole. Bye, now."

Mike stood on the porch and watched Stinky drive off. The nickname seemed even more apropos than before.

Then suddenly his thoughts turned to the present —to the dwindling population, to Becker buying up thousands of acres in the parish, and in this age of overt permissiveness, to the beer joints all closing down, and finally to the strange statement of his lawyer, Wallace. And why had Bonnie cleaned up his house? Why had she warned him to be careful? And how had she known he was even returning?

Odd occurrences. Damn sure was a funny kind of homecoming.

Strange

He picked up the many sticks and stones and soft drink cans that had accumulated in the yard, cranked the mower, and cut the grass. He spent the rest of the afternoon trimming around the sidewalks and house and repairing, at least temporarily, the broken steps and railing.

As he worked, no one waved to him as they drove past; certainly no one honked their horn. And no one walked the sidewalk in front of the old two-story home.

Mike straightened up from his labors and looked around him, enjoying the glow, the satisfied feeling one gets after he or she has done a good day's work and is happy with the efforts expelled.

Definitely a place to be if one wishes solitude. Mike smiled, wondering if Bonnie indeed had thought of everything.

He went into the house, looking around, finally locating the phone. It had been moved from its nook by the basement door and replaced in a small area just off the den. He picked up the receiver; a hum greeted him. He looked at the phone book; it was new, this year's edition. Becker Communications System. Not Ma Bell.

Now why, Mike mused, would a man spend hundreds of thousands of dollars, millions, probably, installing his own system in a seemingly dying part of the parish?

Or was it dying?

He lifted his eyes, letting them roam down the polished floor of the hall that led to the kitchen. They settled on the door that led to the basement. He was walk-

40

ing to the closed door, his hand on the knob, when the phone rang.

"Yes?"

"Get out!" the whispered voice said. A young man's voice. "Get out before it's too late. Leave us alone."

"Who the hell is this?"

"Get out! Don't be a fool. You cannot change what you do not understand. It is beyond your grasp. Get out!"

The line went dead.

Clicked. Hummed.

Something clunked in the house and Mike felt just a light shiver of apprehension tingle down his back. He tossed the feeling aside and slammed the receiver back into its cradle. "Crazy kids!" he said.

He tried the door to the basement. Locked. He went through all the keys on the ring Wallace had given him. None of them fit the lock.

"Crap!" he said, then gave it up and went upstairs to take a shower and get ready to go out to Rana's. Just the thought of her made him feel better. It also produced a slight erection as he showered, his mind playing with erotic mental pictures of the blonde.

Mike was singing in the shower when the basement door opened just a crack. Eyes looked out into the hall. The door closed silently.

The lock clicked.

It's funny, Mike thought, as he drove the parish road to Rana's farm, mention Louisiana to people and they immediately think of swamps and bayous and rice and alligators. Most folks out of state don't realize we have rolling hills in this state. He smiled, recalling an event of years past. He had mentioned he was from Louisiana to a group of guys in the barracks down at Fort Bragg.

One of them had asked him to speak some French. At that time Mike was having trouble with English, much less a second language. He had laughed and tried to explain that not all people in Louisiana were Cajun.

Then he had to explain what a Cajun was.

"Got to go see mother and dad's graves tomorrow," he muttered. "Should have done that today, I guess. Get some flowers, straighten up the site. Better take some clippers with me for the weeds."

He drove further into the parish, noticing, on this warm late May day, a great many houses along the way. All empty, deserted, lonely-looking. There was the Ferrel farm—empty, windows all boarded up. The Manning home—deserted. Half a dozen others, all empty and forlorn-looking. Silent reminders of the people who had poured their sweat and youth into the land and now had moved away.

Or were dead; that thought popped into his head.

And if they left, moved, did they leave willingly?

"Hell, Folsom," he said, disgusted with himself. "Why would they not leave willingly? Damn, boy, you're getting paranoid."

He made a mental note to ask Rana about the deserted farms and houses. Also in town.

He checked the rear-view. That same car was still behind him, way back, but still there. He had noticed it as he was leaving town, and it was still there. Tailing him. Odd. And Mike did not like to be tailed.

He had been too long in and too well-trained in the field of intelligence not to almost immediately pick up a tail. He thought of the big .41 magnum in the glove box.

"Not yet," he muttered.

He pulled onto a dirt road, backed around until the nose of the Jag was facing the blacktop, and waited.

The late model car topped the hill, noticed Mike's

Jag parked, and braked, stopping on the gravel of the shoulder. It watched and waited, the headlights like huge glassy eyes, never blinking.

"Facedown," Mike said. "Well, to hell with you, whoever you are." He pulled back onto the blacktop and drove on.

The car followed, maintaining the same discreet distance as before, hanging well back.

Mike punched open the glove box and took out the big .41 mag, laying it on the seat beside him. The car behind him suddenly accelerated, coming up very fast. It roared around him, kicking up bits of gravel as the left rear tire slipped off the blacktop and onto the shoulder. The rearend slewed, then straightened. It was soon out of sight.

The driver had been Lennie Ellison. He had not looked at Mike, did not acknowledged his presence.

Mike softly cursed, knowing that sooner or later, probably sooner, he was going to have real trouble with Lennie.

And Mike also knew that when it came, he was either going to stomp the shit out of Lennie—or kill him. And it really didn't matter much to Mike which way it went.

Just thinking about kicking the crap out of that ignorant redneck made Mike feel much better. He stowed the .41 mag back in the glove box just as he was pulling into Rana's drive.

The lawn was well-kept, almost manicured in its neatness, with flowers of many types in bloom, the colorful profusion adding not only a rainbow cast to the green of the lawn, but a touch of nature's perfume to the soft, warm air. Mike remembered the huge old oak trees in the front yard and was relieved and happy to see them still alive, shading the lawn with giant arms.

Rana was standing on the porch, watching him as he pulled in and slowly got out of the Jag. She was dressed in faded Levi's and checkered cowgirl shirt. She did things to that shirt that made Mike's mouth suddenly go dry. Tennis shoes on her feet. As he had observed before, the jeans outlined the shape of her womanhood. He pulled his eyes upward to her smiling face. Her hair shone with health. Light honey-colored.

He suddenly recalled Chief Ford's parting remark about Rana and realized he did not like the man.

Rana held out her hands and he took them. He was almost overwhelmed by a sense of at last being home. After wandering about the world for twenty-five years, he was home. The theme from *East of Eden* suddenly played briefly in his head. "I Am Home." He had the tape of Placido Domingo singing that song—among others—and it was one of his favorites.

Mike could not recall ever experiencing such a strong and positive feeling of being where he belonged. He stood for a few seconds, holding the small soft hands, content to gaze into the lovely blue of her peaceful eyes.

She smiled back at him. "What's the matter, Mike? You have such an odd expression on your face, like you've seen a ghost."

He grinned boyishly. "Rana, if you're a ghost, you're the prettiest ghost to ever walk—or float, hover, whatever they do—on the face of the earth."

"Oh, go on, you!" she protested, but enjoying the words. She pulled him to the porch, and just for a moment his hands rested on the gentle beginning curve of her hips.

The feeling to his hands was almost electric.

He dropped them quickly.

She opened the screen door and motioned him inside. "It's no mansion, Mike, but it's paid for and all the land is, too."

"It's very nice, Rana," he said, looking around the large, comfortably-furnished den. The furniture had

44

that homey, lived-on look. "I Am Home." He shook his head.

"Something wrong, Mike?"

"Oh, no," he smiled. "Everything is A-okay, believe it. Rana, how many acres do you actually farm?"

"Waall," she drawled and grinned, that action making her look about eighteen years old. Her reply was an exaggeration of the southern drawl, and when she finished, Mike was laughing at her. "Ah got me 'bout half a dozen of them little ole oil wells. Pumpers. Each one of 'em pumps out 'bout two hundred barrels a day—crude. 'At's on the land next to Barber Parish. Ever' third barrel is mine. I farm two hundred and fifty acres of feed grain; run 'bout three hundred head of cattle. Just me and a couple of hands, suh. Yawl is lookin' at a real farm gal."

"You're kidding!"

"No, suh, Colonel, suh. Ah hire me a couple of extra hands ever' now and then, but mostly it's jist me and Walt and Roy. Real farm gal, 'at's me."

"Corn-fed and hand-spanked."

"You got it, baby. What you sees is what you gets." They were both slightly uncomfortable for a moment, the double-edged statement and the heavy feeling of closeness touching them. Then she laughed at herself and took Mike's arm, leading him to a massive leather sofa. "Sit down, Mike. How about a drink? What's your poison?"

He sat down on the couch, the leather creaking. "How about a martini, on the rocks?"

"Super. That's my drink. Vodka?"

"Nothing else, Rana."

"We're right in tune," she said, then reddened and quickly turned away to the wet bar.

As she moved around fixing the cocktails, Mike again studied her, reviewing her charms, and Rana

45

had many charms to inspect. Once she looked up, catching him watching her. She smiled.

Mike could not remember any Carl Drew. "You mentioned a child, Rana."

"My daughter, Lisa. She's dressing for—church," Rana put a derogatory slur on the last.

On a Monday night? Mike silently questioned. Must be a revival.

She walked to him, handing him his drink, then sat down beside him, a respectable distance between them.

Mike sipped the martini, his tongue detecting immediately the quality taste of Polish vodka. Perfect. "Just the one child, Rana?"

"We had a boy. Carl, Jr. He's with his father. They live in Butler. Just outside of Butler, actually." He looked puzzled and she explained, "It was an ugly divorce, Mike; and even he agreed it was all on his side. Infidelity, drunkenness, and finally a lot of abuse— physical. He put me in the clinic twice. It's a terrible thing for a mother to say, but I didn't want the boy. His father turned him against me. I got both kids, at first. But Carl kept running away, back to his father. Finally I let him go live with the bastard. Excuse me, but that's the way I feel about my ex. Neither of them speak to me, haven't for years. Carl, Jr. is—thirteen, now. But," she sighed, "I hear they've changed, going to church now. A lot." She said the last with a large dose of ugliness in her tone.

Mike did not pursue the source of the ugliness. "I am sorry, Rana—in a way." He softened that with a smile and she touched his arm in understanding. "My kids do write, at best, sporadically, but their mother hasn't poisoned their minds toward me."

He sensed there were questions she would like to ask, so he cleared the air between them, knocking down any invisible barriers that might hinder any type of upcom-

46

ing relationship.

"Full divorce, Rana—years ago. It wasn't just the military life, even though it can be a tough one for a woman. I was in Nam—more or less," he grinned, "when the final breakdown came. It was another man, but I don't blame either of them, not really. At least not now. Hell, I was over in that area for years."

"You must have liked combat." It was not a question.

His smile was twisted. "That's both an odd and interesting statement. I liked the challenge of it. I spent most of my time behind the lines, so to speak; sometimes, hell, most of the time, the lines weren't clearly defined. Working with Special Forces people: Rangers, LRRPs, SEALs, Air Force Intelligence types. Silent Ops, HALO work, body snatching, that type of work—"

She laughed. "Mike, I haven't understood a damn word you've said!"

He shared her laughter and it was a good feeling. "Well, we felt the war was a just one, and it left a bad taste in my mouth the way we just turned tail and ran like a pack of thieves in the night."

"Whose fault was that, Mike?"

"Oh, Congress, the press, the liberals. Believe me, Rana, you don't want to get me started on that subject. I'll bore you to tears." He sighed. "Anyway, it's over, I'm a civilian, out of it, away from it, a private citizen, and I'll miss it—for a time."

"For the rest of your life," Rana said quietly.

"Yeah," Mike agreed. "I guess you're right about that."

Lisa walked into the room and Rana introduced her. Mike sized her up quickly. She looked like her mother, with a woman's body and a mouth made for kissing. There was a pouty look to her lips and face. Sexy, in an

47

almost-woman way. About five feet three inches of dynamite. Trouble with a capital T.

She's discovered what's between her legs, Mike thought, and has got an itch she can't scratch enough.

He recalled his own daughter and the hysterical phone call he received in Saigon from his wife. Their oldest was pregnant. Been seeing a married man. Screwing at fifteen. God! What to do?

"Arrange for an abortion," Mike had told her. Hell, he was as hurt as a man could be, but much more a pragmatist than his wife.

"If you'd been here looking after us instead of fucking off all over the world playing hero, this wouldn't have happened!" she had screamed accusingly at him.

And the conversation had deteriorated from that point.

Mike brought his attention back to the present. He was shocked to see the kid flirting with him. He tried to ignore her.

"Who is coming out to get you?" Rana asked her daughter.

"Jimmy. And that is becoming a bother, Mother. I ask again, when do I get a car of my own? And don't give me that old crap about can't afford it; that's B.S. and we both know it."

Mike watched silently as Rana struggled valiantly to hold her temper in check. The kid definitely had a smart mouth on her. "When you're old enough," Rana said.

Mike could feel the tension between mother and daughter. He wondered why.

"You're so archaic in your thinking, Mother. That means I'll be toddering about with the Geritol set before I get some wheels of my own. I can see it now, headlines in all the papers: GRANNY LISA FINALLY GETS OWN CAR."

"I would suggest you watch your mouth, young lady," Rana warned her daughter, a bit of color fanning her cheeks, spreading out rapidly.

The girl opened her purse and removed a small pocket mirror, staring intently into it—looking at her mouth.

Rana moved toward her, blue eyes flashing.

Mike stepped between them, putting a gentle but restraining hand on Rana's shoulder. "Anything I can do in the kitchen?" he volunteered.

He could feel the heat of her through the thin shirt and her struggle to retain control. When she looked up at him, he could see the leading edge of tears in her eyes.

She blinked them back and touched her fingertips to the back of his hand. "No, Mike—it's all under control."

Another double meaning?

"May I stop looking at my mouth, now, Mother?" Lisa asked.

"By all means," Rana said. "You want something to eat before you leave?"

She looked at Mike and grinned lewdly. Mike flushed under her knowing stare. She laughed and said, "No, thanks. We'll eat at the church."

A car horn sounded in the driveway.

Again Rana flared. "I wish to *hell* that boy had the manners to at least knock on the damn door for you!"

"Careful, Mommy-love. Don't want to spoil your image for your—" she looked at Mike, far too much knowledge in those blue eyes, "—*friend*." She emphasized the last.

"When will you be in?" Rana asked, clipping the words.

"When I get damn good and ready." Lisa turned and gave her trim little ass a vulgar shake. She grinned and looked back at Mike. "Looks pretty good, huh, man?" She laughed and walked out the door, slamming it behind her.

"Jesus Christ!" Mike blurted. He caught himself and looked at Rana. He felt his face burning with embarrassment. "Sorry," he apologized.

The woman shrugged, an almost defeated gesture. "For what, Mike? The truth? I've had her on birth control pills for the past year. Jack Geraci told me there isn't one—not one!—girl in this community over fourteen that isn't on the pill. Mike, it's wholesale fucking!"

"Easy, babe," he said, putting a big arm around her slender shoulders. She turned and came into his arms, fitting herself against him, filling a void needed in both their lives. It was as natural as breathing—for both of them.

After a moment of almost silent weeping, she pulled away and put both hands on his chest, palms pressing lightly on his shirt front. She could feel the slow beating of his heart. "We'll—talk about it, Mike. But not for a while. Let's have a fun evening first; God knows I could use one. Let's have another drink; you fix them, I'll fix myself and get composed." She smiled up at him. "Then I'll drag out the scrapbooks."

"I thought you were kidding about those!"

"No way, hero. I told you I've been lusting after your bod for years," she winked up at him.

"This promises to be an interesting evening," he said. "In more ways than one. And I do want to talk, Rana, about you and this community."

"We will, Mike. But first I'll ply you with home cooking and watch you fall asleep on the couch."

"I might fool you, Rana."

"That is my fervent hope."

He arched an eyebrow.

She gave him a quick kiss on the lips and then left the room, calling over her shoulder, "Fix us some drinks, Mike. Back in a couple of minutes."

"Who belongs to the Jag back there?" Jimmy asked.

"Some guy named Mike something-or-other. Mother's friend. She's got the hots for him so bad she can't hardly stand it. She's probably been playing with her pussy all afternoon."

Jimmy laughed and put his right hand between Lisa's legs. "And you, Lisa?" His tone held just a touch of jealousy.

"Relax, Jimmy. This guy is as straight as an arrow. Besides, you know what Director Egan says, 'Fucking is a good and natural thing. We give our hearts to the Master, but our bodies are our own.' Anyway, I came on to the dude and he about shit."

Jimmy's eyes narrowed. He liked to think of Lisa as his very own private pussy. Which she wasn't. "What do you mean, you came on to him?"

"Come on, Jimmy. Put a lid on it. I don't belong to you."

"How old is this guy?"

"Old—old. Forty-something, probably. You wanna drop the subject, Jimmy?"

"You gonna tell Director Egan about this old dude, Lisa?"

She put her blues on him. "Sometimes, Jimmy, you're a real pain in the ass. Why should I run to Egan about it?"

"You know what he says about strangers coming in."

"Naw. This guy lives here. He was born here. Came back after he retired from the Army, or something like that."

"Okay." He fished in his pocket and took out a fat joint. "You wanna smoke?"

"Sure," she said, taking the joint. She lit up, held the smoke, and passed the joint to Jimmy.

They smoked and drove in silence for a few minutes, Lisa finally pointing to a clump of trees. "First time I ever made it with you was right over there. Place still looks pretty good. You remember?"

"How could I forget, baby?" he grinned and glanced at her. "From where I am, Lisa, everything looks good."

"Did you bring the blanket?" she asked. "Last time you forgot and we got chiggers all over us."

"Yeah, I got it." He turned off onto a dirt road and pulled into a thick stand of timber. "You suppose your mother really believes that shit about us going to church to praise—you know," the boy was wary of even speaking the word God, "that other Master?"

"What's the matter, Jimmy?" she grinned. "You afraid of speaking the word God?" When she got no response, she said, "Oh, man, yeah. She's stupid. You got another joint?"

They spread the blanket, lit up, and smoked, the buzz gently floating them. Lisa opened his pants and played with his stiff and swollen manhood. He opened her shirt; she wore no bra. He sucked at her nipples until they were taut with passion. One hand was busy between her legs, her jeans unzipped. She wore no panties.

"Lisa . . . ?" he questioned, running his finger into the crack of her ass, touching the tiny hole.

She brought his fingers back to her wet mons Veneris. "I told you before, Jimmy, no! I like to fuck with you, but my ass is my own."

"I bet it'd be tight," he said wistfully.

"You'll never know, man. Bet on that."

"I got some KY Jelly with me, Lisa. Come on, baby, just let me get a couple of inches in?"

"Jimmy," she pushed him away and held him there. "My ass is cherry and it's gonna stay that way—until I say so."

"You'll give it to someone else," he pouted. "Then it won't be the same."

"Oh, Jimmy, don't be stupid! You think you're the only one fucking me? You know what Director Egan says, 'we've all got to share with the other.' "

"You like to make it with girls, Lisa?"

"Not too much. Oh, it's all right, I guess. But I'd rather have a stiff cock." She glanced at him. "You like making it with other guys?"

He shrugged. "I don't mind it. Director Egan says it's all right. But I didn't like it when he gave me to Lennie."

"Was Lennie rough?"

"Yeah, and so was you-know-who."

She pulled his head back to her young breasts. She was thinking of Colonel Mike Folsom as Jimmy greedily sucked her nipples. She bet the colonel really knew how to fuck. She'd give her ass to him if he'd just ask for it. She almost came thinking about it. She pushed Jimmy's head down lower.

"Eat me, Jimmy."

THREE

The Church of Friendship, Fellowship, and Faith was housed in the old Butler Country Club. There had been a few improvements made over the years. About a quarter of a million dollars of improvements.

The dance area of the club had been enlarged considerably, turning it into an auditorium. It would seat five hundred people comfortably. There were two other auditoriums located on the huge grounds, with closed-circuit TV linking them. There were many smaller rooms, some of them sound proof. The rooms held everything from cots and beds to whips and chains.

Something for everyone's tastes.

The director of the Church of Friendship, Fellowship, and Faith, the Most Reverend Ron Egan, checked his wristwatch. Another hour before his disciples would be arriving. He laughed as he stood behind the pulpit, gazing out over the dark, empty chairs. His laughter echoed hollowly back to him, enveloping him in an evil shroud.

There was no point in any further pretense; everyone who was joining the church had joined. He reached behind him and turned the Cross upside down.

Everything was going well. Becker said the Evil Old One was pleased. Another month, maximum, perhaps as brief a time as two weeks, and Butler would belong to the Master.

Yes, everything was progressing quite smoothly.

Becker had told him just the week past that the Third Master in the Order of Evil was pleased with Egan. Most pleased.

Actually it was down to only a matter of hours. Plans for the College were off the drawing board and in the hands of the builders; the ground had been broken just outside of town. A small beginning, certainly, but it would grow and grow and grow.

Egan howled his laughter. Oh, my, yes, how it would grow.

"Director?" A young girl's voice came to him through the echoing laughter and the gloom of the huge room.

"Yes, my child?" Egan said, his eyes searching the darkness for the source.

She came closer, walking slowly down the lushly carpeted center aisle. Egan recognized her. Cindy.

"I thought perhaps you might need some assistance in preparing for the ceremony this evening," she said. "I came to offer any help I might give."

"That's very kind of you, Cindy." He could see she wore no bra beneath her thin cotton shirt. Her breasts were almost at full maturity, the nipples aroused, threatening to burst through the material. "But I don't think preparing for the worship was what you had in mind, was it, girl?"

She came closer, her eyes traveling over the burly man's body. His shoulders and arms were packed with muscle, his waist trim, and his legs ridged with solid meat. He did not look at all like a minister.

56

In the Christian sense of the word, he wasn't.

The Church of Friendship, Fellowship, and Faith worshipped Satan.

"Then why did I come so early?" she asked, her big brown eyes innocent.

He laughed.

She climbed the steps and stood beside him, sighing as he put one big arm around her shoulders, a hand cupping a young, firm breast. "Do we have time?" she asked.

"Oh, yes, my dear," Egan assured her. "We have time."

"There you are." Rana pointed to a fading, yellowing clipping. "In your football uniform."

"Well, I'll just be damned," Mike grinned. "Boy, I was a handsome devil, wasn't I?"

"Actually," she said with a straight face, "that was the time you were going through your pimples stage."

"I never had pimples!" he protested. "Besides, you're too young to remember."

She giggled at his expression, the giggling not at all unbecoming or childlike in the adult woman. "Come on," she closed the scrapbook, "let's eat. I'm starved."

Standing over the well-set table, it was as if Mike had been dropped into a time warp and catapulted back to his childhood. He stood by the table for a moment, savoring the sights and smells. His mother used to set a table just like this.

Only in the South, he thought. Nowhere else that I've been able to find. Only in the South.

Finally, he said, "Rana, it all depends on the mess sergeant, but for the most part, garrison troops eat pretty damned well. But—"

57

She finished it for him. "—It ain't home cookin'.' "

"Damn straight on that." He pulled back a chair. "Let's eat."

She laughed at his eagerness.

After eating in silence for a few moments, he said, "You cook just like my mother used to."

"It's all part of my plan, Colonel."

"Oh? Do I get to hear the rest of your plan?"

"I think I'll just let you sweat it out," she smiled.

"That's a good old military expression."

She watched him gobble his food. "Don't eat so fast, Mike. It's not good for you."

His eyes were particularly void of expression as he lifted them and looked at her.

Hunter's eyes, she thought. No—warrior's eyes, she amended her thought.

A slow warmth gradually spread through the cold eyes. He grinned. "Yes, dear."

After two martinis, two helpings of everything on the table, and a huge chunk of home-baked apple pie, Mike was in no condition to do anything except sit on the couch and wonder how long he could keep his eyes open.

"Oohh," he groaned.

"You're the one who made the pig out of yourself," she teased him.

He nodded his head in agreement and patted his stomach in satisfaction.

Rana had curled up at the far end of the couch and was sipping her coffee. "Plans, Mike?"

"I don't know yet," he said, leaning forward and pouring a cup of coffee from the service on the low table. He sugared it and stirred, leaning back. "I'd like to go into some sort of business, but hell, all I've been doing for years is gathering intelligence and killing people."

His remark did not seem to bother her, and Mike looked closely at people when he made that statement. Most were repulsed. He dismissed them as candy-asses. The ones who realized a nation must have men who are willing to kill to survive usually became, if not friends, at least close acquaintances.

"Both of those talents might come in handy, Mike. Sooner than you think. One never knows."

Strange thing for her to say, he thought. "In Butler, Louisiana, Rana?"

She smiled, but it seemed forced. "What do you think of Butler, Mike, after having been gone all these years?"

"It's changed, that's for certain. Seems to me the friendliness is gone from the town. And the town is smaller."

"Sure is. Went from twenty-eight hundred to sixteen hundred in about ten years."

He whistled. "That's one hell of a drop." He looked at her, questions in his eyes.

She shrugged.

Mike got the feeling she was holding back from him. But why? "Why does ten years ring a bell with me? Something Don Ford said to me, I think."

"He came to see you?"

"This afternoon. Apologized for one of his cops getting out of line with me."

"Lennie."

He met her eyes. Lovely eyes. A lot of banked fire hidden in the azure. "I gather by that you know Lennie?"

"*Everybody* knows Lennie, Mike. He's Chief Ford's muscle boy."

"Rana—this is going by pretty fast for me. Muscle

boy? What is this, New York? In Butler?"

Her smile was knowing. She laughed, then abruptly sobered. "They're lovers," she said flatly.

"Lovers? Who are we talking about?"

"Don Ford and Lennie Ellison."

"You're kidding!"

"No. Stinky came out of the closet about ten years ago. Admitted it. I mean, don't get me wrong—I don't care. I'm not so down on gays as a lot of folks. It's just another piece of the puzzle that I put together."

"Puzzle? Rana—wait a minute. The people keep electing him chief. In Butler? Conservative Butler? I find that—well, odd."

"The people, as you put it," she said, and Mike thought that odd, as well, "elect him overwhelmingly. Every time he runs. The last two times, no one ran against him."

"Well, I'll just be damned," Mike said softly, his voice low-pitched. "Ted Bernard."

"He's a puzzle," Rana admitted. "Showed up here one day and the next day he was on the force. Gay? I don't believe so. I don't know what he is. He's a mystery man. But he's one of Becker's people, though."

"Hold that thought, Rana. You said Stinky came out of the closet about ten years ago. Ten years keeps popping up in my mind."

"Everything, as far as I'm concerned, and a few others, as well, believe that things really started going to hell around here ten years ago." Rana hitched herself closer to him. "But—at the same time, Mike, as contradictory as it sounds, things started getting better for those who stayed."

"That doesn't make any sense, Rana."

"Well, look at it this way, Mike—for the people who stayed in this community, things are better."

"How so?"

"Let me finish. We have no crime; no one is hungry or has bad housing; and this might be hard to believe, Mike, but no one, regardless of income, and I mean *no one* is ever denied admission to the Butler Hospital."

"Hospital? I knew we had a small clinic, but I didn't know anything about any hospital. I didn't see any signs pointing one out."

"Damn right, you didn't. And that's very odd in itself. The hospital is located way to hell and gone out in the parish. About six and a half miles from town."

"Which direction?"

"North."

"Then that would be out near the old Blake mansion."

"You got it. Just a little over a mile away."

Mike's expression was quizzical. "I—got the distinct impression from Stinky—Chief Ford," he grinned, correcting the nickname.

His grin was not shared. "Stinky is just fine. He wears it well. He's a despicable man, Mike, and being gay has nothing to do with it. There's a lot more I plan to discuss with you, but go on with what you were saying."

"Well, I was going to say that I got the impression this Becker fellow seems to crave solitude."

"Yes, that's true. So?"

"Why would he move so close to a busy hospital?"

"Mike, he didn't move close to it—he *built* it!"

Mike's short laugh was not one of amusement. "Things just don't add up around here, Rana. Tell me this—who first asked Stinky to run for Chief of Police?"

"I heard it was Becker."

"Why?"

"I don't know, Mike."

"Ummm."

61

"What's in that intelligence-gathering mind of yours?" she asked.

"Nothing concrete, that's for sure. But this much is for sure. I'm getting that little tingle that used to tell me when I was on the trail of something phony—something hot."

She smiled at him.

"That's not what I meant, Rana!"

She laughed softly and moved to his side.

All of a sudden Mike felt warm. "I think I'll get a glass of that good iced tea of yours."

"Mike—" the word was a whisper, but it held more hidden meaning than a wall full of hieroglyphics.

He turned; her face was only a couple of inches from his. Her breath was warm and sweet on his face.

"I don't want you to get the wrong idea of me. About me. I—I'm coming on pretty strong, aren't I?"

He sighed. Moment of truth. "To be honest with you, Rana—and don't take this the wrong way, please —I've seen armored personnel carriers that were more subtle."

She smiled. "Honest Mike. Never changes. Can I level with you, Mike?"

"You know you can, Rana."

"No, Mike—that's wrong. I don't *know* that. I don't *know* who I can trust in this community. Not anymore. Only a few of the people I can trust, only a few who really share my views. But that's not what I was going to say. Carl and I busted up six years ago. There have been only two men in my life in all that time. And they were very brief affairs. I'm being totally honest with you. I have not been with a man—sexually—in over four years. I got pretty soured with men after dealing with those two I just mentioned."

"Divorcée just can't live without it, huh? Got to have it—all that type of redneck bullshit?"

Her smile was rueful. "That's it. But I *can* live without it, Mike. I have been. It's not easy, at times." She laughed and then flipped open the scrapbook, to the last half dozen pages. "Talk about honest, Mike; there is total honesty." She pointed.

Cutouts from the Army Times covered the pages. Mike being mustered out at Fort Bragg; pictures of him receiving the Congressional Medal of Honor; the Silver Star (he had three); the DSC and many more pictures.

"How long have you subscribed to this paper, Rana?"

"Ever since your divorce."

"But—how could you have known of that?"

"Just before she died, your Aunt Bertha told my Aunt Cecilia. Aunt Cecilia told old man Rambo down at the filling station. He told Mrs. Berwick; she told me."

Mike laughed. "Talk about a roundabout method of receiving information. What a system!"

"Women will go to all kinds of lengths to get what they want, Mike."

"Maybe I'm not what you think I am, Rana, not what you want after all. You don't know me. I'm not the Mike you thought you loved in your adolescent years."

"I didn't think I loved you, Mike. I knew I loved you. Period. Truth time again? I still do. Always have. Who do you think you are, Mike?"

He leaned back against the couch, the iced tea forgotten. Who was he? Good question.

He felt her eyes on his face.

Where to begin?

Detective Sergeant Bill Cummings walked into his captain's office in Kansas City, Missouri. He carried a

63

file folder with him.

The captain looked up, questions in his eyes. It was late, past time to go home. Everybody was pulling too much overtime. Got to cut it somewhere; but where?

"That Lewis woman who was reported missing by her husband last month?" the sergeant said.

"Yeah. What about her?"

"Texas Rangers found what was left of her 'bout noon today. They ran her through the tapes. Kansas just called us. Found her right on the Texas-Louisiana border."

"I presume she's dead?"

"You presume right."

"The kid?"

"No kid."

"What? She was nine months pregnant when she was snatched, or whatever happened to her. She had to have had the baby by now."

Cummings shook his head. "The kid was taken."

"I beg your pardon?"

"This is wild, Harry. Gruesome."

"Do I have to get down on my knees and beg your highness for information, Bill?"

"Prelim reports show she was cut wide open, from breast bone to pussy. One very expert cut, with a very sharp knife. The unborn child was then removed, still in the sac."

The captain looked shocked. "Are you serious?" he asked, his voice quiet.

"Yeah, serious as a crutch. The Texas cops are digging, literally, around the area, but they're almost certain the baby—whatever you want to call it—was carried off from the scene of the crime."

"How did they arrive at that?"

"Talking to people who live down the road. Folks said they remembered seeing one of those city-type emergency vehicles drive down that road, then come back out about an hour later."

"What are you saying, Bill?"

"Maybe life-support systems."

"Jesus! That's sick!"

"I'm not sure I want to hear it."

"Well, I got our boys in the computer room to run all this stuff up and shoot it into the big computer with FBI data first, and then I hooked up with Interpol—"

The captain arched an eyebrow but said nothing.

"About ten years ago, give or take a few months, there was a rash of pregnant women vanishing around the country; they were never found. Understand, now, this is worldwide. Same with twenty years back, same with thirty years back. That's as far as I could go."

"Worldwide?" The captain leaned back in his chair, hands behind his head. "How many, all told?"

"One hundred and eighty-eight."

The captain lunged forward so violently he almost fell over onto his desk. "A hundred and eighty-eight!"

"Yeah. And it's cute the way it stacks up. Each group falls into a pattern. Sixty-six. Sixty-six. Sixty-six. But it was worldwide, like I said."

"Let me guess how many countries: sixty-six?"

"Right on the money. Odd, isn't it?"

"Odd! It's grotesque! What in God's name would people do with a hundred and eighty-eight unborn babies?"

"Only God would know."

"Or the devil," the Captain added with a smile.

"Yeah," Bill laughed.

"Well, let's bring it back to home. How many were taken out of Missouri?"

"None."

The captain spread his hands. "And the Lewis woman was taken from . . . ?"

65

"Just across the line, Kansas."

"All right, it's out of our hands, but we'll cooperate best we can. Call the Kansas boys; tell them what you've found, and the FBI. I'm sure they'll be interested."

"You still going on vacation tomorrow?"

"Hell, yes! Three glorious weeks."

"I'll get on this thing first—"

"Let's go!" the call was shouted in the outer office. "Hostage situation in an apartment. Guy's got an M-16 and is threatening to kill his wife and kids."

Sergeant Cummings, in an attempt to dodge a hail of lead from the gunman's M-16, slipped and broke his ankle. A compound fracture. Putting out his hand to soften his fall, he took all his falling weight on his right hand. The wrist popped. He would be in the hospital for several weeks, in traction. The report would lie on his desk for several weeks. Captain Harry Randolph would be gone on vacation for several weeks.

By then it would all be settled in Butler, Louisiana. More or less.

FOUR

"I think I've seen too much of the world, Rana," Mike said. "It's difficult for a highly-trained combat man to explain without sounding like he's proclaiming himself the roughest, toughest man on the face of the earth; and that isn't what I mean. I just don't react to crisis situations like—normal people, if you will."

"In other words, you go in for the kill?"

"Yes, Rana, that's it, exactly."

"So what?" she shrugged.

Mike looked at her, sudden, renewed interest in his gaze. This one, he thought, just might be strong enough to live with me. "Well, there is more, Rana. I've become a cynical, embittered man. And I'm pushing—hell, I'm past!—middle age. I—"

"You're making excuses, Mike." She touched his face with a soft hand. "Look at me, Mike. Am I too pushy for you? Is that it?"

"No," he said quickly. "That isn't it. I don't like whiny, helpless, submissive women. I like a woman who won't fall to pieces in a really bad situation. Hell, look what you do out here on the farm. I'm sure you drive a tractor and assist in the feeding and caring of your stock. You've pretty much been on your own for years, singlehandedly raising a child—''

"And failing miserably there," she interrupted.

"Maybe." His reply was honest, as was his way. She did not take offense. "And maybe not. Didn't you tell me a couple of hours ago that most of the young girls in this community are on the pill?"

"Yes, but—''

"No buts, Rana. You didn't fail. The community did."

That tilt of the head as she stared at him. "You want to explain that, Mike?"

"Not until I have more information. When's your chick due back in the nest?"

"Mike," she sighed audibly, "*if* she returns, it will be very late."

"*If?*"

"As I told you over dinner, Mike, this has turned into a very strange community. Many odd things happening. No, the kids pretty much do as they damn well please. And I think it all started when the new families began moving in. I know it did."

"I thought you said the town had shrunk, not grown?"

"The town of Butler, proper, did shrink, but these new people moved out into the parish. To a private facility for children."

Mike's turn to sigh; too much was being thrust on him in too short a time. "*What* facility for children? No! Let me guess. Becker built it."

"Give the man a cigar."

"I smoke about ten cigarettes a day—usually less." His reply was automatic. "I hate cigars. What kind of facility did Becker build, why, and what the hell do you mean, the kids pretty much do as they damn well

68

please—and what about these new people?''

"Do you realize how many questions you just asked me?'' she smiled, leaning back on the couch. The movement stretched her shirt across her full breasts and stretched Mike's nerves to near the jangling point. His eyes followed the movement. The jeans she wore didn't help, either. Her womanhood was practically leaping out at him.

But he realized the movement was not intended to tantalize him.

Or was it?

Damn women! A man just never knows for sure.

He reluctantly lifted his eyes from her body and his green eyes met the blue.

He realized that any further moves were to be initiated by him; she had done all she intended to do.

Or had she?

He fought back a sudden desire to place his big hand over her denim-covered crotch and gently squeeze.

There had been, after his divorce, many women in Mike's life—casual affairs, at best. He could not remember any woman, ever, who affected him as Rana was doing.

She began talking. "Becker built the hospital first, bringing the construction crews in from out of state; his own people, so I'm told. The hospital—I won't set foot in it . . .''

"Why?''

"Because I'm afraid, that's why. People aren't the same coming out as they went in.''

"Tuck that statement in the back of your mind and hold it there; I want to return to it. Go ahead.''

"As for the kids, Becker built recreation facilities for them. I'd have to say they're the best in the state—best I've ever seen. They're at the old country club site. They're run in conjunction with the church.''

"Becker's church?"

"In a manner of speaking, yes. At first a lot of parents raised a howl about their kids—how can I put it?—about the kid's activities. That didn't last long. After a few sessions with Director Egan—"

"Who the hell is Director Egan?"

"The pastor, for want of a better word, at the Church of Friendship, Fellowship, and Faith. He is the Most Reverent Ron Egan."

"Very impressive title."

"He's an asshole!"

"Very ladylike description, as well," Mike said dryly.

"There is a time to be ladylike, and a time to be honest. Besides, Mike, have you ever known a female who was ladylike when the lights went out and the sheets were pulled back?"

He had a quick mental flash of Rana, naked, on the sheets, legs spread wide, his face pressed against her— He quickly put that thought out of his mind. "Friendship, Fellowship, and Faith," he said. "I don't recall ever hearing of that particular church before."

"I would say it's novel, at least," she replied. "But anyway, after the parents spoke with Egan, everything quieted down. Kind of like a valve was shut off in their minds."

"Interesting way of putting it, Rana."

"But true, I believe. I just can't convince most of my friends, that's all. What few I have left, that is. Mike, I attended one of Egan's gatherings at the church. I felt—I can't really put it into words—odd. He doesn't preach the Bible, not really. He takes selected passages and twists them all out of context. And the feeling I got was that—I don't know—like I was being hypnotized, mesmerized. Scented candles, soft East Indian-type music in the background; the whole hippie bit, right

70

out of the sixties. I got up and walked out. Never went back.''

She refilled their coffee cups and as she leaned forward, Mike caught the scent of her perfume. He didn't know what brand it was, but whatever it was, it was perfect for her: light and delicate, yet sexy and arousing. It touched him intimately.

"As to why he built the facility, for the good of the community, of course. If your kids are giving you trouble, just take them to the Glennwood Institute for Troubled Children. I guarantee you, within three to four weeks your 'troubled child' will be getting straight A's in school; they'll have good manners, the best of behavior, and they will be attending church every Friday and Saturday night.''

"Not on Sunday?''

"No. Never. Director Egan graciously left that day open for the other religions.''

"Hold that thought, too, Rana. Look, what kind of shit is this? I mean, I'm not putting down the Jewish Sabbath, but how many Jews do we have in this parish?''

"None around here. This church hasn't anything to do with the Jewish faith, Mike. And no, before you ask, I have not even entertained the thought of putting Lisa in Becker's Institute for Troubled Children. You should see the kids that come out of that place. They're like—machines! If one did not know them before they went in, why, the results would be astonishing. Well-mannered, well-behaved, neatly groomed, bright-eyed and intelligent. But, if you knew them before, there is a subtle change in them. Not as bad as the old people—''

"Old people, Rana? What old people?''

She looked at him, her eyes serious. "I keep forgetting you've only been back a few hours. All right. If they let us, we'll drive out there tomorrow. I'll show

71

you what I mean about the elderly. They're zombies.''

"If they let us, Rana?''

"Becker's people. You're in, Mike. You probably won't be allowed out.''

He laughed at her because he didn't think she was serious. "I'd like to see the hoss who'll try that.''

"You think it's a joke, Mike. It isn't, believe me.''

"All right, Rana; let's drop this for a time, get back to what you said a moment ago.'' He was really seriously beginning to question her sanity. "What about the kids and the old people? Are you suggesting some sort of mind control?''

"You think I'm nuts, don't you, Mike. That's all right. I don't mind; I'm used to it—in a way. Yes, to your question. I did some reading up on that, before the library was closed and Becker built the town a new. one, stocked with selected reading, of course.''

He studied her closely. He said, "You're really serious, aren't you?''

"As serious as I have ever been in my life.''

"I'm beginning not to like what you're telling me, Rana.''

"Good. That's one of the reasons I asked you out this evening.''

"And the other reason . . . ?''

She kissed him.

The music playing held a hynotic melody, an East Indian trance-producing sameness that soothed and calmed and quieted the nerves. As the music played, the Most Reverent Egan, dressed in a robe of dark velvet, spoke.

"Members of his fold, worshipers of his way, believers in the only True Way—hear me. Let my words by him be your words, my thoughts from him be your thoughts, my actions by him be your actions. And let us worship the Third Master in his name."

Someone began humming.

Egan said, "Let me hear all your thoughts rise to life as we worship him."

The humming became louder as others joined in. A satanic sound.

"Excellent, my children. I know he is pleased."

The humming grew more intense.

"Can you feel the power of him penetrating your inner beings?"

The humming changed into a word: "Yes!"

The music became a few decibels louder.

Scented candles were lit, their fragrance wafting through the huge room, filled to capacity. The odor of jasmine, lightly scented with sulfur, entered the nostrils of those in attendance. A thousand eyes were closed; five hundred throats hummed out in unison, all seeking the same goal: evil Karma with the Master.

"Tell me who is your only true Master!" Egan shouted, sensing the moment was at its zenith.

And they told him. Profanely.

The suddenness of her kiss stunned him into immobility for a few seconds. But only for a few seconds. His hands found the slender waist and the flaring hips and pulled her to him.

He had been wrong in his assumption that it would be he who would have to initiate any further moves.

"Rana—"

She shushed him with what the kids called a soul kiss. Back in Mike's petting days it had been referred to as French.

Vive la France!

Rana's tongue was a passion-driven wet, hot organ

73

that touched his mouth, leaving a searing yet painless burn as it contacted his lips and sought entrance past.

"Lisa—" Mike managed to say, lips on hers.

"If she did come in—which she won't—she'd probably ask you for some."

Mike pulled back, shocked. "That's a terrible thing to say about your daughter!"

"But true. Want to see the vibrator and King Dong dildo she thinks she keeps hidden from me?"

"Not particularly."

"Good. Then shut up and make love to me."

Mike could not imagine his own daughter shoving a rubber cock up in her. He hoped she didn't, at least.

She rose from the couch and Mike leaned forward, kissing her denim-covered crotch.

"God!" she whispered.

Very light thunder rolled faintly across the sky.

Putting his big hands on her buttocks, Mike pulled her to him and pressed his face against her lower belly, feeling the heat of her through the fabric of the jeans.

She worked her hips, her hands behind his head. She shivered. "I just came, Mike!"

"Let's see if we can't set some records," was his reply.

The previous evening he had tossed restlessly and alone in the bed at the motel in Baton Rouge. Now he had in his hands, and his face, probably the most beautiful and desirable woman in Chatom Parish.

The gods work strangely, he thought.

At his thought of gods, thunder rolled across the heavens, shaking the windows of the house.

"I thought it was clear out?" Rana said.

"It was when I came in."

And they thought no more of it.

* * *

74

But miles away, in the Blake mansion, Becker heard the rumblings. And he thought long and hard and deep about the source.

Come! the message was flung into his brain.

Becker rose from his desk in the study and walked to the steps that would take him to the basement.

The scent of her filled the bedroom as she undressed. She did so before his eyes as he sat on the bed, too enthralled at the sight of her to further undress himself. He sat holding one shoe in his right hand, watching her beauty unfold before him.

Her breasts were mounds of tanned ivory, tipped with erect, taut nipples set in half-dollar-sized circles of dark reddish brown. Her skin, as she peeled off her jeans, was without blemish. She was evenly tanned over her entire body, and Mike realized when she sunbathed, it was in the nude.

She turned, facing him, and his eyes were fixed on the honey-colored pubic hair. The dim light in the room glistened wetly off the light moisture that beaded the opening of love.

"Mike? Aren't you going to get undressed?"

"Huh?" not the most intelligent of replies, he thought. "Sure!"

She laughed at him, then knelt down and unbuckled his trousers, pulling them from his muscular legs. Next came his shorts. His maleness sprang free, hard and swollen.

She grasped the hot muscle, working the foreskin back. Then she lowered her head and nibbled and nipped gently with mouth and tongue.

Mike thought the top of his head would fly off.

When the sweetness of her mouth took him, the sensation in his mind was of crystal shattering.

They were on the big bed and his shirt was gone. He could not remember taking it off or what he did with it.

He didn't care.

His mouth found a nipple in the instinctive mother-seeking way of man, and she lifted a heavy breast to his lips, suckling him, moaning as his tongue and lips tightened and swelled the nub of life.

His hand found her downy wetness and a finger sought entrance. The folds parted and the finger plunged into satin darkness, his thumb working at and enflaming the clitoris.

"I—can't—wait!" she said, and mounted him, guiding him into her, crying out as his long bulk filled her.

With her hands on each side of his waist, she worked up and down on him. Tears rolled down her face, streaking the beauty as a climax gripped her and shook her in a firm but gentle hand. She bit short a howl of pleasure and then decided to hell with it.

She screamed as one climax followed another. The juices flowed from her, wetting Mike's belly as he gripped her buttocks with his big hands, holding on for the duration. He felt as though he was trapped in a willing snare of wet heat as she plunged downward, taking all he offered her.

Rana shook as the sweat rolled from her body. Her breasts bounced as she rode him like a jockey, her eyes closed in an ecstasy of sex she had forgotten existed; indeed, if she had ever known it like this.

Mike could hold back his own boiling juices no longer. She sensed it, leaning forward with his maleness inside her, flattening her breasts against his chest, enjoying both the pleasure and the slight pain this position offered her. She fitted her mouth to his just as he erupted in a hot burst, his semen filling her, spilling out on bare skin and damp, rumpled sheets.

She sighed as he softened.

Mike felt that to ask her if she enjoyed their bed session would be more than a trifle superfluous.

She slipped from her jockey position to stand by the side of the bed. ''God!'' she said. ''You must think I'm awful!''

''No,'' he grinned up at her. ''I just think you like to fuck, that's all.''

Thunder once more rattled the windows in the house.

''I guess we're going to have one of those early summer storms,'' Rana said.

But had either of them elected to look outside, they would have found the sky filled with stars, not a cloud to be seen.

And no lightning with the thunder.

FIVE

Mike awoke with that feeling of slight panic when one awakens in a strange bed.

Then he felt her satin warmth lying close to him, and he felt a peace that he had not experienced in years. Not even with his ex-wife. He looked at his wristwatch—three o'clock. He gently pulled her to him and she murmured softly in protest.

"Rana?" he whispered. "I gotta go, babe. It's three o'clock in the morning."

"Whatchit?"

"Wake up," he shook her, attempting to dislodge her from the sex-induced almost trancelike sleep.

She stretched and the sheet slipped down, exposing her breasts. He kissed one nipple. That helped wake her.

"Mike, God! You're insatiable."

"Honey, I couldn't get an erection if you threatened me with death. I'm an old man, remember?"

"For an old man, dear, you sure know how to please a young woman."

They had made love twice more before finally falling

asleep in exhaustion, dozing and resting between sessions. The last time had been the best: a slow, measured lovemaking. And they had climbed the ladder to climax together, finally collapsing on the stained sheets to sleep as if in a stupor.

Mike sniffed and wrinkled his nose. "I smell like a whorehouse," he said bluntly.

"Oh?" she looked at him in the dim light of the hall nightlight. "Well, having never been in a whorehouse," she said primly, "I wouldn't have the foggiest notion what you're talking about. Why did you wake me up?"

"It's three o'clock in the morning, Rana. I have to go."

"Why? If it's that late, she isn't coming home."

"Rana," he lay back, his head on the pillow, "I don't understand any of this."

"Well," she grinned impishly, grasping his soft penis, "Daddy gets this all hard, and Mommy—"

He kissed her to shut her up.

She said, her mouth to his, "She's staying out at the church, that's all."

"And doing what, for God's sake?"

"She isn't doing it for God's sake, Mike," Rana said. "And she's probably screwing someone."

"Good Lord, Rana! How can you be so nonchalant about it?"

"I've accepted it, Mike. Look, what would you have me do? Just listen for a minute; you really don't know what you've gotten into here."

He grinned lewdly.

"I'm serious, now! Come on, let's get some clothes on and have some coffee. Just lying here next to you is turning me on."

"I think whoever turned you on, Rana, forgot to turn you off."

"Notice, please, how I'm convulsing with hysterical laughter."

"Maybe you'd better go borrow that vibrator and dildo you told me about?"

"Don't think the thought hasn't occurred to me, baby."

"You are a horny bitch, aren't you?"

She jabbed him in the ribs and rolled away before he could retaliate. "You know, Mike, you're right about one thing."

"Oh?"

"You do smell like a whorehouse."

They had showered, separately, her idea, and now sat in the den, sipping coffee. It was fast approaching four o'clock in the morning.

"I used to dream about this." She admitted her secret thoughts to him. "No—I suppose fantasize was more like it."

"About drinking coffee?" he smiled.

"Big ox! No. About being with you, watching the sun come up with your arms around me."

"Well, it'll be up in about two hours, and if you like, I'll sure have my arms around you."

"I like. But it was in some far distant country, not here in Chatom Parish."

"Then I suppose I'll have to take you to some far distant country, then."

"You've been everywhere, and I've never been anywhere," she said, a wistful note in her voice.

"Some would say, many, probably, that you're the lucky one of the two."

"You asked, Mike, so I'll level with you. About Lisa." She abruptly shifted subjects. "Let me tell you the way it is. Have you ever dreamt you were on a deserted island, and the island was completely surrounded by huge sharks? Well, that's the situation here."

"Rana." He touched her hand.

"No!" She jerked her hand away. "Twice Egan has been to see me about putting Lisa in that horrible institute. The last time I drove him off at the point of a .38. I did! And if he comes back, Mike—I'll shoot him. I mean it. She's one of the few kids in this area that hasn't been put in that place, so she's still got some human in her."

"Human?"

"Okay, wrong word. They haven't completely taken control of her mind. But they've got a good part of it, Mike. But if I put her into that institute, she's theirs. Believe it."

"Rana—you make this sound so ominous."

"Baby, it is ominous. Let me lay it all out for you. Listen to what I have to say, then make up your mind. You were in Military Intelligence for a time; so you put it all together for me. But now, bear this in mind. I'm pretty much alone in many of my views.

"The Butler Motel? It's closed. Shut down about seven years ago. And it was doing fairly well for a town of this size. Had a nice restaurant and lounge. They went too. Then the Butler Theatre was shut down. No warning. One day it was open, the next day it was closed. Several plants were supposed to come in here. Things were even past the planning stage, the land was bought and being cleared. It all abruptly fell apart. We had a nice little small town newspaper here—you remember it. That's gone. All the advertisers—the big ones that kept it going?—pulled out. Then after a time, only Jack Geraci's drugstore, Louis Weaver's feed and seed store, and two or three others, remained. The paper had to shut the door. With me so far? Okay.

"Becker, and I have never seen the man, set up his own phone company. He or his henchmen run the schools. Yes! He built a new school, all private, absolutely *no government* interference at all. And it's for both blacks and whites. We have no racial problems in this part of Chatom Parish. None! Brothers and sisters, baby—all the way. He built a fine apartment complex for the elderly several miles out of town—out of the way. They get the best of care, Mike. Don't want for a thing. And the poor old people don't even know they're in this world. They're zombies. Period. The doctors at the hospital? All first rate. That's the best-equipped hospital in the state. Now I haven't seen it, but that's what people who have seen it tell me. And that includes Doctor Luden. There is more, but with that knowledge, Mike, what would you say about Butler?''

Mike thought for a moment. He sipped his coffee. ''Well, at first glance, I would say that somebody, probably this Becker person, got rid of everybody he didn't want, and then made things so attractive for those who were left, they couldn't find anything better no matter where they went. That's at first glance, now.''

''That's what I think too. Well—we, but mostly me. I'll get to the 'we' part in a minute. Tell me, what did Stinky Ford have to say to you this—yesterday, I mean?''

''Well, let's see. He told me the night spots were gone. No horn-honking allowed; cost five dollars if caught. Couldn't imagine why I would want to come back to—in his words, 'hicksville Butler, Louisiana to live.' And he mentioned something about this Mr. Becker. Oh, yeah.'' Mike grinned. ''He also said that I shouldn't wear out our little Rana—words to that effect. Said he'd lick your ass just to get to see the little puckered hole.''

She glared at him, fire blazing in her eyes. ''That no-good, cocksucking son of a bitch!''

''You can become quite eloquent at times, dear.''

"Fuck Stinky Ford!"

"Maybe he swings both ways, Rana?"

"He damn sure won't swing on my tree, boy!"

"I think we'd better get off the subject of Stinky."

She took a deep breath, calming herself. "Did you drive by any churches today, Mike?"

He shook his head "Well, to tell the truth, I wasn't really noticing, Rana. Why?"

"They've changed, too, Mike. None of the old ministers are left. They were dismissed years ago. All new people fill the pulpits."

"Again, let me guess: they were brought in by this Becker?"

"That's my theory. True or not, they are all close friends with Ron Egan."

"Our church, Rana?"

"We're down to less than thirty members, Mike; that's counting the kids, and most of them are regulars at Egan's church."

"The kids?"

"Yes. Father Grillet believes me, but he doesn't know what to do."

"Grillet is your—our priest?"

"Yes. Real nice fellow."

Mike's emotions had run the gamut this evening. At first he had thought Rana a person with an overactive imagination. Now he had swung full-circle. He believed something was drastically wrong in Butler.

But what?

Mike was silent for a moment, then told her of Lennie following him out into the country and of the strange phone call he had received. He said nothing of Bonnie.

She sighed and slowly nodded her head. "They didn't waste any time getting to you. The bastards!"

Mike looked at her. She was serious, deep in

84

thought. "Who didn't waste any time, Rana?"

"Them!"

"Them? Rana, what are you talking about? Them?"

"You're not going to believe this, Mike. But I've got to say it, get it out in the open. Everything points to John Becker. Everything evil that's happened."

"Evil? Rana, just who, or what, do you think this Becker represents?"

"Mike—I think he's the devil."

The girl swung slowly from the rope, her toes just an inch off the polished floor. She had long ago ceased trying to relieve the pain by touching the floor. Her arms were swollen from the weight of her body. She was sixteen. She was crying. She was frightened. She was naked.

One single bulb hung over the girl, its light creating a small pocket of illumination in the otherwise dark room. A man stepped out of the darkness. He was naked. He held a short whip in his hand.

"You've been a very bad girl, Ava," the man said. "You know that, don't you?"

"Yes," she whimpered.

"Why have you been bad, Ava?" He ran the leather of the whip over her nakedness, allowing the tip to brush her nipples.

"I don't know," she cried.

"Haven't we taken good care of you, Ava? In all the years you've been with us?"

"I—don't think so." She found the courage to speak her mind.

That reply got her a vicious slash from the whip.

She screamed as the mark reddened on her buttocks. A thin trickle of blood oozed from the cut. She swung slowly at the end of her rope. Tears rolled down her

85

cheeks.

The man said, "We took you when you were merely a child. We schooled you, cared for you, taught you the way of the only True Master, and this is how you repay us?"

"I was only reading the Bible!" the teenager wailed.

"Only reading the Bible," the man mimicked her, a sneer in his voice. "Girl, the Bible is forbidden reading, you know that. Don't lie!"

"Why is it forbidden?" she cried, now only a short distance from becoming hysterical.

The man shook his head. "I was afraid of this. You have to be punished. You have to be taught the way of the Master." He hefted his thick cock. "No," he mused, "that would pleasure you. We can't have that."

He smiled as he reversed the whip handle. He walked closer to her and began forcing the leather-covered handle of the whip into the girl's anus.

Her screaming was hideous.

The audience, cloaked in darkness, laughed and clapped their hands at the action.

"More!" a woman's husky voice called. "Shove it all the way in."

"No," the man said. "That might cause permanent damage. We don't want her dead. Just punished."

He cruelly twisted the girl's nipples. "How would you like me to take a hot pin and pierce your nipples, Ava. I could put some nice earrings in them. Would you like that, dear?"

Ava could but scream her fear and pain.

"But I won't do that," the man said. "This time," he added. "We'll leave you alone for a while. When we feel you have repented, we'll be back and tend to your slight—indignity. Then we'll take you to the institute and make certain you never again transgress."

She screamed her protest at this. She had resisted that place because she knew what would happen to her there. She wanted God and silently prayed to Him.

The naked man laughed and jiggled the handle of the whip.

Ava screamed hoarsely as pain lanced through her slender body. The crowd of men and women, all naked or clad in the barest of clothing, laughed at the girl's wailings.

"Hurry up, Al," a woman urged. "This has got me all sexed up. Let's go to the barracks and fuck. I want you to fuck my ass."

Al goosed her in the anus with a blunt finger. Her coarse laughter was filled with evil.

The room emptied of people. It grew silent as the door closed. The only sound was the weeping of the young girl as she hung from the rope. The rope bit into her wrists. And as she cried and moaned and swayed, the rope bumped the light, causing it to cast weird shadows against the wall of the dimly-lit room which was at one end of the main building of the Church of Friendship, Fellowship, and Faith.

With the whip handle jammed into her anus, the short leather whip dangling down like the tail of some monstrous creature, the silhouette, swaying with the movement of the light, resembled a deformed caricature of Satan.

"This man, this Colonel Michael Folsom." The voice was deep and hard and demanding in tone. "Where did he come from? Why is he here? And why did you not know of his coming and tell me?"

"I knew nothing of it. Neither did Wallace. He was shocked to see him. He thought Folsom would sell the house by long distance and not bother coming here at all. The man has no people left in the parish. Wallace came to me as soon as Folsom left his office."

"You spoke with him?"

"Yes, Mr. Becker. Says he came back to his roots. His words. Came back here to stay, to live."

"He is with the Drew woman this night." It was not a question. "And she is trouble. She should have been taken care of long ago. All right. This Folsom, is he a likely candidate for our Master?"

"I—don't believe so, sir. I would have to say no."

"Then he cannot be allowed to remain. We can't have it. *He* would not like any interference, not this close to triumph. It is only a matter of days now. Two weeks at the most. Victory has eluded us for so long. This time, we must not fail."

"We won't fail, sir. I give you my word."

"*Your word?* Bah! Your word is a fart in the wind. It does not fill me with confidence. We must be very careful in dealing with Colonel Folsom. We must not alarm him so greatly that he calls for help; and he is a man who would have many friends—some in high governmental office. He is not an unknown. He is a genuine hero in the eyes of many. I will speak to the Third Master of this. Then I will think about it. We will have our little corner of the world, Ford. Right here in this miserable parish. The third set of young are soon to be birthed. All the others are here or arriving soon. From this place," he thumped the polished desk top, "we will send out our disciples. *We will not fail!* That is all. You may take your leave."

Ford nodded and left the room, walking swiftly out of the house. He was glad to be dismissed. Glad to be leaving the house, to get away from the aroma of burning incense that never really covered the smell of death, of rotting flesh. Of stinking blood. Of evil.

Not that Chief Ford minded the evil part of it. He

didn't. He enjoyed the favors of the young boys with the sweet cocks and the tight assholes. He could have all he wanted of them, and pretty young girls, as well. The younger the better. And he enjoyed the feeling of power the Evil Old One had bestowed upon him. Well—not exactly the Evil One himself—itself; Ford had only met the creature once. He hoped he would never have to meet him again. The agent for the Third Master of Evil was close enough—too close, at times. Once, just once, Becker had put his hand on Ford's arm. It had not hurt, but it had left a mark for days. Stinky shuddered when he thought of that touch. It was—was—he didn't know how to describe it. He just wanted it never to happen again.

But it seemed like the only thing the Evil Old One had on his mind these days was women. Forget finding a virgin—not in this day and time. And of late he had been forced to bring the Old One younger and younger girls. And Lennie kept wanting to taste their cunts.

The two-timing bitch! And after all Chief Ford had done for him, too.

Stinky had just about given up hope for Lennie. He was going to have to take Lennie to the Old One some day—soon. Becker had told him so. Just one more time; if Lennie stuck his cock into just one more little girl's cunt—a girl chosen for the Old One— Lennie might very well end up on the Old One's dinner table.

Stinky giggled. He was amused at that thought. He didn't think Lennie would like that very much at all.

Rana noticed his slight smile and stiffened beside him, thinking the smile a silent mockery of all she had told him.

When she spoke, it was testily. "Why are you

smiling, Mike?''

"It's not at you or at anything you've said."

She relaxed, putting a soft hand on his thigh.

He said, "I was thinking. Even after all you've told me, and yes, I do believe something is out of kilter in this part of the parish—but I was thinking how good it is to be back. To be here, with you, specifically."

"Flatterer."

"I mean it." He smiled. "Back in Nam, I'd have to say you have great sleeve, baby."

"Mike, God! That's crude. Sleeve!"

He laughed at her and she stuck out her tongue at him. "Rana, you mentioned two things that intrigue me: We and Them. Care to elaborate?"

"Well—the We I was referring to are members of the church. The same church you are still a member of, I might add."

"How do you know that?"

"I looked on the church rolls," she smiled sweetly.

"Please continue."

She laughed at his expression. "Most of them were not Episcopalian originally; they joined after they grew dissatisfied with the changes occurring within their home church. But I'm the only one who believes the devil is behind all that's been happening. The rest believe it's some sort of sex cult."

"Rana—you really believe this is Satan's work?"

"With every fiber in me, Mike. Yes!"

"All right," he said noncommittally. "What are the ages of those in your group?"

"Oh, from about thirty-five to forty-five. Most are your age, I guess."

"Old dudes," he smiled.

"Sure," she said dryly. "Anyway, there's Jack Geraci. You remember his wife, Ann. Louis Weaver; he married Barbie Jenkings. Burke Rider from the bank; he married Vera. You knew her. Sam Marshall. I don't believe you knew the gal he married: Paula Bartlett. She's very nice. David Babin; he and Dee Dee finally got together. Edward Coder and Marge; they're my age. Then there is Father Daniel Grillet. He's married to a real nice lady, Nickie. I'll introduce you to them.''

"The kids of this group?"

"Like I said, most of them are regulars at Egan's crappy church.''

"I still don't understand how it happened so easily. Losing control of your children. I—just can't envision it, Rana. I'm sorry, but I can't.''

"Oh, it didn't happen suddenly, Mike. No, not at all. The first stage of Becker's plan, his people, came in here with him. They were—oh, about twenty years old, I guess. They talked quietly with the kids—our kids. You know how kids are; they formed little harmless clubs and secrets among themselves. But the young people with Becker always came to the parents and told us the secrets. So we believed. We had some good laughs. Turned out the laugh was on us, though.

"It was just—at first—a subtle working on the mind, a little each day, each week, each month. Little presents, little inexpensive toys and gifts that no parent could object to their kids having, especially after the parents met with and talked with the young people. They were all, boys and girls, such *nice* young people; so caring and helpful and sincere, and so—so all-American types. Wholesome. We all just simply fell in love with them.

"Mike, they would baby-sit for us and feel hurt if we offered them money. They would do *anything* to help! We just loved them all. That's how it happened. Over a period of years. Like a slow cancer."

"And then when you—those of you who are free of

91

this Becker's control, as you call it—confronted your kids with your suspicions?"

"Last year, Mike. Last winter. Oh, Becker's people were smooth with it, baby. They had years to work on the kids and the adults. Smooth as silk and honey.

"When I confronted Lisa, she laughed at me. Asked me what I intended doing about it. Said there wasn't a thing wrong with sex. It felt good. I said I'd go to the authorities and try to have some investigators brought in. She said I'd better not do that; she wouldn't want to see my face get all kicked in. I slapped her."

"It didn't faze her, Mike. She just stood there looking at me, the blood from a cut lip running down her chin. She said, 'Go ahead, Mother. Do what you think you can. It won't make a bit of difference.'"

"And?" Mike pressed her.

"Well—this is not really getting off the subject—you noticed the roads in this part of the parish, Mike?"

"Yes. Damn few of them."

"Becker's doings—with the full permission of the people in this community. Bridges condemned, so forth. He's pretty slick, Mike. For a fact, he's got us boxed in."

"Back to Lisa."

Rana shrugged. "Nothing much happened. I called our state senator and representative, and they came over at my request. I've known them both for years. They even brought with them an investigator from the Attorney General's office. They talked with me for a long time, then went out and saw Becker."

Her laughter was bitter-sounding. "Of course, you know—or maybe you don't—that Becker is worth hundreds of millions of dollars. I'm not saying that money bought those men off; it didn't. It just helped pave the way for a smooth ride for Becker and Egan.

"Boy, you talk about getting my name all smeared

with dirt. They came back and told me Becker was the finest man they'd ever met, and so was Reverend Egan. Look what Becker had done for this part of the parish: a school, a hospital, a library, phones, recreation facilities for the kids, an institute for troubled kids. And what in the hell was the matter with me? Trying to smear the names of those good men?

"Then they talked to the people—give them credit for a fair job—at random. But, Mike, ninety-nine percent of the population goes to Becker's Church. That was the easy part. All of them were full of praise, of course. They went back to the Church of Friendship, Fellowship, and Faith. Egan charmed them. Told them he had been worried about me for some time. He was afraid I was suffering from some sort of mental disorder. Boy, did he stiff me."

"Why didn't you tell them to talk to Jack or Burke or some of the others you mentioned?"

"Oh, I did, Mike. But by this time I had lost so much credibility. Well," she sighed, "to give the men credit, they did try to talk with those on my side. The gods of fate, Mike. Burke was out of town at a banker's convention. Jack was up in Shreveport, visiting his mother at the hospital; she was dying of cancer. Jack wouldn't even consider putting her in the hospital here. It seemed to me that everywhere I turned, the gods of fate were lined up against me. It was almost as if . . ." She let it tail off into a heavy sort of silence.

"As if what, Rana?"

She shook her head. "You'd only think me a bigger fool than you already do."

"I *don't* think you a fool, honey. Finish what you were going to say."

"That is—that it—the devil was one step ahead of me all the way!" She finally managed to blurt out the words.

Mike thought about that for a moment. He slowly nodded his head. "I don't know about the devil, Rana. But somebody was damn sure one step ahead of you."

"Or some *thing!*" she added.

SIX

"Then you're beginning to believe me?" She curled up close to him.

"Yes," he said. "Yes, I am—to some degree."

"Even one degree would be a start."

"Oh, it's more than that. I don't know that the devil is behind it, but it's definitely some sort of mind control. I'd bet on it." He reached for the phone on the coffee table, then drew back his hand. "Before I call—"

"Don't call from this phone or any other phone in the Becker System," she warned.

He glanced at her, his eyes narrowing. "The phones are not secure?"

"If by that you mean are they bugged? Yes. They know a lot about the goings-on of those not yet in Egan's Church; some of it would have to come from private phone conversations. One time Ann and I set up this phony meeting between us, talked a lot about meeting with this fictitious private investigator from New Orleans—all make believe stuff—just to see if our phones were tapped. We didn't mention his name. Just that he was a private investigator. Our phones were tapped, all right. We both were followed everywhere we went; that went on for days. Finally, just to stop the snooping and following, we talked on the phone about how angry we were that the guy didn't keep his appointment and maybe we were wrong about Becker; better drop the whole thing. We weren't followed after that. That tell you what you want to know, Mike?''

"Sure does." Mike drained his coffee cup. "And it tells me I don't like what's going on around here worth a good goddamn!''

She patted his muscular arm. She could feel the power in him, the rage suppressed. His arm was as hard as stone. "Settle down, old warrior," she smiled. "I feel better with you just being here. So don't go off half-cocked."

He calmed himself, returned the smile. "I couldn't even quarter-cock it, now."

"Sex fiend," she laughed, and poured them more coffee.

"How about the mail service? Surely he hasn't infiltrated that?"

Her glance told him he was wrong.

"None of us figured out until early this year that our mail was being opened and checked at the post office. All the people there are members of Becker's church. The other side, if you will."

He could only look at her, not wanting to believe it, but knowing it was all probably true.

"Oh, I haven't even begun, Mike. Believe me."

He sighed. "There's more?"

Her chuckle was grim. "Ron Egan? The so-called 'pastor' of Becker's church? Well, before Jimmy Grayson was killed—"

"Jimmy's dead! God, I went to school with Jimmy."

"Yes, I know. Without a home-town paper being

published, you wouldn't have known about his death, would you? He very mysteriously lost control of his car one night and flipped over, out at Verrin Curve. You remember that curve; the 'chickie-run curve' some of the kids used to call it. Chief Ford, who is also a deputy sheriff in this parish, as are all his deputies—gives them jurisdiction outside the city limits—said Jimmy was drinking, that the blood test showed a high alcohol content. He was raging drunk.

"Well, Mike, you know that's a bunch of crap; even when Jimmy was a kid, he didn't drink like most kids. He was raised in a home where both parents were alcoholics; turned him against it. Anyway, Jimmy was the one who first became suspicious about Becker and Egan. He did some checking on Ron Egan's credentials. And there is this. Jimmy came into a lot of money and land and oil leases from his parents—"

"When did they die?"

"About nine or ten years ago. Right after Becker came to town and bought the old Blake mansion. Yes, Mike, it gets curiouser and curiouser."

He recalled using those same words only hours before.

"You see, Mike, people are signing over to Egan, or Becker, same thing, all their worldly possessions—to the church. In return, he pays them a good salary, takes care of their needs, medical, personal, educational, so forth. And there is no law against that that any of us could find. The church—Becker—*owns* Butler, Louisiana. But he's smart." She held up a finger, a cautionary gesture. "He contributes most generously to the right causes, the right politicians; he is a known philanthropist—worldwide. Not a black mark against him. Nothing but good."

"I saw a lot of boarded-up houses and businesses in town, and a number of farms that appeared deserted on the way out here. How did he manage that? What happened to the people?"

"Mike, Becker owns retirement villages all over the country, especially in Florida and Arizona and California. It was easy for him. He just bought them out at twice what the land or business was worth, sold them a house or condominium in one of his senior citizen villages—which will revert back to Becker upon their death—and they gladly sold out to him and moved out. Mike, he even paid their moving expenses!"

"Slick," he muttered. "Smooth as honey and cream." He patted her leg where the robe had fallen open, and the touch of her soft skin aroused him. He slipped his hand upward, the robe parting in the path of his fingers.

"Don't start something you can't finish," she warned him. "It's been a long time for me, and you hit it on the head when you said I was horny. Believe me, baby, I am one horny lady."

He heeded the advice and removed his hand. "You're right. I'll have to remember I'm a middle-aged man and you're too much woman for me to handle."

"Crap!" she said, quite unladylike.

"I'll ignore that. Okay, let me put the rest of this— horrible story together, Rana."

She leaned back on the couch, smiling at him. The robe remained open. Mike had to force the thought from his mind that she was wearing nothing under it.

As if she had the power to read his thoughts, she laughed at him.

"Bitch!" Mike grinned.

"But good when I'm bad, right?"

"No comment. All right, Rana, all of Jimmy Grayson's wealth went to the church?"

"In a manner of speaking, yes. But Mike, unlike some other—cults, legitimate religious organizations,

Becker's books are open for public inspection. He really does take a great deal of the money people give the church and funnel it into worthwhile programs, charities, feeding the hungry, and so forth. He is a mystery man, never seen in public, but nevertheless, a well-thought-of man.''

"How did the monies get to the church, to Egan and Becker?"

"Egan produced papers showing that Jimmy had joined the church several months before his death. It was all legal and notarized, with the proper signatures—including Jimmy's. He was a bachelor, had no other heirs. Everything was very legal and above board."

"His attorney? No! Let me guess—young Mr. Wallace, right?"

"Right on the money, honey."

"But you're still holding out on me?"

"Correct—to a degree. Not that much left to tell."

"It deals with those who refused to sell—at first?"

"Right. But that gets into a real gray area, Mike. People who owned businesses—those who wouldn't sell out to Becker, or Becker's people, I should say. He was *never* personally involved in any of this—suddenly found out that what they had to offer to the public was very unpopular. One man fell from a ladder; broke his neck. Two died from very sudden illnesses. Becker was so heartbroken, so overcome with philanthropic goodwill, he paid all the medical expenses and saw to it the widows got moved out of here at no expense to the ladies, straight to one of his retirement villages. One man's place burned down; faulty wiring. Becker did the same for him; that man has nothing but true love and goodwill towards Becker. All very smooth, but very nasty when you think about the lengths to which this church will go to attain their goals.''

Mike rose from the couch, a quick movement, cat-like, to pace the den. Rana watched him, sensing the power and brute strength within the man. He walked like a great caged cat. For a reason she could not explain, she sensed the ability to kill was very strong in him, but always under control until needed.

"My parents, Rana?" his voice was odd-sounding, choked with emotions he had never released.

"We believe, now, their accident was rigged. That's something we all agree on. Your father told Becker's people to kiss his ass and get out of his store."

Mike had to smile. That would be right in keeping with his dad. "Did you go to the authorities?"

"No. Not at first. By the time we all got together and began comparing notes, feelings, suspicions, they'd been dead for years. Besides, this is Judge Bret Morris' parish."

"Moonshine Morris? That son of a bitch is a *judge?*"

"You've been gone a quarter of a century, Mike," she reminded him.

"That makes me feel very old. All right, this Morris is a member in good standing of the—church, for want of a better word?"

"One of the first converts. He is a perverted old man. Likes little girls and little boys."

"He always did, Rana; you're just too young to remember."

She shrugged and softened that with a smile. The movement lifted her breasts, the nipples outlined under the thin robe.

"Everything seems to be all neatly tied up in a box, doesn't it?"

"It's what's in the box that stinks, Mike. And it really does smell."

"I agree. The state police did investigate the accident?"

100

"Trooper Duval did."

Mike sighed. "And Trooper Duval just happens to be a resident of Butler and a member of Becker's church?"

"You're putting it all together very well, love."

"Goddammit! This—situation is almost too smooth; perfectly put together. But there has to be a flaw somewhere. I don't mean to offend you, Rana, but I don't buy your theory about the devil. I think money is behind it all."

"The man is worth millions, Mike! Hundreds and hundreds of millions of dollars. That line of reasoning doesn't make any more sense to me than my theory does to you."

"All right, before we get into an argument, let's move on to something else. No. Let's get back to Jimmy Grayson. You said he investigated this Egan fellow. So what did he find; what was uncovered?"

"Jimmy didn't do it personally, Mike. He hired a private cop—investigator—to do that. What the investigator found, before he was mysteriously killed—he was killed in a small plane accident; wasn't very nice—was that Egan really is a minister, with all the degrees that go with it, Ph.D type for a fact. But his ministry is marred with—well, ugliness. At first it was just women; then it was boys—he's a pretty slimy character, Mike. He was defrocked, or whatever you call it, and then made a one hundred and eighty degree turn and became obsessed with the devil. Formed a church out in California that worshiped the devil, right down to live sacrifices—human, a few people told our private cop— but he couldn't dig up any proof of that. He could find proof of Black Masses, but no one was willing to go on record about the purported sex acts that went with the mass. Torture, the whole bit. Former members would admit that it did take place, but refused to come for-

101

ward, go public with it.

"Well—we thought maybe we had enough proof, enough evidence to do—hell, Mike!—to do *something!* But no, we didn't. It seems that Egan renounced all that before coming to Louisiana. Openly talks about his past; told the people I called in all about it. Said it made him a better minister of the Lord to have participated in all that evil. Another dead end for us."

Mike rubbed his temples; his head was beginning to ache. "All this is mind-boggling, Rana. Too much in too short a time. It's giving me a hell of a headache."

She rose from the couch, getting him two aspirin and a glass of water. He thanked her and said, "Look, on a somewhat less macabre note—" He paused, wondering how to phrase it, not wanting to break his word to the lady. "Have you seen Bonnie lately?"

Rana sat straight up on the couch, her back stiff. "Bonnie?"

"Yeah. Bonnie Roberts. I don't know her married name."

"Mike, that is not in the least bit funny."

"Funny? It wasn't meant to be funny, Rana. I was just curious, that's all. She cleaned up the house for me—must have worked for days doing it. The place is spotless. All the drapes and curtains were washed and ironed. Clean sheets on the bed; the whole nine yards."

"No—no!" Rana shook her head violently, blonde hair flying about her face, which had suddenly turned deathly pale. "You must be mistaken."

She rose from the couch, walking to him in a peculiarly stiff, robotlike manner.

"Honey," Mike took her hand. It was cold. "I spoke with Bonnie this—I mean, yesterday morning. In my kitchen. We talked for maybe a couple of minutes. Sounded like she had one hell of a cold. Bad one. For sure, she had a great tan. What's the matter with

102

you, Rana?"

"Oh, my God! My God, my God, my God!"

"Hey, Rana! Easy, honey." He took her in his arms and she fought him, struggling to break free of his grasp.

She pushed him back and freed herself. Her eyes were wide and wild.

"Hey!" Mike shouted. "What in the hell is wrong with you?"

She screamed at him. "She was the very first to go, Mike! Bonnie refused to sell to Becker's people. She and her husband owned Cedars Motor Company, a Dodge/Plymouth dealership. It's closed now; been closed for ten years. She had just lost her husband in a car accident, and maybe Bonnie was the first to put it all together—what was really happening. I don't know!" Rana shook her head. "You talked to *Bonnie?*"

"Yes, baby," Mike replied, something cold and slimy crawling all over his skin.

Rana screamed, the wail turning Mike's skin clammy.

Rana cried, "Bonnie was nine months pregnant. Someone strangled her with a wire of some sort. Her face was awful, a dark blue-black. And the baby was cut from her. She was cut from her neck to her—to her vagina! Mike—Bonnie Roberts has been *dead* for ten years!"

She fainted.

The only sounds in the room were faint bubbling noises: the sounds of liquid being pressure-pushed through sterile tubings.

The room itself was more than sterile, more than merely antiseptically clean. It was a near vacuum; almost an air lock, the temperature kept and maintained at a constant eighty degrees. No germ could live in this environment. It would not dare. The Prince would not have allowed it.

The room was lined with womblike glass containers, each filled with heavy liquid, life-supporting food and blood pushing through tubes into the artificial wombs. They were as yet unborn, but the receiving and comprehending brains of the babies were quietly but constantly fed information through electrodes attached to the heads as they floated comfortably in the thick liquid inside the glass wombs.

God is shit!

Reject all His teachings.

Your Master is the Prince of Darkness. Only the Prince is your Master. No one else.

The sounds clicked off, music taking its place, a soothing voice reading over the music. Readings from Crowley and Kellner and Faust. The unborn were taught Tantric ritual, the meanings of the 'left-hand' path of Durga and Kali, that violent sexual orgies were in teaching with their Master's views.

The music stopped; the voice faded. Other information was fed into the electrodes, the unborn brains ingesting and retaining forever the Satanic messages. There would be no further need for brainwashing when they were allowed their births.

They would already belong to the Prince.

The tapes rolled.

God is shit!

You are here to serve Satan.

You are born to serve Satan.

A slight pause, and the sounds of screaming filled the unborn brains. The moaning and panting of a man and woman in heavy climax charged through the young brains. Brain waves took the shape of pictures, force-fed into the minds of the unborn: scenes of mass-rape and torture, human orgies, of women receiving men in every opening, of men loving men, of women loving women, of women receiving dogs and goats.

Music replaced the sex-filled dreams.

Then they rested; slept; nurtured.

Soon it would begin again.

Over and over and over . . .

Ava left the operating room after having stitches taken in her anus where the whip handle had torn flesh and tender membrane as it was brutally forced up her ass.

The girl's wrists had been cared for and bandaged, and she was heavily sedated as she was wheeled to a private part of the institute.

A very private part.

Not too far from the area the doctors referred to, but only among themselves, as the Womb-Room.

Of course the Evil Old One and his Master, Satan, knew of the doctor's slangology—they knew almost everything—and neither objected to it. Even those who worship the devil have a sense of humor.

As long as it didn't go too far.

Ava was placed in a bed, her arms and legs loosely secured by thick canvas straps; they really were not needed, for she would be heavily sedated during her entire stay. Electrodes were placed at her temples, attached to a small machine by her bedside. The machine was turned on. It was directly hooked into the main computer-tape room, the same room that fed information to the Womb-Room. An I.V. was inserted into Ava's arm, the drip started.

She would remain thus for several days—longer if necessary. Then she would be given shock treatments and the entire procedure repeated for a full week.

Then she would be his.
Totally.

The town kids were having a grand old time with the senile man. He had wandered away from the senior citizens' home and had found himself in the middle of a road. Then the young people, having just left the Church of Friendship, Fellowhip, and Faith (where they had been fucking all night) found the old man.

Yes, Becker's plan, as Mike had put it, was almost perfect. And yes, as Mike had suspected, it was flawed: the brainwashing, the mind-control, had been too successful, far more than even Becker had dreamed.

The young people had no love left in them, no compassion, no feeling that even resembled pity or love or like. They did not even like themselves. The dark side of young, undisciplined minds had surfaced under the proddings of Becker's people.

They were nothing more than savages.

The crowd of young men and women, all between the ages of fifteen and twenty, stripped the senile old man of his pajamas and then, without passion or mirth or really entertainment, tortured him to death.

Something to do, man.

Mike gently placed Rana on the couch and lifted her feet up. Her skin was clammy. He put a blanket over her, then went into the kitchen and dampened a cloth.

As the water ran from the faucet, he thought: Bonnie has been dead for ten years? Impossible! But was it? That certainly had been Bonnie in his kitchen yesterday; he was sure of that.

But had she returned from the grave?

Mike shuddered, shook his head in disbelief, and

went back into the den. He placed the cloth on her forehead and began briskly rubbing her hands and arms.

After a moment, she stirred, groaned, and opened her eyes, looking about in confusion.

"You fainted," Mike said.

She lay back, her head on the arm rest. "And after all the bragging you did about me being able to cope with a bad situation."

"This is not a bad situation, Rana. This is a fucking nightmare."

She sat up, flinging off the blanket, ignoring Mike's pleas to stay in a reclining position for a few more moments. She rubbed her face with her hands and looked hard at him.

"What you said, Mike, about Bonnie—that's true?"

"On the level, honey. She was in my house, in my kitchen, yesterday. I thought she was drunk, talking in riddles. She—her face was very dark. Tan, I thought."

"Dear God in heaven," she said, and began weeping.

Mike patted her on the shoulder and took her into his arms. She wet his shoulder with tears that, he suspected, she had held back for far too long. Finally, she wound down and he felt her relax in his arms. He looked toward the draped picture window. There was faint light in the east.

He gathered her up in his arms, lifting her to her feet. He kissed her mouth, tasting the still-warm salt of her emotions. "Come on." He gently led her to the door. "Let's watch the sun come up."

"Oh, Mike," she said softly.

"That's what you wanted, wasn't it?" he smiled.

"Only with you," she replied.

"Well, looks like you got me, Rana."

Mike opened the door.

Rana began screaming.

A dead dog hung from a wire attached to a hook in the ceiling of the porch. The animal's stomach had been cut open, its entrails hanging from the bloody cavity. Blood stained the porch, the screen door, and the front door.

"Oh, my God!" Rana said. "That's old Lightning. The kids grew up with him." She turned her face from the ugliness.

"I'll take care of it," Mike said grimly. "And then, by God, I'm going to find out what the hell is going on around this place."

SEVEN

The Old One was awake; the Third Master in the Order of all that is Evil had roused himself from his almost deathlike slumber and was not in a good mood.

But then, when one is thousands of years old, one should be allowed a testy moment or two every now and then.

"I had a very disturbing dream this night," John Becker said.

"Tell me." The heavy voice reverberated through the draped room in the basement of the mansion. The only light was a single candle, keeping the big room in near-darkness, except for a small puddle of flickering light at the base of the candle. The shadowy room could not have been more in keeping with the evil it held.

The odors of death and centuries of rotting flesh clung to the velvet drapes, the velvet a dark crimson, the color of fresh blood.

Somewhere in the house a young girl was weeping almost hysterically.

"Bonnie Roberts and Jimmy Grayson are walking the earth."

"Yes, I know," the deep echolike voice whispered. Even in a whisper it was an awesome sound, belched from the depths of hell. "And so are M. C. and Grace Folsom. But why should that concern me? I am hungry."

"There was more to my dream vision."

"Relate it to me and then satisfy all my hungers."

"The Roberts woman visited Colonel Folsom."

"And?" The voice was impatient.

"I—believe we should cease all activity until this matter of Folsom is settled."

"That was in your vision?"

"No. But after careful thought in the darkness of early morning, that is what I believe."

"You have been a good and faithful servant, John. For how many years, now?"

"Twelve centuries, Master."

"We have seen much together."

"True. And there is much more to be seen together."

"Hopefully," the Old One said cautiously.

Becker stood silent.

"Have Folsom's parents visited their son?"

"Not to my knowledge. I did not know they were walking."

The Evil Old One laughed, the satanic mirth rattling the table and causing the drapes to quiver as if in fear. "Why should you know? They only left their satin and velvet homes a few moments after I awakened. I received the awareness then."

"I see," Becker replied, relief in his voice that his own powers were not diminishing.

"This man, this Folsom; I have not had the time nor the inclination to study him. Is he a Christian?" The Evil One spat out the question as if the word Christian left a bad taste in his rotting mouth.

110

Which it did.

The Old One belched, noxious odors wafting through the closed room.

"No. That is to say, he does not attend church on a regular basis. Records show he was baptized in the Episcopal Church here in Butler as a child. After that—he drifted away. He is a warrior, though."

The Old One was thoughtful for a time. "Do you believe him to be God's warrior?"

"Not—yet," Becker answered, a note of warning and caution in his voice.

The deep voice once again spoke from the shadows. "I wish you had used more discretion with Grayson."

"So do I, Master."

"Umm." The man behind the rumbling voice, if the creature could physically be called a man, rose from his massive chair. He walked slowly, laboriously across the room. He was naked except for a loincloth. "Well, what is done cannot be undone. Except for the powers of the True Master, should he choose to intervene; and he will not."

The Evil Old One was hideous.

His skin was mottled and peeling, raw and rotting. It was colors of black and gray and red and putrid white; the hands, fingers, feet, and toes were rotted from centuries of time. The lips had long since decomposed and fallen away, leaving the mouth a round ugly hole, covered with pustules. The tongue was a sickening yellowish-red. The teeth were long and fanged. The Old One, the Evil One, was a multicolored personification of ugliness, well over seven feet tall. He was utterly hairless. He towered over Becker. The Old One slumped wearily into a heavy oak chair by an ornately designed dining table.

"I am tired of moving from place to place," he said. "This," he thumped the table, "is to be my home. Our

111

Master has so ordered. We will proceed as planned."

"Yes, Master," Becker bowed.

"You have done well thus far," the Old One complimented Becker. "It has taken years to construct your
empire and your monies. Your reputation is spotless.
There will be no trouble from this Folsom."

"Yes, Master. He is but one human being."

"Correct. Now, blood," he rumbled.

Becker poured blood from a silver pitcher into a tall
goblet and the Old One drank greedily, drops of crimson leaking from his lipless mouth, falling to his chest,
sliding down his rotting belly-skin, into his crotch.
"More." He held out the goblet.

When he had drunk his fill, he said, "Meat."

Becker opened a trunklike box, and the stench of
rotting human flesh rose and filled the room. Neither
man noticed the odor. The Old One dug his hands into
the box, stuffing his mouth with what remained of a
body recently removed from a cemetary in another
state. When he had glutted himself, the creature
belched and smiled. "Now, John, a female. A girl-
child. You have procured more for me?"

"Yes, Master, I have, and I have more in reserve.
This one is very young. A girl of eleven."

The ancient, ageless, Evil One smiled. "Very good,
John. Bring her to me and get out."

The screaming began shortly after Becker entered
the dark room with the frightened, naked girl. It
intensified when he placed the hysterical, kicking child
into the lap of the Old One for his rotting fingers to explore her young flesh and his lipless mouth and putre-
fying tongue to kiss her skin. Becker paid no attention
to the wailings. He quietly closed the door and walked
up the stairs. He had long ago grown accustomed to
that shrieking. It was his dream-vision that bothered
him. The man Folsom bothered him even more.

John Becker sat behind his desk in his well-lighted study. He had sprayed his clothing with a cologne in case someone other than the servants entered the mansion, which was highly unlikely, since Becker was more of a recluse than even the late Mr. Hughes. But still, one could not take a chance.

He was almost a handsome man, John Becker, appearing to be in his late fifties. He was, in fact, many years older, having been blessed, in a manner of speaking, by the Master of Darkness, King of the Pits, the only Prince of Evil, Satan, in what is now called Germany, a mere twelve hundred years ago.

He was a muscular man, with gray tinting only the temples of his dark hair. His face and eyes were too eastern European to make him truly handsome, and the slight cast of his eyes gave him a somewhat cruel heavy slavic look. But for a man his age, he was in marvelous shape.

He was also a warlock and a bloodsucker, to mention only a couple of his more diverse personality traits. A warlock because Becker was practically immortal; a bloodsucker of his own choosing.

He ordered tea and scones sent in, and only after the servant had brought his snack and departed as silently as he had entered, closing the heavy doors behind him, did Becker begin pondering the issue.

The Evil Old One was growing very, very old. His time was rapidly coming to its conclusion. Not death, for the Evil One had died more years in the past than even Becker could comprehend. He could not die again; but he could be murdered in his sleep-period. Soon, very soon, the Old One would have to sleep for a long time, regaining his strength. Perhaps a year, perhaps five or ten years; perhaps more. Only the Old One knew for sure. His safety was of the utmost concern, placed squarely in Becker's hands. And that was why

Folsom, the stranger, worried Becker.

Nothing must prevent the operation from its unnatural, evil conclusion. Nothing.

The Old One would have to be carefully oiled for hours preparatory to his long sleep. He would have to be force-fed blood for hours, and then living human beings would be placed next to his body before they were all wrapped, mummylike; the living would melt into the Old One's flesh over the long months, helping him through his long ordeal of deathlike repose. And his place of entombment must be perfect, for he could not be disturbed during his sleep-period. The deep sleep would allow him to become as he once was.

Nothing must stand in the way of that—nothing. For the Prince himself had so ordered it. And one very simply did not disobey the Prince of Foulness, Lord of Darkness, when he ordered that his friend, the Master on Earth of all Things Dark and Ugly and Evil and Profane, be cared for.

And if one did disobey the Prince—one did so only once.

And then one died ten thousand times a day—for all eternity.

This town, this community, the planned college—all that would become a part of the Darkness.

At any cost.

Becker sighed. Even at the risk of his own life.

In the depths of the huge mansion, the screaming intensified, the girl's agony a long wall-piercing wail of pain as the Evil One penetrated her with his massive organ. When he was finished, he would drink the blood from her body, and then strip the flesh from her bones, feasting, cracking the bones and sucking the marrow for dessert. Then he would sleep.

It was a cycle, Becker thought. Like all things on both sides of the Valley of Light and Dark. The Old

One's strength was fading quickly. It was almost time for him to join the forces of Od, in a comatoselike sleep.

The Evil Old One was not unique on this earth, not the only one of his kind. But he was the oldest and the High Priest of all Evil on earth. Not even Becker knew how old he was. Only the Prince knew that.

Yes, this town, this community—it must be theirs. Too many years had been spent in planning, in the setting up and building of Becker's legitimate empire. Too many dollars had gone into those disgusting Christian programs to be wasted. It would be enough. A little blood here, a little there, and this town would grow like a beautiful cancer of evil, the college spewing out young evil to travel the land, taking jobs in all states, quietly disseminating the word of evil. It had been a long time in the making—and they could not, must not, fail.

He wiped his chin of any crumbs that might linger there and leaned back in his chair, sipping his tea. His thoughts were suddenly of the Drew woman.

Yes, Rana. All sweet and blonde, with hidden fire in those blue eyes. Yes. It was time to be thinking of just one woman. He could keep her as she was—ageless and beautiful—if she would agree. He could keep her a pure human for his pleasure. Perhaps a deal could be arranged between them: her pussy and her ass for her life—eternal.

But his dream-vision returned to disturb him. He had seen it happen before. For Bonnie Roberts and the Folsom people were walking out of the grave. That just might mean He was interfering. Again. The Pure One. That simpering wimp of love and charity and compassion. Damn Him—always meddling. It would be like Him to sit back and watch through the long years, allowing Becker to get this far, this close, before stepping in and fucking everything up. Everything in the world was His fault to begin with. Why couldn't He be satisfied with what was His and leave the rest to Them? But no, it all had to be tested, played like some children's game. Sometimes they won; sometimes He won. Most of the time He won. He and His simpering so-called Son of Jew whore.

Becker wondered if Jew-boy had ever gotten any pussy during his short stay on earth?

The heavens rumbled ominously above the mansion in the slight valley.

"Fuck You!" Becker said contemptuously.

Lightning licked across the sky.

A voice boomed in his head: *Don't press your luck, John. You know what He is capable of when angered.*

Becker knew where that voice came from.

Yes, sir! Becker flung the thought. But he smiled. His suspicions had been confirmed: the Mighty One was near. Watching. Waiting. And probably looking about for a mortal to tap on the shoulder, choosing that man to act as His warrior in the upcoming fight.

Very well. So be it.

Jimmy Grayson was walking. So he had managed to slip past the Gates of the Damned. Well—in all fairness, that was not Grayson's fault; Grayson was what Becker himself had made him—that night. While his heart was still pumping feebly. Just one taste, that's all Becker had wanted, craved, needed, taken. And another undead had been created.

Impetuous fool! He berated his actions of ten years ago.

That had not been like him. Not at all.

Becker sat and sipped his tea and nibbled at the last small cake. He contemplated the future as the wracking cries of the girl-child penetrated the thick walls of the mansion. They went unnoticed by the man deep in thoughts of the darkest evil.

What if? he sighed, mentally playing the ageless

116

game. What if Folsom had been tapped by the hand of God? It had happened before, and the subject did not even know of it for days, weeks, even, once, almost twenty-five years. What if? What if? That game was beginning to wear thin with Becker. If Folsom had been tapped by Him, it would have been a silent tap, probably. The man would not know he had been touched by Him. Every game has its rules. So too, did this one. Since the beginnings of time.

Becker allowed himself a thin smile. It would be interesting to challenge the man. God's warrior.

Becker howled his contempt of Him, his laughter ringing above the child's screaming in the lonely house.

No! The voice that only Becker could hear ripped through his head. *It is not time for that. Your first concern is the well-being of the Old One. If it must be, delay until this Folsom is placated.*

"Yes," Becker said aloud. "I understand."

Mike had removed the dead dog and hosed off the porch. Before he had done any of that, he had gone to his Jag and taken out his pistol, shoving the big magnum into his belt.

"Coming to that, is it, Mike?" Rana asked.

"I hope not," was his reply. "Rana? You're a farm gal, so I would imagine you've got favorite weapons. I saw quite an arsenal in the gun cabinet. Get your favorite pistol and rifle, a shotgun if you have one. Put them in the trunk of the car."

"Mike—"

"Don't interrupt. Then pack some clothing, yours and Lisa's. Enough for several days. I'm getting you out of here."

She had dressed in jeans, a western shirt, and cowboy boots. She stood on the porch for a moment, looking at him. "All right, Mike," she finally said. "You're the boss."

The phone rang in the den. Rana answered it and stood arguing for a few moments—Mike guessed it was Lisa—then she slammed the phone into its cradle. She stalked back to the porch, boot heels hitting the wood floor with authority.

"Lisa?" Mike questioned.

She nodded. "Told me she was spending the day with friends. Said she'd see me tomorrow."

"What about tonight?"

"I've learned not to ask."

He looked at her as if she was a fool. "Rana—"

"I don't want to hear it, Mike. You still don't understand what's happening here. Still won't, for some reason, believe it."

His temper flared. "Then, Goddammit, Rana, show me. Physically show me!"

Her eyes flashed anger. "You got a date, baby!"

EIGHT

She had packed a few things and tossed the two small suitcases in the trunk of the Jag. A rifle, shotgun, and several boxes of shells followed the clothing. Rana slipped a .38 snub-nose revolver in her purse, then plopped her butt in the seat beside Mike.

"House locked up?" Mike asked.

"Don't sweat it, Colonel. Just proceed."

"Rana—"

"Drive the damn car, Mike!"

A grim set to his jaw, Mike backed the Jag out of the drive and headed down the highway. "Any particular direction?"

Her smile was grim. "Just try to leave the area."

"Your wish is my command, dear. We'll spend the night in Shreveport."

"Bet a hundred dollar bill on that, Colonel?"

"You're on!"

Ninety minutes later, Mike pulled over to the shoulder and dug for his wallet, handing Rana a hundred dollar bill. He didn't believe she'd take it. She fooled him, tucking the bill into her purse.

"Bitch!" Mike muttered, not unkindly.

"I won't say I told you so."

"Thank you for that, at least."

Wherever they had driven, they had been watched and followed. The roads that Mike remembered as a boy were all closed; the gravel road shortcuts were no longer in existence. Five times he was stopped by various deputies and checked: driver's license, car registration, inspection sticker. Each time he was turned around in the direction he had just traveled.

And always he was followed.

"It was never this bad before," Rana said. "Something's up, something big. They're setting something in motion."

"Who?" Mike said wearily. "And what?"

"I don't know. But I'd swear it centers around you. Wanna make another bet?"

Mike said an extremely ugly phrase to her proposal.

"Boy, what a sore loser."

He started the car, pulling back onto the blacktop, driving aimlessly. Out of the corner of his eye, he thought he saw a body, a naked body, lying in the ditch beside the road. He dismissed it as his imagination. Then he slowed, stopped, and backed up.

"Oh, good Lord!" Rana said, looking once at the tortured old man, stiffening in death. She turned her head away from the sight as Mike got out of the car, walking up to the body, naked and pitful in death.

The man had at least a hundred cuts on his body, but had probably died from a combination of shock, exposure, and loss of blood. Mike looked up the road at the car that had been following them. He motioned for it to come on. The car pulled up alongside Mike.

Mike pointed to the body in the ditch. "Someone needs to notify the sheriff's office."

"Why?" the man on the passenger side asked.

"Because—" Mike was shocked. "Hell, man, that's a body!"

The man shrugged. "The Lord giveth and the Lord taketh away. Ain't that what it says in your Bible?"

"It isn't your Bible, too?"

The man laughed nastily. "You have to be kidding!" He jerked his thumb at Rana, sitting in the Jag. "She got pretty good pussy?"

Mike held his temper in check. He said nothing.

"We'll get around to her," the man promised. "Her time's comin'."

"You'll have to go through me first," Mike told him.

"Piece of cake." The driver spoke for the first time.

Mike squatted down on the shoulder, looking inside the car. The man looked familiar. "Didn't I go to school with you?"

"Yeah. So what?"

"Al Springer?"

"That's right."

"Al—what's going on around here?"

"You were told to get out yesterday, Folsom. You should have taken that advice."

One mystery solved: the phone call. "That's what I'm trying to do now," Mike said.

"Too late." He backed the car up the road, pulling over on the shoulder. Waiting.

Mike felt a sudden chill wash eerily over his body, bathing him in a cold invisible aura of foreboding. He could not remember ever experiencing anything like it.

He got back into the Jag. "Both of those men were armed," he told Rana.

She nodded. Mike noticed her right hand was in her open purse. "If they had tried anything, I was going to kill Jake Harris first."

Mike sat dumbfounded, staring at her. Slowly, the

121

truth came to him. "You've been boxed in here for how long, Rana?"

"Loosely, for several months. Never this bad, though."

Mind-boggling, he thought. Unbelievable. But it's happening! Here. Now. To me. Us. Jesus! "Have you, any of you, tried to run? Crash these blockades?"

"Not since Pauline Jefferson tried it."

"Pauline. She married Ralph."

"Right. He went over to the other side five years ago. Took the kids with him."

"What happened to Pauline?"

"She is officially listed as a runaway; deserted her family."

"But you don't believe that?"

"Not any more than I believe the Lord God has forsaken us and left us to cope with this horror without His help."

"You believe He is going to send a sign of some sort, Rana?"

"No. I believe He is going to send help. I believe He already has."

"What kind of help?"

She looked at him. "You."

They drove in silence for a time, Mike no more believing he had been God-sent than he believed he could pick up the Jag and carry it around on his back.

He found himself on the road to the cemetery, and when he came to the open gate, he slowed and pulled in. He stopped, getting his bearings, then remembering the location of the family plot, slowly drove to his parents' graves.

Rana was strangely silent as he got out to examine the plots.

When Mike returned to the car, his face was ashen in color and he was trembling with anger. "Their graves have been desecrated; caskets broken into. They're gone, Rana!"

"Were the caskets broken into or out of, Mike?" she asked.

"What?"

"You heard me."

He got into the car and stared at her. "Rana—now I know all this has been a strain, but you've got to get hold of your emotions. You—"

She slapped him, rocking his head to one side with the force of her open-handed blow.

He almost tore her head off. He caught his blow at the last moment, checking it.

"Now, you listen to me, Mike Folsom." She wasn't about to back down. "You said you spoke with Bonnie yesterday, didn't you? Well, she's dead! Been dead. Now she's out walking around, trying to help. Your parents couldn't do the same? Sure, they could. Why not? If we're to believe Bonnie is—with us, in some form, why not your parents?"

Mike could but shake his head.

"You don't want to believe it, Mike. My God, do you think I do! You don't know what it's been like around here. A nightmare. One horrible never-ending nightmare.

"You think you just happened to get out of the Army at this time? You think you just happened to come to Butler in the nick of time? You think the net closing around us is just by chance? It's all too iffy, Mike. No." She shook her head. "You were sent here. You have a job to do."

"What job?" Mike shouted the words.

"You'll be told," she said, certainty in her voice.

"You were saving this little trip for last, weren't

you?''

"Yes, I knew you had to be convinced, knew you had to see it with your own eyes; my telling you would not have been enough. I planned to show you we couldn't get out even before we both lost our tempers back at the house.''

Mike slumped back in the seat. "I—better report that dead man.''

"To whom?'' Rana asked.

"Well, Jesus Christ, Rana! The police.''

She smiled. "This ought to be interesting.''

"Is that right?'' Chief Ford said, a smile on his lips. "A dead man in a ditch? Well, I'll send some boys out that way directly, Mike.''

Mike stared at him, not believing Stinky's attitude. "Don, that's a dead man I'm talking about. He was tortured to death.''

The Chief shrugged. "Probably just some kids havin' a little fun, 'at's all. No big deal. The old fucker was nuts, anyway. No big loss to anyone. Right, Mike?''

Lennie snickered off to Mike's left.

"Kids having fun?'' was all Mike could blurt.

"Sure.''

Another cop leaned against a filing cabinet. His eyes explored Rana's body, settling on her crotch. He licked his lips.

"I'm being followed everywhere I go, Don,'' Mike said. "I don't like it.''

"Ain't no law says a man can't drive on a public road, Mike, It's probably your imagination, that's all. Is there anything else, Mike?''

"I'm being prevented from leaving the parish, Don. At least this part of it. Anything you can do about that?"

"Now, Mike," the Chief said soothingly. "Who in the world would want to keep you from leaving this part of Chatom? Boy, you been under a strain, I reckon. Why don't you and Rana jist go on home and get some—rest," he giggled.

He stopped giggling abruptly when Mike said, "My parents' graves are open, Don."

The chief said nothing. Lennie stiffened. The third cop in the room was fantasizing about Rana sucking him off.

Mike took Rana's arm. "See you around—Stinky."

"Git out there and pick up the body of that old fart," Chief Ford told Lennie. "And find them damn kids."

Ted entered the room. "The young people are arming themselves. They've already shot old man Simpson and taken his wife out to do who knows what to her." The cop wore a strange expression on his face.

"Shit!" Stinky said. He looked at Lennie. "Go on, do what I told you."

Lennie looked at Ted, hate in his eyes.

"Get out and go on!" Stinky shouted.

Lennie left the room.

"How many kids is armed?" Stinky asked Ted.

"Seventy-five to a hundred, I suppose. Maybe more. Most aren't doing anything, though. They're just riding about."

"Well, it'll probably blow over," Stinky said. "Kids will be kids, you know."

About a hundred young people, evenly divided between boys and girls, had gathered in a wooded area a few miles outside of town. In a clearing in the timber, they positioned their portable tape-players all around them and inserted the same tape. Rock and roll music blasted from the dozens of speakers. The young began to dance, slowly at first. The dancing was obscene.

It was only the beginning.

NINE

Mike drove to his house. He had not spoken since leaving the police station. Pulling in the drive, he said, "CB radios."

"What?" Rana looked at him.

"CB radios," he repeated. "I'll get a CB radio, drive as far as the—they'll let me, as close to the Parish Seat as possible, and start broadcasting on Channel 9. Call for help."

"There are no CBs in this town, Mike. The people voted years ago to ban them. Too much profanity on the air. It was a unanimous vote. Good idea at the time; all the trashy-mouthed truck drivers. No CBs, Mike. Forget it."

"It's moot, now, Rana, but I don't think that ban would hold up in court."

She shrugged. "Like you said, Mike, it's moot now."

He looked at his watch and was shocked to see it was only a little past nine. "Where would Lisa be right now, do you suppose?"

"She was probably lying about spending the day

with friends. At the church, I would imagine."

"All right. Then let's go to the church and get her out of there."

"They'll never let you have her, Mike."

His eyes were cold as he looked at her. "Would you like to make a wager on that?"

She declined.

"She will leave when she is ready to leave," Mike was informed by a burly man standing in the door of the main building.

Mike smiled at him—sort of. It was the smile of a shark looking at lunch. "How would you like to have your throat ripped out of your neck and handed to you?" he asked the man.

"Sir?"

"And then all your fingers broken—slowly?"

The man backed up. He understood violence, and sensed this man was ready to do all that he promised. "Perhaps there has been some sort of misunderstanding . . . ?"

"The only misunderstanding around here is this so-called shitty church of yours and the fact that if Lisa Drew is not standing in this door in one minute, I am going to personally tear your fucking head off and hand it to you."

Mike sensed more than saw the man come up quietly on his right. Another man behind him. The man behind him said, "Sir, we really don't condone violence here. We are a house of worship. However," he smiled as Mike turned slightly, keeping the man in the door in his line of sight as well as the man to his right, "I have adequate personnel here to physically dissuade you should you threaten us further."

Mike took the man in the door out first. He caught

him in the throat with the knife edge of his left hand, sending the man to the floor, choking and gasping for breath. He would be out of action for more than a few minutes. Without losing momentum, Mike spun and kicked the second man in the groin, then on the side of the jaw as he was bending over, howling in pain. The jaw popped like a pistol shot. Mike faced the third man, who had not moved in the three or four seconds it had taken Mike to put two men out of action. Mike opened his shirt, exposing the butt of the .41 mag.

Ron Egan smiled. "I get your point, sir."

"Get Lisa Drew or the next point you'll get is me gut-shooting you."

"I believe you'd do it, too, sir," Egan said. He clapped his hands and a man appeared at his side almost instantly. "Get the Drew girl and escort her to this—gentlemen's automobile. Promptly!"

The man was gone at a trot.

"Chief Ford will not like this action of yours, sir," Egan said.

Mike smiled, very unpleasantly. "I'll worry about Stinky. You just worry about yourself, pal."

Egan laughed. "Why, sir, I believe I like you. A pity we can't be friends."

"I'll talk with you any time you choose."

"Name the time and place, Colonel Folsom."

"My house. Tonight."

"Ah—but I'm sorry. I have an engagement. How about tomorrow evening, about sevenish?"

"Fine. I'll be there."

"Oh, I'm sure you'll still be around, Colonel." Egan looked at the men on the ground. "These men may be seriously injured."

"I'm sure I've killed better men in my time."

"No doubt." The reply was dryly given.

Lisa was escorted to the Jag and put in the back seat.

She offered no protest or resistance.

"See you tomorrow night," Mike said, then turned and walked away.

Egan watched him drive off. He smiled, a peculiar tilt to his head. "A formidable foe," he said. "Yes, indeed. This one won't be at all easy." He looked at the men. The one with the busted jaw was unconscious; the first man down was struggling to get to his feet. "Idiots!" Egan muttered.

"Hey, man!" Lisa said. "This car is really something. What is this thing, anyway?"

"Jaguar. XKE-150."

She ran her young hand over the leather. "Smooth, man. I bet for an old dude, you get lots of pussy with this wagon going for you, right?"

Mike said nothing.

Lisa laughed at him. "Will it go fast, old dude?"

"Fast enough," Mike said testily. The girl stank of sex.

"You look pretty satisfied, Mother. You get some cock last night?"

Rana turned to slap her, but Mike's hand was swifter, stopping her before she could get turned and in position. "Easy, babe."

"Oh—babe, huh?" Lisa grinned. "How about that. I guess you old folks still like to fuck, huh?"

Neither Mike nor Rana chose to reply.

"I got some," the teenager said. "I got a bunch. I must have cum twenty times. Tell me, Mother, did you suck his cock last night. I'd like to have seen that; I might be able to learn something from you. I'm still pretty young. Tell me, do you real easylike play with his balls while you got it in your mouth?"

Out of the corner of his eye, Mike could see tears running down Rana's face. She kept her face averted from the back seat, eyes straight ahead.

"Girl," Mike warned. "Watch it."

"Watch what, man?"

"The way you speak to your mother. And the way you speak to me."

"And if I choose not to obey your orders—and you really have no right to give me any orders—what happens then, dude?"

Mike started to tell her he would be only too happy to backhand her into the next parish. Instead, he sighed heavily and said nothing. But oh, what he was thinking.

"Yeah," Lisa laughed. "I thought it might be that way—all mouth and no do."

At that moment, Mike made up his mind that when they got to his house, he was personally going to take a belt to this smart-mouthed kid's behind. And he was going to enjoy doing it.

But he was wrong.

Rana took a small handkerchief from her purse and dabbed at her eyes. Mike thought the entire scene completely wild, since he could see the butt of Rana's .38 sticking out of the purse.

Pistols and tears, he thought.

"Aww!" Lisa drawled from the back seat. "Did I upset Mommy-dear? Gee, Mommy, I wish I could say I'm sorry, but you know how it is. When you're hot you're hot."

Mike ground his teeth together.

Rana broke into his anger. "Back at the house, Mike, you started to call someone, then decided against it. Who were you going to call?"

Using his chest as a shield against Lisa's eyes, Mike pointed a finger toward the back seat. "The State Police," he lied, showing Rana his crossed fingers. "I'll call them later, maybe."

"I—see," she said, a confused look in her eyes.

"Oh, boy," Lisa gushed. "The State Police. Well, that's okay, dude, you'd never get the call through, anyway. I don't believe I'm telling you anything a real smart dude like you hasn't already figured out, but you're boxed in here, man. No—way—out! But I really caused quite a stir, didn't I? Little old Lisa. Mommy-dear, would you really have the Super Cops put me away?"

Rana refused to even look at her daughter. She cut her eyes to the side mirror. "We're being followed, Mike."

"Yeah, I know."

"Better get used to it, folks," Lisa said. "That's the way it's gonna be from now on."

"Shut up, girl!" Mike said, and something in his tone warned the teenager she had best do just that.

She did not utter another word until they reached Mike's house.

"You can't keep me here," she said. "I'll run away, back to the church. You'll have to chain me. I mean it."

"We're going to talk," Mike told her. "The three of us. Try to understand where we're all coming from."

"Oh, heavy, old dude. Heavy."

In spite of the situation, Rana had to fight to conceal a slight smile.

It was then Mike noticed the two parked cars. One parked at the north end of the block, the other at the south end, boxing him in. Two men in each car.

"Like I said, man," Lisa said smugly from the back seat. "Boxed in."

Mike ignored her. He was thinking that the cars were not stock; he would bet on that. One was a Trans-Am, the other a low-slung Datsun, the racing model.

But Mike knew his Jag well. He had been on too

many tracks not to know what it would do all-out. He felt there was not a car in the parish that could take the corners any better, certainly none that could catch the Jag on a straight-away.

But, he cautioned himself, what good was the speed if they had no place to run?

From the back seat, Lisa laughed. Rana and Mike looked at her curiously.

"Mr. Egan's people," the girl said, pointing to the cars and the men inside. "If I want to leave now, all I'd have to do is wave to them and they'd come and get me."

"Then why don't you do that, girl?" Mike asked.

The teenager hesitated for a few seconds, and Mike thought that odd. " 'Cause I don't know about you, man. You're weird! I think you'd kill those guys watching us if they tried to take me. I get those vibes from you. I don't know where you're coming from, man, but I think you like to kill people."

She was wrong in that assumption. Mike did not like to kill. It just didn't bother him to do so.

They got out of the car. Mike jerked a thumb toward the house, looking at Lisa. "In the house."

"Aye, aye, Captain!" Lisa tossed him a casual salute and marched up the sidewalk, her mother by her side, ready to grab her if she decided to cut and run.

Mike parked the Jag in the garage, carefully closing and locking the heavy doors, securing them with a heavy lock and chain.

He entered the house through the garage door that led into the hall between kitchen and den. He looked at the basement door. Tried it. Locked. He walked into the den where mother and daughter were sitting, glowering at one another. Mike was tired, irritated, somewhat confused, and was in no mood for games. He came right to the point.

"Lisa, there is an old man, dead, naked, tortured to death, lying out in a parish ditch. Chief Ford tells me it was probably kids that did it. What do you think about that?"

Again, she hesitated as the powers that controlled her mind fought with a hidden, but still viable, well of good that was struggling deep within her. The dark powers won. She shrugged. "It don't mean a fucking thing to me, man."

"Oh, God!" Rana said.

"Oh, shut up!" daughter snapped at mother.

Mike said, "Why are you so down on your mother, Lisa?"

Again, the shrug.

"Answer my question!" Mike barked.

For the first time, Mike saw a touch of fear crawl into the girl's eyes. And something he could not pinpoint. Both were gone as quickly as they had appeared.

"Okay, man, don't get hostile. I'll talk to you. I'm not on her case. I just wanna do what I wanna do, that's all."

"You think you're old enough to make all those decisions, Lisa?"

"Yeah. Why not? I'm fifteen. Besides, no one else in town puts up any howl about their kids going out to Director Egan's church. How come I'm the one who gets all the guff?"

Mike said it, and knew the instant the words left his mouth, they were the wrong words. "Because you owe your mother something, girl."

"Shit!" Lisa spat the profanity. "Man, it's the other way around. She," Lisa visually shot daggers at her mother, "owes *me!*"

"All right," Mike said, sitting down across from the teenager, "let's explore that. Tell me, what do you think your mother owes you, and why don't you owe her anything?''

"Hey . . . !" Lisa blurted, then leaned back on the couch and stared at Mike. She sighed. "Okay, I'll play. What's wrong with sex?"

"Nothing," Mike said honestly. "Providing both people are old enough to understand what it's all about and all that goes with the act. Don't worry," he assured her, "I'm not going to start quoting the Bible to you. I'm not that big a hypocrite."

Lisa narrowed her eyes, not believing him.

"But having sex with a special person is one thing; having wholesale group sex is quite another."

"That's your opinion," the girl challenged.

"That's right. But give me credit for having learned something over the years."

That infuriating shrug.

"Tell me," Mike tried to gently shift the direction of the conversation, "what does this Director Egan teach at this church?"

Mike watched the eyes of the girl darken momentarily. He knew she was going to lie to him. "Oh—standard stuff, man. Except that what we do with our bodies is our business, and there is nothing wrong with screwing. It's not only fun, it's good for you, too."

"And . . . ?"

"What difference does it make, man? You people aren't going to get out—ever."

She might not be lying about that, Mike thought. But if she really believes it, why did she lie about what is taught at the Church of Friendship, Fellowship, and Faith? "Come on, Lisa," he urged. "I'm at least trying to understand and level with you. Won't you do the same for me?"

But he felt her withdraw, and felt, too, something alien in the big room. Lisa inwardly pulled away from him. She was silent.

"Lisa . . ." Rana leaned forward, trying to take her daughter's hands.

What in the hell was in this room! Mike thought. Whatever it was seemed to be growing stronger.

The girl slapped her mother's hands away, striking out at her, hitting her on the arm with a balled fist. "Keep your fuckin' hands to yourself and off me!" she snapped. She turned to Mike. "And I don't need your goddamn sermons, either, man. So just butt out."

Mike took a chance. "You think the devil's going to win this one, don't you?"

"I don't know, man!" she blurted. "I'm not really into that heavy stuff yet."

She stiffened on the couch, her eyes changing, transforming into something wild. Her smile was savage.

She cursed him until she was breathless.

That strange, unexplained force was still present. Mike shrugged it off as a change in the atmosphere.

When Lisa was through, panting and red-faced, Mike said, "I honest to God believe what you need is a good old-fashioned spanking, Lisa. And I don't believe very much in manhandling kids. But in your case—"

She cut him off, screaming at him. "Then do it, you mother-fucker!"

Mike rose slowly to his feet, loosening the buckle to his leather belt. "Get up! By God, I'll beat some sense into you." He was so angry he was trembling. "No kid talks to me like that."

The girl rose without hesitation, glaring defiantly at the man towering over her. "Well, baby, let's just get it on then."

"Mike," Rana said.

"No way!" he said, his temper boiling. "I'd do the same if she were mine." He pushed the girl toward the basement door. "Move it, girl."

She quickly obeyed, a smile on her lips, heading for

the door.

Mike remembered the door was locked and he did not have the key. He started to tell the girl to stop, but she had already opened the door.

Strange, Mike thought. I *know* that door was locked. "The light switch is just inside the door."

"BFD," Lisa said.

"What?"

"Big Fuckin' Deal."

The basement was just as spotlessly clean as the rest of the house. Not a cobweb or a speck of dust anywhere. Crates and boxes were neatly stacked, the contents of each printed on the side.

Mike pointed to a table that needed refinishing badly. Something for me to do, he absently thought. Then he caught himself. Brought himself back to the present. He pointed again. "Bend over that table, girl. And hang on."

"Yeah, man," she sneered at him. "I know. This is going to hurt you worse than it does me and all that happy horseshit."

Then she smiled.

That force again. We must be really coming in for a bad storm, Mike thought. "You think this is funny, Lisa?"

Rana stood quietly to one side, arms folded under her breasts. She said nothing.

"Now I get it," the girl said. "Oh, I read you like a book, man." She unzipped her jeans, smiling lewdly at him.

"Keep them on!" Mike snapped.

"Oh, no way, man. You want to see the pussy, don't you. Get all turned on looking at the young cunt. That's the point of this whole thing, isn't it, man?"

"Keep your jeans on, girl!"

But Lisa calmly dropped her jeans to the floor. She

stepped out of her panties. She smiled, her fingers lightly caressing the honey-colored patch of pubic hair. "You like this, man? Come on, let's get us a threesome going. I'd like to watch you and Mother fuck."

"Turn around and shut your mouth!" Mike told her.

"I bet you got a nice cock on you, man. Come on. How about it?"

Mike's face was flaming crimson. *"Turn around!"* he roared.

She laughed and turned, bending over the table. "Okay, give it to me, Dad."

Rana was silently crying.

Mike raised the belt. He couldn't do it. He shook his head in disgust.

"Come on, you son of a bitch!" Lisa yelled at him. Filth rolled from her mouth, phrases and expressions Mike himself would not use. She cursed him; she cursed her mother; she cursed Mike's parents. Finally, she cursed God.

Mike swung the belt, the leather popping against her bare buttocks.

"Oohh, man!" Lisa moaned. "Do it again. Goddamn, do it again."

He swung the belt.

Lisa screamed, but it was an odd scream.

At the strange scream, Mike stopped. He looked at Rana, questions in his eyes. She blinked away the tears and shook her head. "I don't know, Mike."

"Hit me again, man!" Lisa hollered. "I'm cummin', baby. It feels good."

There was horror in both Mike and Rana's eyes.

Lisa yelled, "Director Egan says pain and sex are like one and the other. This is good, man. Hit me! Don't leave me like this. Help me cum!"

Mike's arms hung by his sides. The belt dragged

limply on the floor.

The teenager reached behind her, parting the cheeks of her ass. "Look, man; see my hole. It's cherry, I swear it. No one's ever balled me there. I'll give it to you, Pops. Come on. You don't even have to get any KY Jelly or anything. Just wet me from my cunt and give it to me. I promise you, man, it'll be good. Tight. Please!"

Mike was openly crying as he threaded the belt back through the loops in his trousers.

"Don't leave me like this, man!" Lisa yelled. "You got to make me cum! I'm hurtin', man!"

Mike and Rana walked slowly up the steps to the main floor.

Lisa was cursing them both.

They put their arms around each other and held on tightly.

For the first time in his adult life, Mike knew real fear.

Rana broke away from him and walked to the picture window, overlooking the silent street.

Mike put his hand on the mantel, his fingers touching a book resting there. The strange force withdrew.

Neither adult could hear Lisa crying and begging in the basement.

Rana turned. "Mike, what am I going to do with her?"

He hesitated. "You want the truth, Rana? And I mean the truth?"

"As you see it, yes, I do."

Mike stepped away from the mantel, from the book his fingers had touched. "Rana—I think if she was a horse, I'd shoot her."

TEN

Rana had not taken offense at Mike's remark, merely nodded her head in agreement, saying, "Maybe, Mike, but let's see if we can't find a somewhat less drastic alternative."

She fixed them an early lunch, then took Lisa a tray of food. The teenager refused to leave the basement. She cursed her mother and threw the tray of food at her, the milk splattering on the wall, the glass breaking.

"Get out of here and leave me alone, you bitch!" she screamed at her mother. "You're in trouble, goddamn you—you're really in trouble. Don't you think for a minute Egan is gonna let me stay here. He'll send somebody for me. He'll—"

Rana turned her back and walked away from the ugliness and profanity of her screaming offspring. Lisa picked up an old vase and threw it, the vase hitting Rana in the back, almost knocking her down. Her mother knew that beating the girl would be useless. She straightened up and kept on walking, closing the basement door behind her. Her daughter's screaming and cursing carried through the door, a steady stream of profanity.

The screaming finally wound down; Rana could not hear her daughter's begging for help.

Rana sat in the den, looking at Mike.

"I don't understand how things got to this point," he questioned, as much to himself as to Rana. "Outsiders have to come in here every day. Supply people, salespeople, relatives and friends. Fresh bread and milk has to be delivered—"

"No, they don't," Rana broke in, contradicting him. "We have our own dairy and bakery. I say we. The town, I mean. A lot of supplies, like clothing and building materials and canned goods and furniture— items like that—are off-loaded at a warehouse miles from here, brought in by train. No heavy trucks are allowed in Butler. The town council passed that ordinance years ago."

"And Becker owns the spur line railroad," Mike said. Not a question.

"Right."

Mike studied the road in front of the house, cutting his eyes first to the Trans-Am, then to the Datsun. The men inside the cars had not moved.

"What are we going to do, Mike?"

"I don't know," he admitted. "I think—I'm pretty sure—I can get you and Lisa out of here. . . ." He paused, a curious look on his face.

Rana read his look and his tone of voice. "But you don't want to do that, do you, Mike?"

He hedged the question, sidestepping it skillfully. "I want you to be safe."

"But running galls you, doesn't it?"

He admitted that it did indeed, adding, "But sometimes it's necessary." He was silent for a moment, then lifted his eyes to hers. "All right, Rana, tell me this. How many graduates of the class of '57 live in this com-

142

munity?''

She thought for a time. ''Well, really I guess, about half of them. I see your point, Mike. Why is Becker allowing the reunion, right?''

''Exactly. How many reunions have been held over the past ten years?''

''I—uh—can't recall any.''

''Interesting.'' He was lost in thought for a moment. He smiled. ''Look, military people aren't that difficult to track down. Yet the first I knew of the reunion was when Jack told me less than twenty minutes after I arrived in town. Then Stinky told me. I got an idea.''

He went to the phone, looking up the number of Jack's pharmacy, and then dialed the number. ''Jack? Mike Folsom here. Sure. No, everything is not dandy. We'll talk about it. Yes, I'm sure you do have some ideas. Look, Jack, how many people from the class of '57 live out of town? That many, huh? Okay, how many are attending the reunion? I see. Well, that's too bad. I would have enjoyed seeing them, I'm sure. Jack, I'll talk to you later. Right, thanks.'' He hung up, turning to Rana.

''How many, Mike?''

''Not a one.''

''They never received the invitations,'' Rana stated flatly.

''No, Jack said they all declined.''

''Someone else declined for them, honey.'' Rana was adamant. ''I told you about the local post office.''

Again, that thoughtful look crossed his face. ''How many grads of that class are part of Becker's Church?''

''No,'' she shook her head. ''That won't wash, Mike; some are and some aren't here in town.''

''Maybe it will wash. Getting us together, I mean.''

''For what reason?''

"I don't know. Where would the reunion be held?"

"At the community center, I'm sure."

"What community center?"

"The one Becker built for the town." She looked at him. "Sure," she said, drawing out the words slowly. "To get you all together to—well, we can only guess at what might have happened."

"Yeah," he said sarcastically. "Back in Nam we used to call it dealing with the enemy with extreme prejudice."

"And that means . . . ?"

"Kill them."

She sighed.

"Okay, Rana, you get on the horn." He pointed to the phone. "Call Jack and all the rest of your friends you believe you can trust; invite them over this afternoon. 'Bout two-thirty or so. That'll give us time to catch a nap, get some rest. Then we'll hash this thing around between us."

"I thought you'd never ask." She moved toward the phone.

Mike's big arm stopped her, gently. He pulled her to him and kissed her. "Time to take a nap—among other things."

She was half-serious, half-joking when she asked, "Did my daughter kind of turn you on, baby?"

"I'd be lying if I gave you an unequivocal no. But mostly I felt sorry for her. And I apologize for my remark about shooting her."

"Are you always this honest?"

"Yes, and it's gotten me into trouble a few times."

She looked up at him, into those cold hunter's eyes. "You don't have to reply, Mike. But I want to tell you something."

"Oh?"

"I love you."

* * *

The screaming woke them.

They were asleep in a downstairs bedroom, just off the den, lying in each other's arms. It was Lisa's screaming, and her wailings were horrible and terror-filled.

Mike jerked on his trousers, jammed his feet into tennis shoes, and ran for the basement door, the .41 mag in his right hand.

The lights were off in the basement. Mike hit the switch just inside the door. But it was already on.

"Lisa!" he yelled.

She was running, bolting for the shaft of light that poured around Mike, standing tall in the open door at the top of the darkened stairs. She flew into his arms, almost knocking him down. He held her and slammed the door shut.

"What's wrong, baby?" he asked, feeling her body tremble against his.

"*Things* down there!" she sobbed. "Monsters and ghosts and—*things!*"

"Monsters and ghosts?" Rana questioned.

"I never seen anything like it," the girl wept, her face pressed against Mike's shoulder. "They were coming at me. An old man and an old woman. And there was this—man, kind of. He had—his teeth were all—pointed! This old couple kept trying to push him back, away from me. They were protecting me! Protecting me. And I don't know why!"

"Could it be, baby," Mike asked, "that you had fallen asleep and dreamed all this?"

"No!" She yelled the word. "No. I swear to God I wasn't dreaming." She caught herself, looked at first Mike, then her mother. "Swear to God," she whispered.

145

The force that Mike had experienced before returned, stronger than ever.

Lisa trembled in his arms. "Make it go away, Mike! Please make it go away."

"What is it, baby?" Rana asked.

"*Him!*" she screamed. "The Prince! Egan's people are calling on him to make me come to them. Please, Mike—I don't wanna go back. I don't want to."

Mike remembered and led the girl to the mantel above the fireplace. He looked up at the book where he had rested his fingers before. The Bible. He touched the Holy Book. The Force faded as abruptly as it came.

"Oh, God!" Lisa sobbed, holding on tightly to Mike. "Help me."

"We'll help you, baby," Mike said. "I promise. Was there anything else that happened in the basement?"

"Well—like I said, this old couple kept trying to push this—whatever it was—back. Then the lights went out. Not like the switch was turned off. I mean—they just slowly faded into nothing."

"Was there anyone else down there, honey?" Mike asked, a sick feeling growing in the pit of his stomach.

All this was too real—too real to deny, too farfetched to believe. But it was happening.

Lisa pulled back and looked up at him. At that moment, she looked so young and vulnerable. So fresh and lovely. "How—how did you know, Mike?"

"What did she look like?" Mike pressed.

Beside him, Rana made a gasping sound. A sound of pure fright.

"How did you know it was a she, Mike?" Lisa asked. "Yes," she said, before he could reply. "It was a woman—sort of. I mean—she was all misty—but God! man, she looked like—I mean, her face was all dark."

Rana backed up against a wall. Her face was chalk

146

white. Sweaty. "Jesus God," she said. "Please help us."

"I don't know who the others were," Mike said, choosing his words carefully. "But the woman with the dark face was Bonnie Roberts. She's been dead for ten years."

Lisa's face turned as white as her mother's.

"Bonnie was trying to help you. She warned me yesterday to be careful. She's on our side, Lisa. That has to tell you something."

"Wh—what?" the girl stammered, almost completely frightened out of her wits.

"That you're not yet lost, that you're worth saving. And probably, that you have not given your soul to Satan."

Rana looked at him curiously, and Mike wondered where the words he had just spoken came from.

Lisa said, "I—I mean, man—dead for . . ." Her voice trailed off into an eerie silence. Her eyes left Mike's face and drifted to the mantel above the fireplace. "Help me," she whispered. "Oh, please help me."

"Baby, what's wrong?" Rana came to them, putting her arms around her daughter.

Mike released the girl and Lisa turned to her mother, throwing her arms around her.

"The pictures!" she wailed. "The pictures!"

"What about them, honey?" Rana stroked the girl's hair.

She pointed to the mantel. "The old couple in the basement—that's them!"

She was pointing to a photograph of Mike's parents.

The picture rested next to the book Mike had touched.

The Holy Bible.

ELEVEN

"I have an appointment with Colonel Folsom," Egan told Becker. "As if you didn't know."

The men spoke over the telephone.

"I know," Becker replied. "Keep the appointment. He'll be there; he's curious about us. Besides, he can't get out. During the course of the conversation, try to detect his weak points."

"He has no weak points." Egan's reply was firm and flat. "He is a warrior. He would have shot me with no more feeling than stepping on a bug."

"The guards?"

"Bruised and sore and out of commission for several days—maybe longer. The doctor said they were very lucky the blows were delivered by an expert, otherwise they might have been killed."

"I have read Folsom's military file. He is an expert in the martial arts. He is a very dangerous man. I have spoken to both Masters. I have attempted to slow matters here. I must proceed with the Old One's sleep-period. I have no choice in the matter."

"We have had exceptional luck in the past ten years,

sir. We—"

"Luck, Egan, has nothing to do with it. *He* simply did not interfere, that's all. Until now." The last was added bitterly.

"Why?"

"Why—now?"

"Yes, sir."

"It's the game They play. It's been going on for eons, ever since our Master was ejected from heaven. And it will continue until this world explodes in nuclear holocaust."

"I'll report back to you after tomorrow's meeting with Folsom."

"Please do."

The phone went dead in Egan's hands.

He smiled and put the plug back in the base of the receiver.

Now he could receive calls in the normal fashion.

Rana had given her daughter a sedative and put her to bed, upstairs. She sat in the den, watching Mike carefully clean and oil the guns she had brought from her farmhouse.

"You can shoot?" he asked her.

"You're asking a farm girl?" she smiled. It was the first smile since Lisa had become hysterical. "I can knock the head off a cottonmouth at fifty yards."

"Ever shot at a man?"

"No."

"It's a whole new ball game." He was field-stripping a military M-1 carbine. His skilled hands worked swiftly. "This is a good weapon for you; light, but yet adequate up to about seventy-five yards. I'll keep this shotgun, if you don't mind."

She didn't. Instead she asked, "How many men

150

have you killed, Mike?"

"Obviously, not enough," he said.

She did not pursue the matter any further.

He stood up, the shotgun in his hand. "I hate to do this to a fine shotgun, but I've got a bad feeling in the pit of my stomach about this—situation we're in."

"Hate to do what?"

"Be back in a second. I'm going to the workshop."

When he returned, he had sawed off the barrel down to the magazine tube, smoothing the bore with sandpaper and grinder.

The weapon looked awesome. Rana said as much, adding, "How much of that did you whack off?"

"It's down to eighteen inches."

"You don't plan to fool around, do you, baby?"

"Not when it's our asses on the line," he said bluntly. "I wish I could get my hands on some kind of automatic weapon. Rana, how about the hands on your place?"

"What about them?"

"How long have they worked for you?"

She smiled. "They started working for Dad forty years ago. They helped raise me. Both are members of the Lone Pine Baptist Church. That's a community about—"

"I know where it is," he returned her smile. "Then you trust them?"

"With my life," she said simply.

He dropped the subject.

"Rana? Is Stinky married?"

She looked startled. "I didn't tell you? No, I guess I didn't. Yes, he's married. Married Elaine Trudeau. They have three children."

"I remember Elaine. Real pretty girl. She's not still with him?"

"Yes, she is. And a few of us admired her for it. I

151

don't believe I'd have had the courage to stay after—well, you know.''

He shook his head. "Yeah. Then she must be a part of Becker's church?"

"No. She's a member of our church. She doesn't attend regularly—maybe once a month. But she definitely is not a part of Egan's—crap."

"The kids?"

"Let's just say the boys are not members of the Episcopal Church."

The way she said it got her a curious glance from Mike.

"Two boys and a girl, Mike. The girl is a real Cajun beauty; takes after her mother. She's gorgeous—beautiful in that dark French way. And she's a good, decent girl. The boys are—nasty. And that's being kind about it. They—well, this is rumor, nothing more, no proof—they've tried to have relations with the girl, Tina. Some whispered comments, even say they've raped her several times. They've even tried to—God! this is awful—have relations with Elaine."

"Their mother?" Mike's unbelieving words were more an explosion from his mouth.

"Yes. It's a real snake pit, Mike. Everything about this town is slimy."

He had to agree. "What are the kids' ages?"

"Wayne Ford is twenty; Sheldon is nineteen; Tina is—either fourteen or fifteen. Stinky's niece came to live with them after his sister and her husband were killed in a boating accident. That was years ago. She's sixteen, I think. She tried to come to our church, but Stinky wouldn't have it. Made her go with him to Egan's church. I really hate that bastard, Mike."

"What's her name?"

"Forrest. Ava Forrest."

* * *

For a few moments, the gravity of the situation momentarily forgotten, it was like old home week at the Folsom house. Mike remembered most of the guests; a few, Rana's age, he did not recall.

After ten minutes of light conversation, Mike brought the group to shocked silence with a blunt remark. "All right, people. Let's can the shit and get down to business."

Tongues ceased their wagging. Eyes swung in Mike's direction. "This isn't the Army, Mike," Jack Geraci reminded the ex-soldier.

"I wish to hell it was," Mike responded. "I wish to hell I could look out that window," he pointed to the front of the house, "and see a full company of Rangers out there. In combat gear."

The men and women shuffled their feet nervously on the carpet, the motion producing static electricity as the soles rubbed the carpet. Jack touched his wife's arm and the current crackled at the touch. Ann jumped about three inches off the floor, slapping at his hand.

Mike didn't let up. His anger was clearly evident and he pulled no punches. "How in the hell did you people let this situation get so far out of hand? Will somebody please tell me that?"

"It just—happened, Mike," Louis Weaver said. Louis ran a feed and seed store. "I know that's probably difficult for you to understand; you've been gone for years. But none of us really had an inkling until—it was too late."

"I don't buy that," Mike said flatly. "Your local post office was opening and censoring your mail. You knew that; you could have called in postal inspectors. You didn't. Why?"

"The calls would not have gotten through."

"Bullshit! Hell with the phones. Why not just get in your car and drive to Shreveport and report it face to face?''

"Jerry Murtz tried that, Mike," Sam Marshall said. "State Police report says he left the road just south of Mansfield. The car exploded and burned. Rana probably told you what happened to Pauline Jefferson. It—well, after that, it just didn't seem advisable.''

"You got scared," Mike said.

"That's right, Mike. We got scared. We got so scared we couldn't even talk about it. Mike," Jack said, "they know every move we make—literally. We're just a few; they're many. You have to understand that. A man from Egan's church came to see me—all of us—about five months ago. He told us there was no need for any of us to ever leave this area; anything and everything we needed was right here. That's when Jerry got mad and tried to make a run for it. You beginning to understand, now, Mike?''

"You mean none of you have been outside this—invisible barrier for—''

"Since before Christmas last," Rana said. "I told you, Mike, I was saving a few last tidbits for you.''

"But this is the last of May!" Mike almost shouted the words.

"Yes, Mike," she said. "Believe me, we know that very well.''

"But—you could have told the hands on your place. You said you trusted them with your life.''

"I didn't want to see them killed." She met his level gaze. "We've all had warnings like that." She looked around the room.

All nodded their heads in agreement.

Sam Marshall puffed on his pipe, resembling a short, stocky steam engine attempting to make a steep grade. "The point is, Mike, now that you're here, what are you going to do?''

They all looked at Mike. "I see," he said quietly, anger in his tone. "Oh, boy, do I see it clearly now."

Rana put a hand on his forearm. "Mike—"

"No." He gazed down at her. "No, I'm not going to play this game by your friends' rules. No way. It's not going to be dumped in my lap. I'll take you and Lisa and we'll get the crap out of here."

"And just leave us for the wolves, so to speak?" David Babin said.

"Well, you're the ones who have sat on your civilian butts and let it happen!" Mike roared at the man.

"My word!" David said, taking a step backward.

"What would you have had us do, Mike?" Sam asked. "We're merchants, not vikings. What would you have us do—take the law into our own hands? Can't you understand, Mike, please? All that has happened was not done overnight. It's taken years of very careful and deliberate planning on the part of Egan and Becker. They—"

Mike waved him silent. "I don't want to hear all that crap from the mouths of *men!*"

"You don't think we're very much, do you, Mike?" Jack asked, a flush to his face.

"Right now," Mike said acidly, "I sure as hell don't."

"Mike," David Babin said, "I'm sorry if we don't match up to what you consider manhood. You've been dealing with violence all your adult life. I've never even had so much as a fistfight. My guns haven't been out of the rack in years, except to clean.

"We've kept up a facade here for months. You haven't been here; you're not now and haven't been standing in our shoes, so don't blame us if we seem uneasy, edgy, and quite unsure as to the right direction to take."

David was the most educated man in the town, and all of his degrees were useless toward making a living or

155

coping with reality. He was born into wealth and his hands were as soft as a baby's palms—and about as useful as a baby's hands in any kind of tight situation. David had never worked a day in his life, and had no intention of doing so. Mike figured David would be about as helpful in a bad situation as a fart in a high wind.

Mike decided to take it from the top. "How many of you people pulled any military time?"

The men looked at each other and uncomfortably avoided Mike's cold gaze. Jack cleared his throat. "Ah—well—none of us, Mike. But what has that to do with this situation?"

"Depending on the unit, I could tell—in all likelihood—how you would withstand pressure."

David's wife, Dee Dee, a stunning brunette with about as much practical sense as her husband, said, "Perhaps, Colonel Folsom, these men saw no real need to offer themselves up to America's reply to governmental penal servitude."

That remark did not endear her to Mike. At all.

Mike's usually well-controlled temper hit the flash point. He was just about to tell the brunette where to go and what road to take in getting there, when the doorbell rang. Mike jerked open the door. Lennie Ellison stood before him, grinning.

"Just wanted you to know, Folsom, we found that old fucker. Tossed him in the garbage dump. But the main reason I come over was to tell you we have an ordinance in this town about too many cars jammin' up a street. You tell them folks in there I said to break up this gatherin' and get their asses out there," he jerked a thumb toward the street, "and move them cars."

Mike looked at the cars in front of his house. They were all tucked in close to the curb, all parked in compliance with the law.

"When I tell you to do something, Folsom," Lennie barked, "you goddamn well do it!"

Lennie felt himself jerked into the house. The movement was so swift, he did not have time to even yell. Dimly, as he was flying through the air, aware of startled eyes on him, he was cognizant of the front door slamming. He hit the far wall with a crash and slid limply to the floor.

Chief Ford, standing by Lennie's patrol car, waved back the men from the Trans-Am and the Datsun. "Stay back!" he yelled. "I warned him. Let him learn it the hard way."

Lennie was shaking his head, clawing at the pistol at his side, when he felt the weapon jerked out of leather and his fingers finding only an empty holster. Something slammed into the side of his jaw and he knew the touch of cold steel. Mike tossed the .357 mag to Rana and she caught it.

Pain began moving through Lennie, coming in flashes, as swiftly as striking snakes. His stomach felt as though it had been struck with an eight pound sledgehammer; then it went numb as nerves protested. His arms were useless as stiffened fingers slammed into nerve pockets, momentarily crippling the cop.

The pain began again, coming in new waves as tortured nerves screamed out. It seemed to last forever, with no end in sight.

Kung Fu, or something, he thought.

He was close.

Lennie wanted to scream, but nothing could push past his lips. Then he wanted to cry, but his face felt made of stone. Nothing seemed to work on or in his body.

Except his bladder and bowels.

To his disgrace, they worked just fine.

Then darkness took him, and Lennie was very happy

to go.

He came to his senses in the street. He was looking up into the angry face of Chief Ford. Ford was speaking to him, shouting at him, spittle from his mouth spraying the younger man.

"Just had to try him, didn't you?" Stinky yelled at the cop. "I tole you and tole you to leave Folsom alone. Them words come from Becker hisself. You're through, Lennie. Done. You tole me you always wanted to meet the Master? Well, boy, you 'bout to git your wish."

Ford waved his hand, signaling to a man in a dark sedan. The car pulled up swiftly. "Take him to Becker," Ford said.

Lennie was tossed into the back seat. He realized, in a moment of clarity, where he was being taken. He began screaming. The slamming of the back door did little to muffle his howls of fright.

Ford stood in the center of the street, looking up at the big house of Mike Folsom. Mike glanced at him through the big picture window and then arrogantly turned his back to the man.

"Well, now," Dee Dee said, her eyes on Mike. "Perhaps I've misjudged you." Body language said the rest, speaking in volumes.

Mike ignored her. He felt better than he had felt in weeks.

"What kind of fighting was that?" Jack questioned, awe in his voice. "Some kind of Kung Fu?"

"Something like that," Mike replied.

"Jesus!" Louis said.

The doorbell rang. Mike looked at Rana. "Tell Stinky to please come in, will you, Rana?"

She opened the door. But this was not the country boy, humble-as-pie Chief Ford of old. She felt herself being mentally undressed by the man. And she did not care for the feeling.

"Come on in, Stinky," she said.

"That's Chief Ford to you, Rana."

"It's Stinky, Stinky. And that's Mrs. Drew to you."

The Chief flushed and stepped inside. He faced the group, nodding his head at them. He fixed his eyes on Mike. "You won't be bothered no more with Lennie, Colonel."

Mike said, "He never bothered me very much to begin with, Don."

Everything is fallin' apart! the words rushed into Ford's head. Everything we done is comin' down like a house of cards in a strong wind.

He looked at Mike, and the words rushed into his brain. I ought to kill him. I ought to jerk out my gun and shoot him dead in his tracks. Right now. Right here in this house. Hell! nothing would happen to me. They can't none of them get out. Can't run. We got all the roads blocked and covered. I'll just shoot the big son of a bitch and Becker will be pleased with me.

He put his hand on the butt of his .38 Police Special. "You think you so goddamn tough, don't you, Mike? You always did think you was better than me. Come on, ain't that right, boy?"

"No, as a matter of fact, I didn't."

"You a liar, boy!"

"Give it up, Don," Mike urged him, "Don't do this—not to yourself, not to this town. Give it up. It isn't too late."

"You're dead," Stinky hissed. "All of you whimperin', psalm-singin' fuckers. You're all dead."

The group of men and women stood in frozen silence, watching the chief's right hand on the butt of the pistol.

"Where is your soul, Don?" Mike asked, his words calmly spoken.

The chief's grin was ugly. "Give you credit for some

smarts, boy. Didn't take you long to put it all together, did it?''

"I had some help.''

The man cut his eyes to Rana. "She got pretty good pussy, Mike?''

Mike said nothing, but a vein pulsed in his forehead.

"Always wanted me some of her; she never would give me no more than the time of day. Acted like she was doin' me a favor with that. Becker's got plans for you, baby,'' he grinned. "For your asshole and your pussy.''

Rana hissed at him, fear in her eyes.

Stinky returned his gaze to Mike. The .38 was half out of the leather. Something moved in the rear of the house, something only the chief could see. His eyes widened and his hand left the pistol

"Don't come no closer!'' he yelled. "Y'all leave me alone.''

No one knew what was the matter with him.

"You dead!'' he squalled. "You all dead. Stay 'way from me.''

He turned, stumbled, the pistol falling from his holster. He ran from the den, screaming insanely. The chief ran out the front door and lunged down the steps, racing for his car. He leaped into it and left ten dollars worth of rubber on the street as he screeched away, the back end fishtailing as he gained speed.

Mike closed the door, then picked up the .38. He looked toward the rear of the house. The polished wood of the hall and the tile of the kitchen were smooth and empty. The door to the basement was closed. He walked up to it.

A slight odor of damp earth filled his nostrils. He knelt down, running his fingertips across the floor.

It was slightly wet.

He looked at the base of the door leading downward.

A thin tentacle of mist was rapidly dissipating.

Mike jerked open the door.

Darkness greeted him.

Total darkness.

"No closer, son," a familiar voice whispered. "No closer."

TWELVE

"What—happened?" Jack finally managed to blurt out the stammering question.

Mike pulled himself together after hearing his father's voice. I imagined it, he tried to convince himself.

But he knew better.

Mike sighed, long and hard. "Stinky probably saw Bonnie Roberts."

Jack's wife, Ann, promptly fainted. Jack grabbed her before her head banged on the floor. He laid her on the couch. Barbara Weaver sat beside her, patting her hand and looking confused. She wished to God she had married that Kealy boy; he was a lawyer in San Francisco.

"Bonnie?" David said. "But—she's dead!"

"She's back," Mike said quietly. "And so are my parents."

They all looked at him as if they were discussing a topic with an idiot. Louis finally said, "Mike, what in the hell are you babbling about?"

Mike ignored him. He turned to Rana. "Bonnie said something to me that I don't understand. I just remembered it. Maybe you can clear it up. She said, 'Jimmy Grayson keeps pestering me.' Real heat in her voice when she said it. Angrylike. Anybody care to explain that?''

"Jimmy Grayson is dead, Mike. You're dreaming all this,'' Jack said. He looked around the room to the others. A few nodded their heads, agreeing with him. The rest remained noncommittal. "Where did you learn to fight like that, Mike?''

"In the service,'' Mike replied wearily. "Let's stay with the subject matter, people, shall we? Okay—now, you people are going to find this hard to believe, and I don't blame you for your doubts. Here it is. My father just spoke to me about three minutes ago—''

Barbara began weeping.

"—And I saw and spoke with Bonnie Roberts just hours ago, about thirty hours ago, right back there in my own kitchen.''

Shock, silence, and the sounds of weeping greeted his words. Louis finally said, "I just don't believe you, Mike. I'm sorry—I really am. But what you're saying is just—well, impossible.''

"Now, wait a minute,'' Jack held up his hand. "Let's hear this out to its conclusion. I think there is something more going on—something more to this situation—than we all believe, or care to admit. For over a year Rana has been telling us the devil is behind all our problems—the problems of this town. Some of us have even openly snickered at her. But now,'' he paused, his face holding a contemplative expression, "here's Mike Folsom, a relative stranger; been gone twenty-five years. He returns and runs into Bonnie, who has been dead ten years, and she tells him something about Jimmy. Look—let's hear it all with an open mind, people.'' He looked at Mike. "Go ahead, Colonel.''

"It's Mike, Jack. Not Colonel. Rana's girl, Lisa, claims she not only saw my parents, but two other—beings, if that's the right word. I suspect she saw Bonnie and Jimmy.

"People, I don't know what to make of all this," Mike admitted. "Perhaps it's all some ugly joke—but I seriously doubt that. I do know this. Butler has changed. It's—" he struggled for the proper word and phrase, "—evil! Someone killed and cut open Rana's dog last night or early this morning; left it hanging on the front porch just in front of the door. That's the first thing we saw this morning when we opened it."

Rana saw questions in all the eyes and said, "Mike spent the night with me. No apologies, people."

Dee Dee's eyes appraised Mike. "None expected, Rana. Personally, I don't blame you."

David cleared his throat. "Well, speaking of personally, I personally think all this devil business is a bunch of claptrap. And I don't believe you saw Bonnie, nor do I believe Miss Drew saw your parents—"

"You weren't down there, you *bastard!*" Lisa's voice rang from the stairs.

Heads turned at the sound of her voice. "Honey—" Rana moved toward her daughter.

"I'm all right, Mother," Lisa said, and Rana was filled with love for her daughter.

The eyes of mother and daughter met, held, and Lisa forced a small smile. "I'm glad," Rana said. "Really glad for you."

"No Mother," Lisa said. "I mean, I'm *really* all right. If you know what I mean."

"Oh, baby, I do!" Rana was crying.

"Now, you people listen to me," Lisa said, walking down the steps. " 'Cause what I'm going to tell you all is—well—unbelievable and disgusting, and you don't know how hard it is for me to say those words." She

165

sighed. "I've—we've—been trained for years not to say them." She went to her mother and put her arms around her, kissing her on the cheek. "I'm so sorry, Mother. There is no way I can make up for what I've put you through." She looked at Mike. "And the same goes for you, Mike."

Mike nodded.

Lisa turned to the group of adults. "Becker is the devil's agent."

A collective gasp came from the mouths of a few. Most wore looks of skepticism. David Babin laughed out loud.

"I've never seen the Old One," Lisa plunged ahead, ignoring the disbelievers, "but I'm told he's at the Blake mansion."

"Two questions, Lisa," Mike said. "What did you mean about, you've been trained not to say those words; and who is the Old One?"

"It began about nine years ago, for those in my age group, Mike. We are trained to worship the—god that Egan worships. It's vague at first; never really clear at all until a person is about thirteen, but most of us figured it out long before then. We are to praise no other god except the Prince."

"The Prince of Darkness?" Rana asked.

"Yes, ma'am."

Rana felt a wave of emotion wash over her; she had not heard "yes, ma'am' from her daughter in more years than she cared to recall.

"The Old One, Mike—I'm not really sure, but I think he's the Master of all that is Evil on Earth."

David snorted. "All this is so ridiculous, it borders on the asinine."

Dee Dee looked at him. "Shut your face, David. For once, just shut your stupid mouth and listen."

"You people are just about all that's left," the teen-

166

ager said. "That's the way I figure it, anyway. Oh, there's about a hundred or two hundred people in town who don't go to any church of—the Lord." She stumbled over the word and smiled an apology. "Sorry about that. And it's gonna go hard for them. I overheard some of the other kids talking. Really hard. I can't tell you what they're gonna do. Don't know. But you can bet it's gonna be rough.

"Anyway, you can forget your kids—they've had it, unless you can figure out a way to get them from Egan. But there really is no way, I reckon. I'm the last of my age group who has not yet been baptized into Satan."

"Black Mass?" Mike struggled to dredge up into his brain all he could recall of devil worship.

"Yes, sir. It used to be sixteen was the age when a person was taken into the Arms of the Prince. All that was kind of moved around some a few months ago. I've been—well—doing some heavy thinking—when the force would let me alone, that is."

"The force we experienced today?" Rana asked.

"Yes, ma'am."

"But—" Jack fought for words to describe his growing horror and the fact that all this just might be true. "—in all the books I've read and the movies I've seen about devil worship, I've never heard anything about a minimum age."

Lisa shrugged. "It all depends on what Master on Earth you serve, I guess."

"There is more than one?" Ann asked. She sat on the couch, her face pale, hands trembling.

"I guess so, Mrs. Geraci. More than a dozen the way I hear it. They're all over the world. There is at least one Order of Evil in every large city, but not all of them are ruled directly by a real Master."

"What is a real Master, Lisa?" Mike asked.

"The undead."

Barbara shuddered.

"Then you have submasters?" Mike asked.

"I—I don't know, Mike. I guess you could call it that. I've seen a Black Mass, but I've never really taken part in one. Other than the sex and stuff that comes after it, that is."

Barbara began to cry. "Then my Cindy . . . ?"

"Oh, sure," the girl said nonchalantly. "She's been fuckin' Director Egan. All of us fuck Egan."

"Dear God in heaven!" Jack blurted.

"What do you mean, child?" Louis asked. "The stuff that comes after it?"

"Well—you know—there's straight sex, and then there's the other stuff. Lot of women in this town like to make it with other women; same with men. Some adults are into S & M, some into bondage—golden showers—so-called kinky sex. It all goes on. Torture, the whole bit. Lots of people into ass-fucking; all that stuff."

She said it with no more emotion than if she were reading the menu at McDonald's.

Sam Marshall walked stiffly from the den into the hall bathroom—holding his stomach. The sounds of being sick drifted out from behind the closed door. His wife, Paula, went into the kitchen and wet a cloth for him.

The Marshalls had two girls, Pam and Nancy, both members of the Church of Friendship, Fellowship, and Faith.

Mike looked at David. The man was very pale and not holding together well at all. He met Mike's steady gaze. "I—don't need to be struck over the head, Mike. I don't believe in this—in its entirety, but I—can't help but believe in it in part."

Mike walked to a bookcase and took down an old high school yearbook. As he did so, he wondered in awe at how long it must have taken Bonnie to do all this. Or, he thought, did she merely snap her fingers and it was done? He shook his head as he flipped through the yearbook. He found a picture of Jimmy Grayson and showed the picture to Lisa. "You ever seen him before, Lisa?"

She recoiled as if confronted by a hissing snake, fangs bared. "Man! That's the guy in the basement! Mike—get it away from me!"

Dee Dee started screaming.

Lennie's bowels had once more released their excrement; urine ran down his leg. He was trembling so violently, he felt sure his bones would crack. He had never seen anything so hideous as this creature before him.

The Old One rumbled his profane laughter. "Do I disgust you?"

"Oh—no, sir!" Lennie managed to gasp.

"Liar!" the Old One roared. "Don't *ever* lie to your Master!"

"Yes, sir!" Lennie screamed the words. "I won't ever do that again, sir."

"What to do, what to do?" the Old One rumbled the words. "What is truth?" he chuckled. He looked at Becker. "Remember when those words were spoken, John?" He shook his ugly head. "No—no, you wouldn't. You were not yet born. What is truth?" he whispered, the timeless ages flinging him back to another land, and, like Pilate, would not stay for an answer. He looked at Becker. "Do with him as you see fit. I am weary. I must rest. Please remove this babbling fool from my sight."

Becker pushed the weeping, stumbling, badly-shaken man from the dark, foul-smelling basement room. He shoved him up the steps and into a bathroom on the ground floor of the mansion.

"Bathe," he commanded him. "And then come to me in my study."

"But I ain't got no clean clothes!"

"Then come to me as you came into this world, you fool."

Lennie stood washed and naked before the man. He could not help himself; he had a slight erection.

The sexual arousement of the man amused Becker. He sipped his tea and gazed at the man. "Always bearing in mind I can read your thoughts, you idiot, what are you thinking?"

"I—want you."

"*You* want *me?*" Becker laughed. "How perfectly droll. I much prefer women. Tell me, what do you have that I might desire?"

And Lennie knew suddenly both the answer and the awfulness that awaited him.

He could not speak of it.

Becker laughed, the evil howling a fan of hot wind on Lennie's nakedness. His erection became full and throbbing, jutting out in front of him.

Lennie looked at Becker's face. It was changing, the lips pulling back, the teeth becoming fanged, the eyes becoming that of an animal. A beast of hell, the words leaped into his mind.

"Correct," Becker said. "Come here. Let your protruding organ guide you."

And Lennie could do nothing but obey.

"Squat," Becker commanded.

Lennie squatted before him.

"You are mine," Becker said. "You are a spawn of my Master. And you have no other Master—ever."

"I understand," Lennie said.

170

Lennie felt the stinking breath of the animal-man on his neck; felt the slight prick of pain as fangs entered a vein; experienced the pull of blood leaving his body. His head felt odd, almost as if life had momentarily left him.

It had.

Visions of horror plummeted through his brain. He saw and physically experienced the pain of the smoking pits of hell; wanted to scream out from the agony of the damned, but the sound would not push out of his throat. Demons howled in his mind as his blood mingled with centuries of evil. Somewhere in the depths of the great house, a shrieking laughter was heard, pushing into Lennie's corrupted brain.

Lennie felt Becker's hand on his stiff penis, and he lifted his face to kiss the mouth of the Destroyer. His hands worked at Becker's fly until the massive organ leaped free. Lennie took the blood-engorged organ into his mouth, sucking as the forces of Satan bombarded the house.

Lennie shifted positions and knelt on the carpet, his buttocks elevated, ready to receive Becker. He screamed as the man penetrated him.

He had never experienced such pain.

It felt so good, he came on the carpet.

"I'm getting out!" Dee Dee screeched. "You're all crazy if you don't come with me."

"Honey." David reached for her hand.

She jerked away from her husband. "Don't honey me! We've got to run."

"You can't get out," Lisa said quietly. "Just ask Mother or Mike. They'll tell you." Her words quieted the room immediately. "I heard them talking out at the church. None of you can get out until it's over."

171

"Until what is over?" Mike asked.

She shrugged. "I don't know. I'm telling you the truth, Mike. I think it has something to do with the Old One. But I'm not sure."

"Nobody tells me I can't leave when I get good and ready to go!" Dee Dee yelled. "Nobody!" She jerked at her husband so hard he stumbled, almost falling. "We're getting the hell out of here, David. Getting the kids and getting out."

Mike watched them leave without comment. He turned to Rana. "Honey, will you and Lisa fix some coffee? I want us all to sit down and talk this thing out. We'll wait here for David and Dee Dee to return."

"But they said they were leaving." Paula looked at him.

"None of us can leave," Mike said quietly. "None of us."

Father Grillet of the Episcopal Church knocked almost timidly on the door. Mike opened it and stood for a few seconds, looking at the young priest. The man had a bruise on his cheek. He was a small, slight man. "Yes, Father?"

"I'm Father Dan Grillet."

"Mike Folsom."

The men shook hands. Mike waved him inside the house. "What can I do for you, Father?"

"I—need to speak with someone and I saw all the cars in front of the house. Recognized them."

"Well, you're among friends, Father," Mike assured the man. "Say whatever you want to say."

Grillet spoke to all present. He wore a confused look on his face, and his hands were trembling. "I don't know where to begin," he said.

Rana smiled at him. "From the beginning, Father

172

Dan.'' She noticed the bruise on his cheek but said nothing.

"Genesis?" the priest tried a small joke. His people smiled respectfully. "I'm—afraid it really did begin there."

"I've just fixed some coffee and sandwiches, Father," Rana said. "Please let me get you something to eat and drink."

He waved away the offer. "Tell you the truth—I'd like to have a shot of booze."

Mike laughed and poured the priest a hefty shot of Seven Crown over ice. Grillet swirled the amber liquid for a few seconds, then downed it, the ice clicking against his teeth.

"Where is Nickie, Father Dan?" Louis asked.

"Why—" the priest looked confused for a moment. "I—at home, I should imagine. My wife was all right when I left her, although I imagine the news I'll bring her will be upsetting." He looked at the empty glass, then at Mike. "Would you be so kind . . . ?" he held out the empty glass.

Mike refilled the glass with a splash of Seven Crown, much less than the first one. Grillet smiled.

"Afraid I'll get drunk, Mr. Folsom?"

"That thought has entered my mind, Father."

"Put it out of your mind, sir," he smiled. "I'm a good priest; I drink, but don't get drunk." He downed the shot of booze.

"Father Dan," Lisa said in a soft but firm voice. "I've committed a lot of sins. I'd like to talk about them with you."

"Anytime, Lisa. And it's good to see you again. I've missed you at church."

The girl began to weep. "And I've missed church."

Rana put an arm around her child's shoulders and once again daughter was close to mother. Rana met

Mike's eyes and said, "Two good things came out of your visit last night, Mike."

"Oh?" Father Grillet said. "You visited Rana last evening, Mr. Folsom?"

"He spent the night," Rana said.

"Oh." the priest said. "Well . . ." He looked down into his empty glass. "I believe one more should do it, sir."

Mike smiled and said, "How about some coffee, Father? Then you can tell us what has gotten you all upset. As if I didn't know."

Priest met warrior's eyes. "Mr. Folsom—you look— oh my!—how strange. Must be the light, I suppose. But—well, it's gone."

Mike had no idea what the priest was talking about. Neither did anyone else in the room.

Only Father Grillet could see the halo of light dimly surrounding the ex-soldier, the light coming and going very rapidly.

Grillet said, "You *know* what has happened to me?"

"I didn't say that, Father. But I'll bet it has something to do with Becker, Egan, and the Church of Friendship, Fellowship, and Faith."

"Why—that's correct."

Mike felt a surge of sorrow for the young priest. "Your first church, Father?"

"Yes. How did you know?"

"Just a guess. What's happened to you, Father?"

Grillet sighed. "A group of men—all local men— you all know them—came to the church about two hours ago. I was in my study. They told me—I could go home. Why, I just looked at them; thought they were joking. Then they began tearing up things. Ripping Bibles and hymnals. They went into the sanctuary and destroyed everything they could get their hands on. It's all ruined. They—urinated on—things Holy. I tried to stop them, and one of them took a pistol from his belt and pointed it at me. I demanded to know the meaning of his action. He—well, he cursed me and hit me. Knocked me down." The young priest touched the bruise on his cheek.

"Who hit you?" Jack's face was livid with rage. "Tell me, Father—I'll kill him!"

Mike looked at the druggist. He sighed. "Ever kill a man before, Jack?"

"Why—ah—no."

"Got a pistol on you, Jack?"

"Ah—no."

"Got one in your car?"

"Ah—no."

"Sit down, Jack," he said wearily. He turned to the priest. "Go on, Father."

"Why are you all gathered here?"

"To compare notes as to what has been and is presently occurring in Butler," Mike said.

"Evil," the young priest said, his voice soft. "Evil from hell."

"If you knew," Mike pressed him, "why didn't you and the others do something about it?"

"Mike!" Rana glared at him, heat in her eyes. "I don't think you have the right to—"

Father Grillet waved her silent. "He has the right, Rana. Believe me, he does. God-given—"

Mike looked at the young man as if he was a fool.

"—And I must accept the blame for at least part of what's happened."

"I was not placing blame, Father." Mike softened his words. "If there was anger in my tone of voice, I apologize for it. I was merely curious as to why a man of God would wait so long before taking some action."

Father Grillet sighed. "I—question just how faithful and competent a man of God I am, Mr. Folsom—"

"Mike, Father. Call me Mike."

"—And I've been doing that more often the past few months," the priest confessed. "Several times I've had my hand on the phone to call for help or at least advice. Each time I said to myself to wait; things really aren't as bad as they seem. Each time I was wrong. Things worsened. Then last week I received a letter complimenting me on not just maintaining congregation strength, but for increasing it several percentage points. Increasing it! What a joke. What a profane, ugly joke." He looked at the coffee cup in his hand and Mike could almost read his mind—wishing the coffee would change into booze.

"The local post office has been altering your reports, Father," Mike said. Not a question.

"Obviously."

"But you still didn't attempt to drive out of here, to speak with the Bishop?"

"No, Mr. Folsom—Mike," he smiled timidly. "I didn't. I'm sure these good people have told you about those who tried to leave. I was frightened. And, like Pilate, chose to wash my hands of the matter and put it out of my mind. I will not be forgiven for that act."

"Don't be too sure of that, Father Dan," Rana said. "We all make mistakes."

"But I'm a *priest!*" Father Grillet exclaimed, considerable heat in his voice. "A priest. And I can't afford to make mistakes."

"Bullshit!" Mike said. "You're a human being, Father. Stop trying to play God. He has enough problems without any of that."

Grillet smiled. When he spoke again, it was as much to himself as to the room of people. "I never wanted to be a priest. My grandfather was a priest; so was my father." He laughed without mirth. "I always wanted to be a paratrooper." This time the laugh had real humor

176

in it. "Can you imagine that? All one hundred and twenty-five pounds of me. I'd still be floating around up there somewhere."

Mike's laughter joined Grillet's. Mike had seen lightweights do just that when an updraft caught the silk and carried the men straight back up in the air.

Father Grillet walked to a corner table near the kitchen archway and set his cup and saucer down. He stood for a few seconds, sniffing, a puzzled look on his thin face.

"Something the matter, Father?" Mike asked.

"I don't mean to be rude, or offend anyone," Grillet said. "But it smells like a freshly-opened grave right here."

THIRTEEN

David and Dee Dee burst in without knocking, their kids in tow. The youngest, a girl of about ten, Mike guessed, looked scared and was offering no resistance. The two older ones, a boy and a girl, about sixteen and seventeen, respectively, wore sullen looks on their faces.

"Every goddamn road in this part of the parish is blocked off!" Dee Dee said. Her eyes found Father Grillet standing in the hall. "Oh—excuse me, Father Dan."

"Perfectly all right," Grillet said. "Considering the circumstances, I'm sure He understands and forgives."

"You sure about that, Dave?" Louis asked. His wife held onto his arm, her face white.

"Damn right, I'm sure. Hell, there isn't but three roads leading out of Butler. We traveled them all as far as we could. And something else—seems like every direction we turned, we saw young people. And they were armed. It was the damndest thing I've ever seen. They didn't try to stop us or shoot at us, but we both," he looked at his wife, "got the impression they'd like to kill us."

"Most young people are savages," Mike said. "And I don't mean that in an ugly way. I believe it was Jung who stated that a young person's mind is, at best, jumbled and disorganized. With all this mind control going on, it would be very easy to take it to an extreme with a young person and turn them into raging savages sure enough. Becker just may have gone too far without realizing it."

No one had anything to add to that.

"How are the roads blocked?" Mike asked.

"Work crews with signs. But I saw a pistol shoved in the belt of one of the men. And he really isn't a workman. He's a guard out at the institute."

Dave's son laughed crudely. "Aw, why don't you old fuckers just cool it and give in?" His words were as ugly as his tone. Before his shocked parents could react, the young man looked at Mike. "And we got plans for you, man. Your ass is deep in a crack, Pops. We gonna nail you to a cross, man; you think you're Jesus, so end up like Him."

Mike took two steps forward and backhanded the young man, knocking him sprawling. Reaching down, he jerked the young man to his feet and began shaking him as one might shake a rag doll. He shook him until the boy's head was bobbing up and down and his teeth were clacking together. Mike finally released him, dropping him casually on the floor. The boy struggled to clear his head. He blinked several times and looked up at Mike, fear in his confused eyes.

"Man—" the kid said. "You're nuts!"

"Get the Bible, Rana," Mike said. "Off the mantel."

"What about a Bible, man?" the kid questioned.

"What's your name, punk?" Mike glared down at

180

him.

"C—Curt."

Mike took the Bible from Rana. He dropped it on the floor beside the young man. Curt recoiled from the sight of it. He shook his head and closed his eyes, blotting out the sight of God's word.

"Put your hand on it, Curt," Mike ordered.

"No way, man," he said, his eyes closed.

Mike kicked him savagely in the side. The father started to protest, but one look from Mike closed his mouth before he could speak.

Curt screamed in pain and grabbed at his side.

"Put your hands on the Bible!"

"You don't understand!" Curt squalled. "If I do that, I'll die."

"Why?" Mike shouted.

"Because—because—" The young man shook his head and rolled over onto his stomach.

"Your soul belongs to Satan, doesn't it?" Mike questioned. "You better answer me, punk; don't make me stomp it out of you."

"Yes," came the damning whisper.

Dee Dee covered her face with her hands and turned away.

Grillet looked at the boy. "Possessed," he said. "Demonic possession." He looked at Lisa. "How did you escape it?"

"I never let them get complete control of my mind, Father Dan. They only thought they did."

"Good girl," the priest said.

David and Dee Dee's daughter suddenly lunged from her parents' side and ran for the front door. David grabbed for her, missing in his haste. "Come back here, Bev!" he yelled.

She was gone, the door banging open.

"Sit on your son," Mike told the father. "If he

181

moves, kick him in the head.''

David looked at Mike strangely.

Mike ran to the window; the girl was running up the street, toward the parked Trans-Am. She got in the back seat.

''Too late,'' Mike muttered.

He turned. Lisa was at his side, looking up at him.

She said, ''It's more than just possession, Mike. It is, kind of, but it isn't. It's—well, complete and total acceptance of Satan—but a lot of it is done willingly on the part of the worshipers. Let me try to explain.''

Father Grillet was listening intently.

''Egan has the minds of his followers. The kids— well, ever since most of us were very young. Hundreds and hundreds of hours of training, most of the time so subtle we didn't even know what was going on.''

Father Grillet said, ''Are you saying he really believes he'll die if he touches a Bible?''

''Well, yes and no. They didn't get that far with me. No, I think Curt's conning you there. What I think is if you try to—what's the word I'm looking for?''

''Exorcise,'' Mike supplied.

''Yeah! That's it. You try,'' she looked at the priest, ''to make him renounce his belief in Satan, he'll die. He really believes it—that's preached into our heads from a long time back. I just never did believe it, that's all. But Curt does. And if you try to exorcise him, he'll die. Bet on it.''

''And the other kids?'' Mike questioned.

''Every one of them.''

''Quite an insurance policy Becker's taken out,'' Mike said. ''But it just might backfire on him.''

Father Grillet was studying Lisa very closely. ''Will you renounce your faith in Satan and profess your undying and eternal love of God?''

''I sure will,'' she said.

And she did.

The priest seemed to grow as Lisa offered her heart and soul to God; seemed to gain strength, and Mike smiled with gladness for both the man and the child.

"Don't ever talk to me about not being faithful to your God, Father," Mike said.

"I do feel closer to Him," Grillet smiled.

"Can we stash Curt somewhere until we can figure out a way to deprogram him?" Mike asked.

"Deprogram?" Dee Dee said. "Oh, my God!" She looked down at her son, still on the floor. "Curt, son—why? Why would you do this to your father? To me? Haven't we given you everything you've ever—"

"Oh, shove it up your ass, you old bag!" the young man said.

David gave him a good kick in the slats for that. Something he should have done years before.

The boy lay moaning on the floor.

"You kicked your son, David!" Barbara said.

"If he speaks to his mother in that manner again, I'll kick his teeth out!" the father warned.

Mike said, more to himself than anyone else, "We could put him in the basement, I suppose."

"Man!" Lisa blurted. "I wouldn't put my worst enemy down there. That damn thing with fangs for teeth will be after him like white on rice."

"I'll get you for kicking me!" Curt screamed from the floor. "You goddamn son of a bitch, I'll get you for this! I'll—"

The sound of a shoe meeting jaw was dull in the room. Curt flopped on the floor and was still. "I warned him," the father said.

"It isn't the boy's fault, David!" Ann yelled at the angry father. "Not really. He—"

"Oh, shut up!" Dee Dee screamed at her best friend.

"*Knock it off!*" Mike shouted the room into silence. "All of you just shut up and sit down."

"I'll get some coffee and sandwiches," Rana said. She tugged at Dee Dee's arm. "Come on, you help me."

Father Grillet looked at Lisa. "What thing with fangs for teeth, Lisa? What are you talking about, child?"

"Jimmy Grayson," Mike answered for her. "She saw him in the basement. Along with my parents, and Bonnie Roberts. I think—God, this is so hard for me to say, much less believe—that Grayson is—what's the word? Undead?"

"Zombie?" Grillet questioned, a note of disbelief in his voice.

"No," Mike clenched his big fists and spat out the word from hell. "Vampire."

Barbara Weaver fell to her knees and began praying almost hysterically.

"You have speeded up the timetable," the Evil Old One said to Becker. It was not phrased as a question. The creature knew everything that went on around his domain, his invisible Evil Third Eye seeing and retaining all.

"It had to be, Master. Folsom is making trouble for us. Any further delays and it could be disastrous for you and us."

"I am not questioning your judgment, John. I never have. It is just that I am very tired. Soon I must take my long sleep."

He had made his decision.

"Yes, Master," Becker said.

"You have found a place for me to rest?"

"Yes. Here."

"I knew. I approve. Very well." He tapped his chest. "Protect me well, good and faithful servant."

"I shall, Master."

The Evil Old One gazed intently at his longtime friend and servant. He looked deeply into the black heart. "I sense you are troubled. Do you wish to talk with me of the anxiety you are experiencing?"

Becker was not afraid of the manlike creature; had no reason to fear him, for in many ways he was as the Evil Old One—almost immortal. He met the creature's gaze. "I sense there may be trouble, and in that respect, I am somewhat fearful for your safety."

"You have had another dream-vision?"

"Yes. While I napped this day."

"I see," the Old One said in a whisper. "Yes, I read your thoughts. You feel this Folsom has been Chosen?"

"I am certain of it."

"I can see you are. That could present a problem. I agree with you. Yes. All right, let me consult with the Prince."

Becker bowed slightly and left the room.

The room began stinking of sulphur.

"Go home," Mike told the women. "Get what kids will come with you and keep them at home behind locked doors. Stay inside." He turned to Louis. "You carry a good line of guns?"

"A very good line. But business hasn't been very good of—"

"I'm not interested in your profit and loss statement, Louis," Mike cut him off. "Is that your pickup out there?"

"Yes," the man said, a puzzled look on his face.

"I'll leave the Jag here, Rana, and go with Louis to

185

his store. We'll take all the weapons and ammo. I have a hunch we're going to need them."

Mike bent his attentions to Curt, still groggy from the kick in the jaw he received from his father. Mike jerked him off the floor and quickly secured him to a straight-backed chair, tying him in to it, then tying the chair securely to a thick support post of the stairs.

Curt cursed him and spat at him, trying to bite him.

Dee Dee wept openly.

"I don't know, Mike," Louis said, after watching and thinking for a few moments. "I got a lot of money tied up in those guns."

Mike's temper exploded. "Then goddamn you all! Now you listen to me, you simpering feather-merchant. Hear me well, all of you, 'cause I'm only going to say this one time. I can make it out of this area. I can take Rana and Lisa and make it out. Don't ever doubt it. 'Cause I will very calmly and coldly kill any one or any thing who gets in my way. I can take materials from your store, Louis, simple nitrates and chemicals farmers use every day, and make enough bombs to obliterate Butler. I've killed with my hands, with a knife, with a gun, with a wire, and with a grenade—to name only a few of the more obvious methods. Believe me, there are many more ways. Now you people seem to be looking at me to help you.—"

"We are, Mike," Jack interrupted, hastening to reassure the colonel. "We are."

"Then goddammit!" Mike thundered. Father Grillet jumped about a foot off the floor. "Don't ever question my orders. Not now, not ever! Is that understood?"

"Mike, you can have the guns!" Louis said. Like most civilians who have no military background, he was in tremendous awe of those select men who wear the berets of Ranger and Special Forces; the Navy men

186

who are the SEALs; the Marines who are Force Recon; the Air Force who are Jungle Commandoes. "I was just thinking out loud, that's all. Forgive me. I'm—scared, and I'm not ashamed to admit it."

"We're all scared, Louie." Mike reverted back to the man's high school nickname.

Louis grinned. "That's the first time I've been called Louie in twenty years. When I went off to college, the nickname dropped. I'm glad it's back. Makes me feel good."

Mike returned the grin. "Then let's get rolling, Louie."

But underneath the grin, Mike was worried. These men had never been tested; had never been pushed to the limits of courage and endurance; never been forced to reach deep inside themselves, to that hidden well, and drink from the cup of inner courage, to take one more step when their feet were raw and blistered and bleeding from marching forty miles through jungle or mountain or desert. They had never leaned into a mountain and felt it tremble under their hands, knowing that there was only one way to go: straight up, for to go down meant failure; Never faced an enemy, knowing that only one of them would walk away. So much these civilians had never done.

And he wondered, if it came to shooting, and he felt certain it would, how many of these men would hold up under the strain?

The thought came to him—some of these people are going to die. And one or two are going to do it badly.

And another thought came to him—when all is said and done, it will all be up to me.

Rana picked up on his silent thoughts; her eyes found his and she understood him. She did not know how she could understand his thoughts, but she did not question the source or the comprehension. She let her eyes speak for her heart and mind.

And as is so often the case, man drew strength from woman.

"Let's go, people," Mike said. "I think time is running out."

Mike loaded the guns and ammunition into the back of Louis' pickup and returned to the house, caching the mound of supplies in a storage room off the kitchen. He had assigned each man a specific task: one to get all the canned foods he could load into his car; another to get tents and ground sheets and rope and pegs; a third to procure medical supplies, five gallon cans of gas, and plastic jugs of fresh water.

To a man, they all looked at Mike curiously, questions in their eyes. But they did as they were told, without inquiring as to why.

And Becker viewed it all with a mixture of amusement and a slight feeling of dismay. So the man was not going to run. Becker did not think he would. Well—not run in the usual sense of the word—out of cowardice. This man would run, but the running would be in the form of attacking. His file read that the man was a guerrilla expert.

All right.

Becker stroked his chin thoughtfully. Perhaps, he mused, he could meet with the man, discuss this situation logically, perhaps work out a plan of—

He rejected that immediately.

Becker summoned all the dark forces at his command, willing them to thrust themselves at the man.

They would not.

Becker chuckled sourly. He thought that would be the case.

So the game had begun. The never-ending game between the King and the Prince.

But Folsom would have to die. Too much had gone into this to allow one man to ruin it. Too much money had been spent. Not that money really mattered. It didn't. His many and varied companies were real and legitimate. His life was open to public inspection. The life the Master had constructed for him, that is. Money was no object; only his Master's safety was paramount.

Back to Folsom.

Becker could destroy any mortal man with no more effort than a wave of his hand. But now he knew he could not kill Folsom in that manner.

That is quite true, the voice rang silently in his head.

Becker could almost smell the burning odor of flesh as the millions charred in the pits; he could almost hear the cries of the damned as their flesh smouldered through all of eternity.

"So that much is firm?" Becker asked the Prince.

Yes.

"Damn that meddling son of a bitch!" Becker slammed a hand on his desk top.

Actually, only part of that statement is true, but that is no matter. What do you intend to do about this Colonel Folsom?

"I intend to stop him, Prince."

How?

"I don't know. His mind, I suppose. There must be a way. I'll find it."

The town is of little importance. I can revert it back to ten years ago with no effort. The Old One has been my friend for— well, time is not the issue. For eons. He is your primary concern. His safety must come first. Always. Above all else. Do you understand?

"Yes, Master."

A pity, though. We almost had perfection.

Becker detected a note of resignation in the hot voice. He said nothing of it. He knew he did not have to

189

speak; the Prince knew the minds of not only every mortal, but also his subjects.

Speak your mind, servant.

Becker spoke the words that left an ugly taste on his tongue. "Have we lost? After all this time, all this preparation, have we lost?"

We never entirely lose; He never entirely wins.

Becker felt the voice and the heat retreat in an invisible swirl of burning wind.

As usual, Becker thought, the Master has left me with a riddle.

Nothing ever changes.

He sat behind his desk and enjoyed the picture his third eye gave him of Rana going to the bathroom.

"Nice cunt," he said.

FOURTEEN

"I'm afraid we're going to have to expedite our meeting, Colonel Folsom," Director Egan spoke over the phone. "Ah—pressing matters have arisen. I do hope you will understand. Do you still desire a meeting with me?"

"I wouldn't miss it for the world," was Mike's reply. "Come on over. I'm sure you know where I live."

"I'll be there promptly." Egan broke the connection.

Mike looked at the bound and gagged Curt Babin. "Your buddy's on the way. I'm sure you'll be glad to see him, right?"

Curt's profane reply was muffled against the gag tied around his head, covering his mouth.

"Just as well," Mike muttered. He walked to a chair and sat down, only then realizing just how tired he was.

And he could not bring himself, his mind, to fully accept all that was happening around him; all that he sensed was true, but yet had such a—a Hollywoodish air to it.

Mike sighed in confusion, allowing his eyes to close.

He dozed for a few moments, sitting in the big easy chair. When he awakened, he felt better, the catnap having worked its magic on him, as it always did.

He was up and moving before the echo of the doorbell's ringing had faded.

Egan stood smiling at him in the dim light of dusk. "You look rather weary, Colonel," he said. "Are you sure you're getting enough rest?"

Mike glared at him.

"I rather doubt you care to shake my hand?" Egan's smile remained fixed in place.

"You got that right. Come on in. Sit over there," he waved.

Egan sat, perfectly relaxed, fully composed, a faint smile on his lips. He ignored Curt.

"Aren't you going to even acknowledge the presence of your parishioner in sin?" Mike asked.

"What a quaint way of putting it. Yes, of course. When I take him with me."

"Curt isn't going anywhere. At least not with you."

Egan's smile widened. "You jest, Colonel? What good is he to you? Surely by now Lisa has told you, or you have put it together, that if you attempt to meddle with the young man's faith—he'll die. Do you really want that?"

"Better he die than live a life of filth."

"Filth? Oh, come now, Colonel, let's not be overly dramatic about this little issue. Why don't you just take your new-found pussy and her turncoat daughter—who really has excellent cunt, I must say, very tight—and just leave here?"

Mike had no ready reply for that question.

"I see," Egan said softly. "You really don't know yet. Well, you will, in time. Very soon, in all probability."

"I haven't the vaguest idea what you're talking

about, Egan.''

''Umm. An honest man, too. I can now see why you were picked.''

''Egan, what in the devil are you talking about?''

Egan laughed. ''How true, that question.''

Mike sighed.

''No matter, Colonel. Let's get down to business. What will it take for you to leave us alone? Take your two pussies and leave?''

''You must think me a fool. I don't believe you people have any intention of allowing any of us to leave. But you're going to regret pushing me to the wall.''

''Oh, Colonel! I must protest. You may leave. You will not be harmed. I assure you of that. Take Rana and Lisa and get out. It's as simple as that. You will not be harmed. I have our Master's word on it.''

''By your Master, I presume you mean the Devil?''

''He is not without honor, sir. Bear in mind he was once one of God's angels.''

''Egan, if you're serious with this proposal, then one of us is an idiot.''

''Why?'' There was genuine perplexity on the man's face.

''Why? Damn, man! Once on the outside, all I'd have to do is tell the press and the authorities about this scheme of yours and it would all come crashing down around your ears. Kaput!''

''Oh, come now, Colonel.'' Egan primly crossed his legs, adjusting the crease in his tailored trousers. ''Now who is assuming the other is a fool?''

Mike stood in the center of the den, looking down at Egan. Slow comprehension spread over his face. ''I see,'' he said. ''At least I think I do.''

Egan clapped his hands gleefully and giggled. ''Oh, I do so love this. Put it all together for me, if you can, Colonel.''

"This is all a joke to you people, isn't it, you fairy? Just one big damn joke."

"Oh, no!" Egan immediately sobered. "It's no joke, sir. I assure you of that. It's very real and taken very seriously, believe me." He sniffed distainfully. "Fairy, sir, is a very outdated word."

Mike ignored that. "All right, Egan, let me put it all together. If I were to agree to pull out," he paced the den as he talked, ";probably within twenty-four hours, maybe less, this town—this community—would be as normal as before. And I use the word normal paradoxically."

"Are you asking me a question, or merely stating your beliefs?"

"Flat out truth."

"You're right on the tweetie, sweetie," Egan giggled. "My, you are a smart one, aren't you?"

Egan's eyes centered on Mike's crotch. Mike shuddered. He said, "And outwardly, there is nothing wrong with this community as is."

"Bingo, Ringo," Egan twittered.

"And if I did leave, bringing the press and the authorities back with me—I'd look like a fool."

"Direct hit!"

"Because everything would be just dandy."

"Bong!" Egan gonged an invisible bell.

"But the people who were here this afternoon: Louie, Jack, David—all of them—they'd be brainwashed, if that's the right choice of words—and all part of your group, by then."

"Bong-Bong!" Egan struck the imaginary gong.

"But for some reason, you people obviously feel you can't work your—black magic on me—why?"

Egan giggled. "I never kiss and tell, baby."

Mike resisted an impulse to punch him out. "How do you propose to fight Bonnie Roberts and my par-

194

ents?''

"You really don't know much about the—ah—supernatural, do you, Colonel? I hate to use that adjective, but in this situation it's the best at the moment."

"I know practically nothing about it."

Egan glanced at his wristwatch. His face hardened for a few seconds. "I urge you, Colonel, take your blonde twits and get out!"

"Sorry. I like it around here. Lots of action coming up shortly; I like action. Used to be a friendly town. Maybe I can bring it back; turn it around."

Egan got to his feet. "Well, I tried. You're making a terrible, horrible mistake, Colonel; you don't realize it, but you are. Your friends are going to die very slowly, very painfully. And I'd think about Rana and Lisa, if I were you."

"You'd let the others live in exchange for their vows to make hell their dismal home for eternity?"

"What a vulgar way of putting it! But—true."

"Tell me something, if you can—or will?"

Egan shrugged.

"Why did you wait so long to put your plan in action?"

Egan pursed his lips, then licked them and smiled at Mike. Flirted with him. Mike kept his temper in check. "Well, Mikey, I suppose I can divulge that. It's really very simple—you were a surprise; not expected."

"Dammit, man! Why me? Why am I the pivot piece in this jigsaw puzzle of yours?"

Egan did a little dance step on the hardwood floor. "Don't you just love a mystery? *Ciao!*" he cried happily, and then pranced out the door.

"Son of a bitch is as queer as a three dollar bill," Mike said, with the usual military man's distaste for homosexuals.

"He swings both ways, Mike," Lisa spoke from the

stairs. "Besides, homosexuality is not forbidden in the Church of Satan."

Mike turned. "Come over and sit with me, Lisa. Talk to me. In some areas, I'm more confused now than before."

Mike sat in the easy chair, Lisa in front of him on the hassock. She looked very fresh, very appealing. Her blonde hair shone with youth and health.

"Mike, I think any normal, healthy person has some sexual fantasies," she said. "But your—our—Bible forbids them. That's why so many people are so easy to convert to Satan's Way. Let me use 'your Bible.' It'll be easier that way—okay?"

He nodded.

"Christianity is filled with hypocrisy; probably always has been. Christians *want* to do right, but your Bible places so many rules and restrictions on them. Most people just can't abide by those rules. They want to, but they can't—not to the letter. 'Cause they're human. And they are not perfect. So along comes Egan with his line of BS, and away they go.

"Christianity had better get its act together, Mike. That's my belief, anyway. And I'm just a kid. But I'm a pretty wise kid in some respects—and you better believe that.

"Just check off the rules your religion has: you can't engage in masturbation; you can't lust after your neighbor's wife or husband or both—even mentally; it's a sin; you can't engage in any type of sex that is considered 'abnormal.' What the hell is abnormal? Man, if it feels good and it isn't hurting anybody—what's wrong with it? But not if you're a Christian, right?"

"But one can try to be a Christian, Lisa." Mike defended his faith. What faith? he silently questioned. How many times have you been to church in the past

196

five years, Folsom? Twice. At the most. Good going, boy. You're a hypocrite. Just like what this child in a woman's body is describing.

"No, you can't, Mike! You can't. You've got to *be* one. You've got to live it twenty-four hours a day, every day, for all your life. If you don't, then you're not a Christian, you're a make-believe Christian. You can't tell a dirty joke—not one; you can't take a drink; you can't place a bet; you can't work on Sunday—the list is endless, Mike. And break just one of those rules, and you're a sinner. It's too much, Mike. Way too much. It's just one big damn hassle and a lot of people are saying piss on it. Saying—literally—to hell with it!

"Those people are looking around and seeing mass hypocrisy. People who are just as sorry as dogshit sitting up in church and acting like they're just as pure as snow, when everybody knows they're dickheads who cheat on their wives or husbands; who screw people in business dealings, every day; who are bigots; who know that fifty-two percent of the world's population goes to bed hungry at night, and they're not doing a damn thing about it; TV preachers who say love God but send your money to them.

"Oh, Mike, you know what I'm talking about; you're an adult, I'm a kid, but I can see where organized religion is off the track.

"Look," she put a soft young hand on his forearm, "I'm not so sure I'm strong enough to resist the pull that is yet to come, really come, from Egan and his dark forces. I mean that. I need help and I want help, but I don't believe now and never will that sex is wrong if both parties are consenting to that act.

"Okay, I'm back now. And I love God, and I'll accept His word—as much of it as possible. And as for the rest of it, well—I'll just have to take my chances."

Out of the mouths of babes, Mike thought. "This

pull you're talking about—what can I do to help you when it comes?"

She looked at him. "Fuck me," she said simply.

"I—can't do that, Lisa."

She grimaced. "You see what I mean? Why can't you just say you're fucking for God?"

"Because temptation is supposed to be resisted, Lisa."

She smiled. "Like you and mother do?"

Mike shifted in the chair. Damn!

"You see," Lisa said. "Restrictions and double standards again. Tell me this—how many men that you know who profess to be Christians would hold back if I offered them some?"

Damn few, Mike thought, but did not put his thoughts into words.

"Damn few, huh?"

"Don't get in my mind like that!" he said. "Lisa, I can't debate the Bible with you, or its rules. I'm just not qualified."

Her smile was mocking, but it was a sweet mocking, not at all ugly. "Really, Mike? You really don't know what has happened, do you?"

"What are you trying to say, Lisa?" Rana asked. She stood in the middle of the stairs, rubbing sleep from her eyes.

Lisa shook her head. She looked first at her mother, then at Mike. "Man, you really are dense, you know that?"

"You've lost me," Mike confessed.

"Mike, you've been chosen. Michael probably picked you as the Warrior."

"Dense? Warrior? Chosen?" Mike almost babbled the words. "Lisa, what are you talking about. Chosen by whom?"

Her smile was very sad. "God," she said.

* * *

Mike stood on the porch of the old home. He was deep in thought, but still very much aware of his surroundings; it was a trick that all professional fighting men soon develop—or they soon become very dead professional fighting men.

He had explained the offer of escape from Egan. They had both rejected it—flatly.

Their answer came as no surprise to him.

The night lay silent and peaceful over Butler, belying the evil and the unspeakable horror that was crouched just below the shadows of darkness, ready and willing to rear its ugly, smoking head.

Mike wondered if Lisa was right in her assumption that he was a Chosen Person. Why? Why him? There was nothing he had done in his life to make him obvious to the eyes of God. He was neither atheist nor fanatic; just a man who believed quite simply that God was the Supreme Higher Power, and believed that in his own quiet, simple way. He had sinned many times in His eyes, in many different ways.

As he stood on the porch, his thoughts were flung back to Southeast Asia in the early sixties, where he had participated in many ambushes, many body snatches, killing and kidnapping cold-bloodedly in the soft heat of night.

And torture, he forced himself to admit in his mental recall.

He thought of the women he'd known sexually down through the long years. He had never even asked some of their names; could not remember many of the faces.

I'd have been just as well off sticking my dick in a warm room and waving it around, he surmised.

He looked up and down the street. The Trans-Am and the Datsun were parked a respectable distance from the house. He could not tell if Bev was still in the Trans-Am. He doubted it. He looked at his wrist watch. Ten o'clock.

And all was not well.

He heard the screen door open softly behind him. Instinctively, he tensed. Rana came to his side, her soft scent reaching him first.

"Lisa is sleeping soundly," she said. "Curt has peed on himself."

"Fuck Curt," Mike said bluntly.

"I feel sorry for the boy," she said, compassion in her voice.

"I did, at first," Mike admitted. "But I'm rapidly losing any feelings of compassion for him."

She looked at him in the darkness. "He's only a child, Mike."

"I was only a year older than Curt when I went through Jump School," Mike said, a hardness in his voice.

"And that proves . . . ?"

Mike was silent for a moment. "It proves I'm a better man than any present boy in this town will ever be."

Every good, decent man has his faults, Rana thought. "Not much give to you, is there, Mike?"

"Damn little, honey. Not when it comes to a man doing what a man is supposed to do."

"Oh, Mike! What a male chauvinist remark. Well, *I* can't place all the blame on the kids," she said stubbornly. "The parents have to take a large part of the responsibility for what's happened here."

"And the courts, and the news media, and the schools, and the federal judges—including the supreme court—and the TV and the radio, for programming the shit they present as entertainment."

Rana laughed at him. "All right. Mike, Enough. I

agree with you. What kind of music do you like?"

"Classical. I grew up on rock and roll and country. But people have to mature in all kinds of ways, broaden their horizons, so to speak. I do like the big band sounds, though."

"In other words, in your opinion, classical music is the ultimate in music?"

"Yes."

She didn't agree with him; but now that she had discovered this hard, unyielding part of him, she knew that to argue further would be futile. Besides, she reluctantly conceded, he was right to some degree.

"What are we going to do, Mike?"

He leaned down and whispered in her ear.

"Mike! That's positively—pornographic!" she giggled. "But it does sound like fun."

She was silent for a time, enjoying just being close to the man she loved, and had loved, in a long-distance manner, for most of her life. Finally, she said, "What if Lisa is correct, Mike?"

"About me being chosen?" He looked at her. She nodded.

He shook his head. "I don't believe that. I think they're wary of killing me—physically removing me— because I'm not an unknown; because I am moderately wealthy; because killing or kidnapping me would probably prompt an investigation.

"There are things that don't add up in this thing, Rana, like who hung the dog on your porch, and why? What—"

There was a rush of wind and a hot, stinking blast of sulphur.

Becker appeared on the porch.

FIFTEEN

Rana almost fainted and Mike almost put a round from his .41 mag into the man.

"Who the hell are you?" Mike shouted.

"John Becker. Calm yourselves," he said quietly. His eyes glowed yellow in the night.

Both Mike and Rana smelled the now-fading odor of sulphur around the man.

"Lennie hung the dog on your porch, Mrs. Drew. Lennie is and will always be, a fool." He smiled. "Among other things, that is. Why he did it is, as yet, and probably will always be, an unknown."

Mike turned to see if the men in the parked cars had taken notice of the night visitor.

"They don't know I'm here," Becker said. "They can't see me. Only you two can see me—among the mortals, that is."

"Where in the *hell* did you come from?" Mike asked.

Becker smiled. "Somewhere in your question lies the answer, Colonel."

Mike decided not to pursue that. Rana came closer to him and he put an arm around her waist.

Becker felt something tug at him as he witnessed the act. He mentally brushed it off. "Were you really going to eat this young woman's pussy, Colonel?" He shifted his burning eyes to Rana. "And why did you think it pornographic, madam?"

"How long have you been standing by the porch eavesdropping?" Rana asked.

"I have never stood by your porch, dear. Actually, I was having a small dinner at the mansion, listening to you two chat. I decided to make an appearance. I do so enjoy a touch of the dramatic. Very good entrance, don't you think?"

"You were listening—from the mansion?" Mike didn't believe a word of it.

"You doubt me?" Becker smiled, but his smile was as cold and as black as his heart.

"I damn sure do!"

Becker looked at both of them, but then shifted his gaze to Rana. "You went to the bathroom this afternoon, late. You were wearing blue panties. The toilet paper roll was almost empty. You allowed your fingers to brush your clitoris while your thoughts were of Colonel Folsom. You shook away those thoughts and rose quickly to your feet, tearing a small rip in your panties as you did so. Left side, near the almost invisible seam. Correct?"

She looked up at Mike and slowly nodded her head.

Mike met the man's burning eyes. "Are you . . . ?"

"The devil?" Becker laughed. "Oh, no, Colonel. Not even my second Master is the devil. But he is— well—close to him, shall we say. I just *possess*—I love that word—certain powers you mortals do not now and never will comprehend, that's all."

"Then you're not human?" Mike could not force himself to believe this conversation was real and actually taking place.

"Not in your sense of the word. But I was at one time."

"How old are you?" Rana asked.

"Oh, about twelve hundred years, give or take fifty or sixty. Birthdays don't impress me much anymore. Not since—oh—Columbus sailed the ocean blue."

"In fourteen hundred and ninety-two," Mike replied automatically, and felt like a damn fool for doing so.

"Oh, my—you are quick, aren't you?" Becker said dryly.

"I don't believe any of this bullshit!" Mike said.

Becker fixed his strange eyes on the ex-soldier. "Frankly, Colonel Folsom, I don't particularly give a twit what you believe or disbelieve. And furthermore, I am growing quite weary of you. I—"

"Becker?" Mike said.

"What, Colonel?" the tone was hard.

"Fuck you."

Mike expected anger from the man; instead Becker only laughed softly. "I see," his tone was considerably lighter. "So the battle lines have been drawn; is that what you are telling me in your vulgar way?"

"That's it, pal."

"Very well. I came here attempting to converse in a civilized manner with a civilized man. You obviously are a person of low degree, without the ability or desire to behave in any sort of refined demeanor." He reached into the night and pulled out a coiling, striking rattlesnake as thick as a big man's wrist. He threw it at Mike.

Rana screamed.

Mike put one boot on the snake's head, reached down, and secured a grip with his fingers behind the snake's head. He released the head and picked up the snake, looking at it while the rattler coiled around his arm, hissing and rattling its fury. Venom dripped from the fanged mouth.

Mike put the snake's head back under his boot, grinding and then crushing it. He jerked, and then separated the snake's head from the body. He looked at Rana. "Rattlesnake meat is very good. I'll clean this and we'll have it for appetizers tomorrow evening." He dropped the still-writhing reptile to the porch floor.

"Very, very good, Colonel," Becker said, approval in his voice. "I am certain you were the hit of the show when you instructed Ranger candidates years ago. You will make me a most worthy foe."

Rana could not take her eyes off the dark shape of the bloody, squirming, headless snake on the porch.

"Look in the house, Colonel," Becker said.

Mike looked. Curt was gone. The ropes lay in a neat pile in front of the chair.

"How—"

"Don't tax yourself mentally, Colonel. It is beyond any mortal's grasp. Just take your two cunts and leave. This will be your last chance for safe passage."

"And if I don't?"

"Then you'll die."

"All right," Mike said quietly. "I'm ready. Do it, Becker."

John Becker's face paled in the night.

Rana gasped in fright, clutching at Mike's arm.

Becker raised a hand and then let it drop to his side. The rage on his face was horrible.

"You can't do it," Mike said. "I don't understand why—but you can't kill me."

"*I* can't kill you, Colonel," Becker said. "Bear that in mine. *I* can't kill you—yet."

Mike kicked the poisonous head off the porch, then spat after it.

"I shall take my leave now," Becker said.

"Good riddance," Mike told him.

"Oh, we'll be seeing each other again, Colonel," Becker assured him. "You may be certain of that. Yes," he chuckled, "*rest* assured of that. And speaking of a time of sweet repose, by all means, people, do rest well this stormy night."

Mike and Rana both looked up at the sky. It was star-filled and there wasn't a cloud to be seen.

Becker was gone as silently and as quickly as he had appeared. The porch was once more tainted with the invisible odor of sulphur.

The couple stood in silence for a few moments. Neither of them could really make themselves believe they had seen what they had.

But both knew they had witnessed a spawn of hell.

"He watched me go to the bathroom!" Rana said. "That's disgusting."

"I turn you on so much you have to play with yourself?" Mike chuckled.

She faced him in the darkness. "I believe you made a proposition to me a few minutes ago, Folsom."

"That I did."

"Then get on with it."

"On the porch?"

Ava finally opened her eyes and found herself in total darkness. She lay very still and counted slowly to one hundred. She was alone in the room, she decided. She turned her head and could see rain spotting the barred window, then sudden flickering flashes of lightning illuminating the sky. She heard someone coming up to the door, and she quickly lay back on the bed, closing her eyes, breathing slowly and evenly—like she had seen people do in the movies.

A single beam of light cut through the darkness,

playing briefly on the girl's face.

"She in there?" a man's voice asked.

"Out like a light," a woman's voice replied.

"Which is what we ain't got," the man laughed. "How long has it been since her last shot?"

"Put your light on the clipboard, Ned. Let's see. Oh, hell, she just got one five minutes ago. She'll be out until daylight, at least."

"What the hell is the matter with that auxiliary generator?"

"Broke down. I know some people who ain't gonna like this."

"How about the Womb Room?"

"It's okay. The backup there is humming."

"Okay, let's check the rest of our patients," she laughed.

Ava was wide awake, but confused. She knew she had not received any shot in the past five or ten minutes—maybe longer. What had happened? She didn't know. All she knew was she was awake, the lights were out in the hospital, and if she was going to get away, this was the time to do it.

She fought the straps that held her wrists and freed herself. Obviously, they had not expected her to be awake for a long time. She removed the I.V. from her arms and jerked the electrodes from her head, wincing as bits of hair were pulled from her scalp.

She slipped from the bed and felt her legs wobble a bit until she regained her strength. Her asshole hurt. And then she remembered the man with the whip. And other things came rushing into her mind. Bits and broken parts of sentences.

"—is shit!" Who is shit? "God is shit. Satan is your Master. Satan is all powerful."

She fought the words from her mind and stubbed her toe on the side of the dresser. She bent over to rub her toe just as the door was cracked open.

"—give this little cunt her shot and I'll see you later," a woman's voice spoke. "I'll meet you in the lounge as soon as the lights come on."

"Right, baby," a man said.

Ava almost panicked. Her hands gripped the dresser, found the knob that pulled the drawer open, and jerked it out. She straightened up, running barefooted to the door, the metal drawer held over her head. The door opened fully, the woman's shape silhouetted in the dim light. Ava brought the heavy drawer down on her head.

She thought she would be sick as the woman's head cracked open from the impact. Ava fought back hot bile as the door hissed shut and the white-uniformed nurse fell to the floor. The top of her head was flattened from the savage blow; blood leaked from both ears and one eye bulged from the impact.

Ava composed herself and laid the drawer on the floor. She stripped the woman of her uniform and struggled to put the woman on the bed, pulling the sheet over her. Ava slipped into the white uniform and jammed her feet into the shoes. They were just a little tight, but Ava didn't notice it; all her thoughts concentrated on escape. She picked up the little tray the nurse had carried, and the flashlight, checking the beam. The flashlight worked, although the lense was cracked.

She stepped out into the hall and ran right into a white-coated man.

"Aw, hell, baby," Chief Ford said to his wife. "Go on and give the boys some pussy. It ain't like they ain't been there before." He laughed at his crudeness and pounded his hand on the coffee table. "I mean, Elaine, they—"

"I know what you mean, Don," the woman said. Her heart was pounding heavily in her chest and she was frightened. But she must not let her fright show; she had to get Tina and get away from this madhouse.

Stinky's sons laughed at their father's joke.

"Yeah, Mommy," Sheldon smirked. "You know what they say—a boy is a lot closer to his mother than to his father. So let's you and me get *rreeeall* close."

This is not happening to me. Elaine fought to keep her sanity. This simply can't be happening.

But it was.

"I'm packing, Don," she told him. "It's been bad before; but at least you tried to stop them," she waved at the boys. "Now you're actually encouraging this— perveted filth. You're sick! This whole town is sick! I'm packing and leaving. Now!"

"You ain't goin' nowheres, baby; 'cept to get your ass bare and get on that bed over yonder. I may decide to knock me off a piece after the boys get through."

The storm built in fury, lashing the earth with rain and wind.

"What's happened to you, Don? This town?" Elaine questioned. "This afternoon I went into town and it's as if I didn't know a soul. The people have all changed. It's like I'm looking at strangers. They've been—queer—"

Stinky gave her a dirty look.

"—before; but this time it's reached ridiculous proportions. And yes, Don, I most certainly am leaving; I'm taking Tina with me. And I want a firm answer from you. Where is Ava? What have you done with her?"

"I done tole you, baby, at the hospital. I checked her in yesterday."

"Again? why?"

"I'm tired of your goddamn questions!" He lunged

210

from his chair and grabbed her, ripping the housedress from her, leaving her in bra and panties. She fought him, slapping him hard across the mouth. He backhanded her, knocking her against a wall, stunning her. He jerked her bra from her and ripped off her panties. He brutally squeezed a breast until she screamed out in pain. Then he hit her in the stomach with his fist.

"Now, you behave, Elaine—you hear?"

She could but numbly nod her head through the pain.

He jammed a finger into her dryness and she moaned from the assault.

"You git yourself wet for my boys, Elaine. Hell, baby, you know you gonna enjoy it." He looked at the young men, open lust in their eyes. "There it is, boys. Jump right in and get you some. And don't bother me none, you hear? I got other things on my mind."

The boys knew what those "other things" were.

"All praise the Prince," Sheldon said, moving toward his mother, unzipping his jeans.

Elaine could only watch in horror as both her sons exposed themselves to her. She knew to fight them would only cause her greater pain. She limply allowed them to position her on the couch. She closed tear-filled eyes and gasped as the oldest took her first.

"All praise the Master of Darkness," Stinky said, moving toward the center bedroom of the house. He tried his daughter's bedroom door. Locked. "Open this here door, girl."

"Go away!" came the timid, tiny plea. "Please, daddy, don't do this to me."

"Open this goddamn door afore I kick it in."

"Are you going to hurt me?"

He grinned. The only time Stinky could make it with a woman was when she fought him—and then only if she was young. The younger the better. But he'd seen his daughter's bush the other day, and it had aroused feelings of lust in him. "No, baby, I'm gonna make you feel good."

"You promise me? What's happening to Mother? Why did she scream a minute ago?"

"Run, Tina!" Elaine's pain-filled voice screamed through the house.

Stinky kicked in the door, splintering it. The girl began screaming as he moved toward the bed. He slapped her back on the bed and dropped his trousers to the floor, kicking off his shoes and stepping out of his pants and underwear. He grasped his erect maleness and skinned it back.

"Look at it, girl. You 'bout to feel something good."

"No!" she screamed.

She screamed as he jerked the nightgown from her. She screamed as he forced her legs apart. She screamed and cried as he bent his head and licked at her womanhood. She yelled in pain as he rammed his way inside her, her blood spotting the sheets.

"Daddy, please stop," she begged him. "Daddy—it hurts!"

"All love the Master," Stinky panted. "God is shit. All praise the Prince."

And in the den, the mother wept from shame and pain and humiliation as her sons took her from front and back.

The scene was being repeated all over town; most of it with willing partners.

A hundred naked teenagers danced in the stormy night. The music had long ceased; they pranced and strutted and hunched to a silent beat, accompanied by roaring thunder and bolts of hard lightning.

The dancing changed, the teenagers forming a crude

212

circle, the young men to the inside of the circle, the young women behind them. They danced first inward, then backward. They chanted as they danced, calling out the vilest of oaths, all directed heavenward, all condemning the Lord God and praising the Prince of Darkness.

And to this scene, God closed His mighty eye. They who dared to profane His name in such a manner—were forever lost.

"Watch where you're going, nurse!" the man said. "Is our patient still out?"

"Yes, doctor," Ava said, deepening her voice, hoping the man was really a doctor. "I was just going—"

"I don't care where you're going. You just make sure Ava stays out and the equipment is running smoothly when the lights come back on." He walked away down the dark corridor, his flashlight lighting the way.

Ava headed in the other direction, using her flashlight sparingly. She found a door marked Exit, paused to look around her, then pushed open the door and stepped into even more darkness than the hall offered her. The door closed silently behind her. She stood very still, attempting to get her bearings.

"Oh, goddamn, baby!" a woman's voice whispered. "That feels so good."

Ava tensed, her back to a wall.

"I thought I heard the door open," a man panted the words.

The voices came from her left, far down in the darkness.

"You heard my door open, baby," the woman said. "Just keep pumpin'."

The wet slap of flesh on flesh resumed.

Ava slipped forward, the rubber-soled shoes making no noise. A few yards away she saw flashes of lightning dance wickedly across the wind-swept sky. She moved toward the storm-produced source of light and freedom. A few seconds later she was outside and knew where she was and how to get to town. She darted across the darkened grounds of the institute and made it to the blacktop road that would take her to Butler. She didn't know where to go once she got to town; she knew that most—if not all—the residents were members of Egan's church.

Then she thought of Father Grillet.

She would go there.

She walked on, oblivious to the drenching rain and the stormy night.

"What we just did, Mike," Rana said. "Was that wrong in the eyes of God?"

His reply was long in coming. "Oral sex? I don't know, honey," he admitted. "I would guess so, but how can I be sure?"

"It felt good," she said.

"Yes," he chuckled. "It sure did."

"Then there is some truth in what Lisa said this afternoon?" She looked at the clock on the bedside table. "Or rather, yesterday?"

He sighed. "There was probably bits and pieces of truth in everything she said. But I can't set myself up as some sort of morality judge; I'll leave that up to these self-righteous political groups that are springing up all over the country, trying to dictate terms to people and run everyone's life."

A hoarse yowl of intense pain drifted up to them, overriding the noise of the storm.

Rana tensed at Mike's side. "My God, Mike—what

was that?"

"It's beginning, honey."

"What's beginning?"

"Hell."

SIXTEEN

Mother and daughter lay naked in each other's arms in a bedroom off the den. The male members of the family were getting progressively drunker, the sex acts more and more perverted.

Jimmy Laplante from the post office had joined them after Don had raped his daughter, and Don had magnanimously offered Tina to the man. Jimmy had graciously accepted the offer and raped Tina. Burke Rider, the stuffy president of the local bank, had joined in the grotesque festivities with his wife, Vera. Burke was now servicing Jimmy from the rear while Jimmy was lapping away at Vera, his head between her widespread legs.

All were far too preoccupied to care about or notice the ravished mother and daughter.

In the dim light from the nightlight, Elaine looked at her young daughter's nakedness and fought back tears. To cry now would be useless. The girl's thighs were streaked with dried blood and semen; her breasts were bruised from many rough hands; and the girl had been brutally raped from the rear—by Trooper Duval, who had since departed after firing his load of sperm up the girl's rectum.

Duval had grinned at the girl's wailing and then withdrew his softening penis. "Got to go back on patrol," he had said, zipping up his trousers. "Start my vacation tomorrow; and you all know what that means." He had patted the weeping teenager on her bare buttocks. "Got some good tight ass, baby," he had complimented her. "Really skinned my pecker back."

His laudatory remark had not been fully appreciated by either mother or daughter.

And from the very darkest depths of hell, Satan had howled his sulphuric laughter, approving of his subject's humor.

The lightning, the thunder, the wind, and the rain had increased into almost gale force.

"Get up," Elaine whispered to Tina. "Be quiet and get some clothes on. Never mind underwear; just slip into jeans and a shirt and put something on your feet that won't slip off. We're going to run for it."

The child's tears wet the mother's breast. "What's happening here, Mother?" the girl cried softly. "Why is all this being done to us?"

"Get dressed," the mother urged her, pushing her from her side. "We'll talk later."

The raped and ravished women dressed quickly and silently, the noise from the orgy covering any sound they might have made. Mother and daughter slipped from the house of ugliness and depravity and melted into the stormy night.

"Where are we going, Mother?"

"I—I think to the Folsom house."

"That's all empty and dark, Mother."

"No, no it isn't. The man who will save us is there, Tina."

"How do you know that, Mother?"

"I don't know. I just thought of it."

"Why did you think of it?"

"Maybe God wanted me to."

"I don't think He likes us here in Butler anymore, Mother."

"Oh, honey! Don't even think that, much less speak it."

"But look what's happened to us this night."

"There is a reason for everything, Tina. And don't ask me to explain that—I can't. Just keep your faith in the Almighty."

"I do try, Mother. But—it's hard to do."

"I know, baby. I know."

The lights sprang at her, catching Ava before she could jump and hide in the ditch. She was headlighted by the side of the road. The car roared through the rainswept night, sliding to a stop beside her.

She looked at the driver, his face illuminated by the glow of dash lights. His face looked savage. His eyes were mean. Ted Bernard.

"Oh, dear God!" She begged for His help. "Please help me."

The strain and the drugs had taken their toll on the girl; she was too exhausted to run. She had been stumbling when the lights caught her in their harsh glare.

The door to the driver's side opened and Ted got out, a billy-club in his hand. He wore a yellow slicker over his uniform. He walked towards her, his eyes taking in her young lushness under the wet uniform. She wore no bra or panties and all of her was visible to his hard eyes.

He reached for her.

She began screaming as his hand gripped her arm and pulled her to him.

She was too weak to fight him off.

The pounding on the front door jarred Mike out of a deep slumber. His .41 mag in hand, he walked down the stairs and looked out onto the porch. He flipped the porch light on. Two women. No—a woman with a young girl. The storm had built into a raging maelstrom while he had slept, the wind howling around the town, tearing limbs from trees and toppling TV antennas.

Mike cracked the door and the wind opened it the rest of the way. He fought to keep the wind from tearing the door from him. "Come in," he shouted, his voice just carrying over the howl of the wind.

Automatically he checked the street, looking up and down; the watchers were still there.

"Mike," Rana shouted from the top of the stairs. "What is it?"

The door closed and the howl and rush of wind abated. Mike turned on the ground floor lights.

"Oh, Elaine!" Rana called, coming down the stairs. "God, what's happened?"

Mike looked at the pretty young girl, noting the darkening bruises on her lovely face. He felt waves of pity wash over him; then anger as the name Elaine sank in and he realized who the mother and daughter were.

"Stinky did this to you two?" he asked.

Rana had gone to the downstairs bathroom, gathering up towels. Mike led the pair into the den.

"Yes." Elaine's voice was dull from fatigue. "Don, my sons, Jimmy Laplante, Trooper Duval, Mr. Rider—"

"Burke?" Mike asked, startled. "Prissy Burke?"

Even in grade school Burke had been a very reserved young man, almost prissy with his aloofness.

"Momma?" Tina said. "I think I'm bleeding again."

"Where?" Mike asked. He could see no open cuts on the girl.

"From my—behind," the young girl said.

"You mean . . . ?" Mike looked at Elaine. "They —there?"

"Yes."

"Good God!" The word exploded from his mouth.

"Mike, call Doctor Luden," Rana suggested, giving the pair of women towels. "When you get him, tell him what's happened. He'll come right out."

"I don't *know* what's happened!"

"It wouldn't do any good to call Max," Elaine said. "He's one of them."

Rana thought of the times Lisa had more than willingly gone to the doctor when she had nothing more than a very minor scratch.

Now she knew why. She silently cursed Max Luden. Then her emotions got the better of her. "That no-good son of a bitch!" she cursed the doctor.

Rana gathered up dry clothing for Elaine and Tina; Mike went into the kitchen to make coffee. He checked his watch. Two o'clock. Well, he'd operated on a lot less sleep. He returned to the den. Lisa had joined the others, rubbing sleep from her eyes.

The rain-soaked women had dried and changed into jeans and shirts from Lisa and Rana. They sat drying their hair. Mike looked first at Tina, then at Rana.

"She—ah—all right?" he asked.

"As near as I can tell. I don't believe it's serious. The bleeding has stopped."

"What is this preoccupation with anal sex?" Mike asked.

221

"Tight," Lisa answered bluntly. She looked up at him. "I mean," she shrugged, "so they tell me."

Mike had grown accustomed to the teenager's frankness. Familiarized to it, but not comfortable with it.

She said, "You mean, Mike, as worldly as you are, you've never gone in the back door of a woman?"

Her mother sighed and shook her head.

"No," Mike replied, his face red.

"That's really wild, man."

"Lisa," he said, "would you please drop the subject?"

"You brought it up," she reminded him.

The storm raged on, the wild howlings of the wind causing the raindrops to sound like a thousand hammers beating on the house in a crazy rhythm, each crystal blow independent of the other.

"I just vaguely remember you, Elaine," Mike said. "And this puzzles me. Why did you come over here, to me?"

She put her dark Cajun eyes on his face. "I received the thought when we," she looked at her daughter, "were leaving the house. At that precise moment, as I recall."

Mike shook his head. "I don't understand. Who was it that told you I had returned?"

"No one told me."

"Then . . . ?"

"I don't know," Elaine admitted. "I was just told to come here."

"By whom?" Mike pressed. He turned his head, conscious of eyes on him. Lisa was smiling sadly at him.

Tina looked at the tall man; her dark eyes were still filled with the horror she had experienced. But behind the abhorrence lay a seriousness. Her reply to his question chilled Mike, weakened him to a point that he had

222

to sit down in a chair before his knees gave way, spilling him to the floor.

The battered, abused, and assaulted child said, "Mother thinks it was God."

"I'm not going to hurt you, Ava," Ted said. "I'm not one of Becker's people. He and Egan just think I am. Get in the car. There's a jacket and an old pair of jeans on the back seat. I'll stand out here until you get changed. Go on."

She struggled into the too-big jeans and jacket and was grateful for the warmth. She tapped on the glass, signaling for him to get in.

They rolled swiftly down the slick blacktop, the wind occasionally rocking the car with sudden gusts. "Where are we going?" she asked.

"I don't know," he admitted. "We sure can't get out of this part of the parish. Becker's people have closed the roads. And I think this storm has just started. I think it's going to get really rough before it's over. And I'm wondering who sent it."

She studied his face. Now it did not seem hard or mean. She decided it was a good face, full of decency.

She hoped.

"What do you mean, Ted?"

"I'm wondering if it came from God, or from the Devil."

She shuddered beside him. "I've—been acquainted with the Devil for some time."

"I know," he said dryly. "Why are you running from your Master now?"

"He's not my Master, Ted. I decided that several weeks ago. Who are you, Ted? You drifted into town last year and the next thing I knew, you were a cop, working for Chief Ford."

He smiled faintly. "I was one of Egan's people in California when I was very young. My parents had me kidnapped from his church and deprogrammed. That was years ago. Then I went to Vietnam and lost God again; again returned to Egan. Well, finally I came back to Christ. I've—changed some over the years. I work for the government, Ava. Don't ask me what department. I can't tell you. When I realized who Mike Folsom was, well—I almost lost my cool and blew my cover. I was, well, afraid the colonel would foul things up for me. I know the colonel's reputation. He doesn't back away from trouble." He sighed. "I was right; Colonel Folsom brought things to a head around here in a hurry."

"I still don't understand," she said.

The rain drummed on the car; lighting bolted across the night sky; thunder rolled, a mad drummer with every percussion instrument available at his command. A cadence from both heaven and hell; one power hysterical with joy, the other furious and wrathful.

"My—superior wanted me to handle this," Ted said. "I have a rather—personal interest in it. I tried to warn Colonel Folsom off; obviously my warning didn't take. I didn't think it would."

"Are we going to this colonel person's house?"

"I think that would probably be best."

"God?" Mike said, a stunned expression on his face. He tried to smile. "You people keep on telling me that and I'm liable to believe it and start acting funny."

"I told you so," Lisa reminded him. "I feel the same way she does."

"If that's true," Mike rubbed his face, the scratch of his whiskers reminding him he hadn't shaved in over thirty-six hours, "he sure made a bum choice."

"No," Tina said softly, her young eyes appraising him. "After meeting you, seeing you, I think He made the right choice."

The water kettle began whistling in the kitchen. "I'll get it," Lisa said. "I'll put sugar and cream and stuff on a tray and bring it in here."

Her screaming brought Mike to his feet, charging into the kitchen.

A man was struggling with the girl, his hands ripping the blouse from her, striking her with his fist. "All praise the Master!" he shouted. His eyes were wild.

Mike stepped in and chopped the assailant on the back of the neck with the knife edge of his hand. The man grunted and fell to his knees. Mike stepped in closer, put both hands behind the man's head, and jerked, bringing his knee up at the same time.

There was a sickening crunch; teeth rolled and bounced like popcorn onto the tile floor. The man was still except for a slight trembling of his legs.

"You know him?" Mike asked.

"Joe Marsh from the post office," she said, holding her torn shirt over her bare breasts. She looked again. "You sure changed his looks, Mike."

The kitchen was filling up with people. Rana took her daughter in her arms, held her for a moment, then led her away to get a fresh blouse.

Mike jerked the man to his feet and held his head under the open water tap for a moment, the cold water reviving the him.

"Elaine," Mike said, "go open the front door and see if you can't hold it open, please."

She looked at him strangely, but did not question the order.

Mike got a running start in the hall, with one hand on the man's shirt collar and the other hand holding onto the seat of his pants, forcing the man to run through the house. When he reached the wet, windy, open darkness of the porch, Mike released him with a mighty shove. The man went screaming out into the night, literally sailing off the porch. He landed with an ugly thud on the sidewalk, one arm broken, the bones glistening whitely in the night; a leg was bent under him. The man lay very still.

Mike closed the door and turned to look at Elaine. She was studying him, inspecting him with dark eyes. "You play rough, don't you, Colonel?"

"At times."

"That man might well die out there; bleed to death; go into shock."

"Then that would mean there would be one less for us to contend with."

She shrugged as only a Cajun can. "*Chacun a son gout*," she said. To each his own taste.

"*Oui, en effet,*" Mike smiled.

"You knew French as a child?"

Mike laughed. "No. Cajun's kind of difficult to learn in redneck country. I spent a good many months with the French Paratroopers—kind of a lend-lease deal. I learned what I know of it there."

"I think you're a good man, Colonel Mike Folsom," she said simply, no other meaning to the words.

"*Peut-etre.*"

They walked into the den, just as Rana and Lisa were coming down the stairs.

The lights flickered once, then dimmed, staying dim as the storm raged on.

Elaine suddenly gasped, looking wildly around the room.

"What's wrong?" Mike asked.

She pointed to the empty couch. "Tina's gone!"

The lights went out, plunging the house into total darkness.

SEVENTEEN

"Stay calm!" Mike shouted down the near-hysteria of the women. He walked through the den, down the short hall, and into the kitchen, opening the drawer that held the emergency candles and the flashlights. As he passed the door to the basement, he again smelled that musty odor. He could not deny he was relieved when the candles were passed around and lighted.

Someone knocked on the door. They had to knock several times before being heard over the roar of the storm. The people in the darkened house tensed, eyes narrowing in strained speculation, their just-under-the-surface fear showing in their eyes in the flickering candlelight.

"Colonel Folsom!" the voice called over the howl of the tempest. "It's Ted Bernard. I've got Ava Forrest with me."

"Thank God!" Elaine said. "One accounted for. But where is Tina?"

"Right here," the girl's voice sprang through the flickering light of the room. "I only went to the bathroom, Momma."

Elaine's laugh was tinged with uncontrolled relief.

Mike flung open the door, again fighting it as the storm had increased in its fury; the wind almost tore the heavy door from its hinges. Again, he looked up and down the street. The watchers were still watching.

The room turned into a babble of voices, with everyone except Mike and Ted attempting to talk at once. Mike looked suspiciously at the cop, still in his dripping yellow slicker.

"You've got some explaining to do, buddy," Mike said.

"Yes, sir," Ted agreed. "And I fully intend to do that. As much as I can, that is."

"Now just what the hell do you mean by that?"

"You are familiar with the military clearance of Eyes, Ears, and Hands?"

"Yes. I have that clearance. Or had it, I should say. It's the second highest clearance in the intelligence community. Only one above it."

"I have that one," Ted said quietly, just loud enough for Mike to hear.

Each man then knew who the other was, or had been. They visibly relaxed.

"It's been hell around here," Mike said.

"Apt choice of nouns, sir, I assure you."

"So you believe in all this, too, eh?"

"Very much so, Colonel. And so does my superior."

"And who might that be?"

Ted smiled. "You do not have a need to know, sir."

"Same old bullshit."

"Never changes."

Mike nodded. "Come on in the den and sit down. Take off that slicker and hang it over there," he pointed. "We'll have coffee and then you can level with me." He looked at the younger man. "As much as you can, that is."

"I am very, very weary," the Evil Old One said, his heavy voice no more than a whisper in the gloom of the foul-smelling basement. "I will have to sleep soon."

"Only a question or two," Becker said. "Who is sending this storm?"

"The gods."

"Both of them?"

"Yes. The King is very angry, venting His rage. Finally. I knew it had to come. The Prince is trying to help us. Tell me how, John."

Becker smiled. "There will be a disruption of services in this part of the parish. Roads will become impassible and the phone service knocked out for several days, perhaps longer. More than enough time. I will call the governor, personally, and assure him that everything is perfectly all right: no injuries, no deaths, et cetera. No need for any outside help. Our Master and his Ageless Adversary will do the rest, although I don't see, at this time anyway, what He hopes to accomplish by this. Whatever it is, I should imagine it will not be to our liking."

"True. He aids Folsom by this. Although the colonel does not, as yet, know it. Very well; there is a chance we still might be victorious. A slim chance. John?"

"Yes, Master."

"At dusk of this day I will be ready for my ordeal to begin. Have you everything in ready?"

"Yes, Master."

"Send the servants in to prepare me."

"Right away."

"You work for what office?" Mike asked.

"The Office of Unexplained Phenomena." Ted

smiled. "Yes, I realize it's rather a paradoxical title, but I didn't come up with it."

"And it's military?"

"To a degree. That's all I can tell you, Colonel. You'll just have to trust me. Please don't press for more."

"I understand the 'don't press for more' part, Ted. What I don't understand is why you people are investigating Becker."

"Oh, we're not the only ones investigating him, Colonel." His replies were glib. Maybe too glib, Mike thought. He didn't trust Ted Bernard as much as he hoped the man thought he did. "The IRS is looking very closely and very secretly into his rather vast holdings; the FBI is standing by, ready to move in—several more government agencies which you would be quite familiar with. I'm just the only—field agent in here at this time, that's all. And," he listened to the howl of the storm, "I'll probably be the only one for several days. Maybe longer. This storm was deliberately sent."

Glib, Mike thought. Very pat. Everything smooth as honey and silk. Are you lying to me, Bernard? "Would you explain that last part, Ted?"

"Either God or Satan sent it; maybe both."

Mike cleared his throat and looked at the man. He sighed, blinked. "All right," he said. "I guess I have no choice but to accept that; too many strange occurrences happening to just brush it off lightly. Back at Rana's house I was going to call some buddies of mine, ask them to come in for a few days." His smile was grim, a death's head grin. "Kind of a reunion, you might say."

"Men you soldiered with, Colonel?"

"Right. But Rana cautioned me about the phones in this part of the parish. So I guess that's out."

"We won't need any outside help," Ted said. "At

least not from your—buddies, that is."

"You real sure about that?"

"Trust me, Colonel."

I wonder. "It's Mike, not Colonel."

"I like Colonel," Ted insisted.

"*Quelque,*" Mike shrugged it off. Whatever.

"*Merci.*"

"You speak French?"

"I speak seven languages, Colonel."

"Very impressive."

Ted smiled. A strange smile, a quick curving of the lips that was gone as quickly as it came. "Not really, Colonel. Someday you'll understand what I mean. Now—why don't you people," he looked around the room, "all get some much-needed rest? I'll stand watch until dawn."

"You're not tired?" Rana asked.

"I don't need much sleep, Mrs. Drew." That odd smile again.

"Conditioning?" she asked.

"Something like that, ma'am. Go on—all of you. I assure you, nothing will harm any of you."

In bed, snuggled up against the bulk of Mike, Rana said, "What an odd young man. I mean, I guess he's older than I am, but he seems so young-appearing."

"I don't trust him," Mike said bluntly. "I just flat out don't trust him."

"Your imagination, honey," she murmured.

"Maybe."

And in the morning, the sun shining brightly, the birds singing happily, not a cloud to be seen in the clear blue sky, Mike drove into town.

It was as if nothing at all out of the ordinary had occurred.

* * *

"Good morning, Mike," Burke Rider greeted him, a smile on his face, open, friendly. He rose to walk around his polished desk, extending his hand. Mike reluctantly took it. "I can't tell you how good it is to see you after all these years."

Mike released the man's hand. "Are you putting me on, Burke?"

The banker blinked. "Why—not at all, Mike. What an odd question."

Mike studied him closely. The banker's eyes were just a bit puffy from lack of sleep; but other than that, there were no signs of dissipation from the previous night's sexual antics.

"How much money do I have in this bank, Burke?"

He was told. It was considerable.

"All insured by the government?"

"Every penny, Mike. Not all of your monies are in the same accounts, of course. Young Mr. Wallace has invested a great deal for you."

"In Becker stock?"

"Ah—yes."

"Get it out. Sell it. Right now."

"Mike—I—ah—"

"Just do it and quit stuttering. You sound like a set of Westinghouse brakes." He took a slip of paper from his pocket and tossed it on the desk. "I have two accounts with that bank. Send the monies to them."

"I'm afraid it can't be today, Mike." The banker's smile was smug, conciliatory. Mike wanted very badly to spread his nose all over his face. "We have no phone service," Burke said, spreading his hands in a helpless manner. "But just as soon—"

Mike was in no mood for games. "Then get papers drawn up—right now—attesting to the fact that I officially requested this action, making you and the board of directors personally responsible should this bank fail.

232

Get it done, get it notarized, get it legal, and get it *now!*"

"I don't care for your attitude, Mike."

"I don't give a flying fuck what you care for, Burke. You just do what I tell you to do with my money, and you do it pronto."

The banker's face flushed crimson. "It will take a few moments."

"I'll wait."

When Burke returned, Mike said, "Elaine and Tina and Ava are staying with me for a time. I think they'll be safer there, don't you? Much less chance of rape at my house."

A vein pulsed heavily in the banker's bloated face. "Enjoy your mood of superiority, Folsom. I assure you, it won't last long."

Mike laughed at him.

"Oh, I'm so looking forward to the next few days," Burke said.

"I'll just bet you are, Burke. Sure is a beautiful day, isn't it, Burke?" Mike smiled. "Considering the violent storm that passed through last night."

"A storm that closed the roads and cut off all communications, I should tell you, Folsom." His eyes were shining with evil.

"In other words, Burke, I can't get out or call anyone, and no one on the outside can get in. Is that what you're telling me?"

His smile was the darkest of evil, a baneful curving of the lips. He did not have to speak.

"Oh, but you're wrong, Burke."

The banker's eyes narrowed.

"There *is* someone with whom I can communicate."

"I'd like to know what that person is," the banker sneered at him.

Mike smiled. "God."

* * *

"Good morning, Colonel Folsom," the lady at the drugstore said with a smile. "Lovely day, isn't it?"

"Just marvelous, ma'am," Mike replied. She looked familiar, but he couldn't place her. She left and he turned to Jack. "What the hell is going on now? Two days ago very few people in this town would even speak to me; now I'm Mr. Popular."

"Mike?" Jack hissed at him, his face chalky with fear. He smelled as though his deodorant had failed him—badly. "We're cut off; can't get out. Mike— we're trapped like rats in here!"

"Calm down, Jack. Get a grip on yourself, man." He brought the druggist up-to-date on the past night's events.

"Burke is one of *them?*" The words were hoarsely whispered, although there was no one else in the store. "Mike, I can't believe it."

"You can believe it. I just left him at the bank. He's one of them." Mike looked around the store. "You run this place by yourself, Jack?"

"No. All my help walked out on me yesterday after-noon 'bout two o'clock." He shook his head. "Mike, what are we going to do?" There was a note of ur-gency, almost panic in his tone.

"For one thing, Jack, you are going to calm yourself. I would suggest you close the store, go home, and take a shower. You smell like a goat in rut."

"I don't—have your courage, Mike. I'm scared."

"Jack, we're all scared. I—"

"No, you're not scared, Mike," the druggist cut him off. "Damn you, you're just as calm as if you were out for a quiet stroll around town. And you know it. So please stop patronizing me—us—all of us who didn't fight in wars and win medals and jump out of airplanes

234

and all the rest of that hero stuff. I'm scared, Mike. Just flat scared shitless.''

Mike stared at the man for a few seconds. "I didn't mean to patronize you, Jack. I really didn't. I'm sorry if you think it was deliberate.''

Jack shook his head. "And I didn't mean to snap at you. You're right. I'm shutting this place down and going home to my family—that's where I belong. I'm going to get my gun and by God, I'll shoot anybody who—''

"Whoa, Jack.'' Mike put a hand on the man's arm. "Whoa, now. Just take it easy. Don't go running around shooting at shadows. Let's take this slow and easy for the time being. What about your kids?''

"All gone. Ann's been crying all day. I feel so sorry for her. I don't know what to do. She's—not well, Mike. Emotional problems. I don't know what this is going to do to her.'' He sighed and took several deep breaths. "My kids just flatly told me to kiss their asses. Then they left. It hurt, at first, then I got mad, then scared, then mad all over again. Hell with them.''

Mike glanced at his watch. Early yet. "All right, Jack. Get in touch with the others. Tell them to pack some things. All of them. Have them at my house at noon. From this moment on, you all go armed. Understand? Good. But let the other side make the first aggressive move before you do anything hostile. I don't know when or how or if this thing is even going to break; but when it does, Jack, I think it's going to pop quickly. Lock up and get cracking, buddy.''

For the first time that day, Jack Geraci smiled. "Yes, sir, Colonel Folsom.''

But Mike could tell the man was very near the breaking point. He wondered how many of the others were nearing their limits of mental endurance.

He stood in front of the drugstore, watching the flow

of traffic, both street and pedestrian. Those on foot were friendly, vocally; but their eyes mirrored none of the friendliness. The eyes were savage and mean.

A young girl, no more than fifteen, wiggled up to him. "Hey, man? You wanna fuck?"

Mike looked at her. He could feel no pity welling up within him. "Go on home, girl," he said.

"Too bad, man," she said. "You don't know what you're missin'."

"I can guess, girl."

"Oh?"

"Several shots of penicillin."

She spat in his face.

Mike wiped the spittle from his cheek and turned his back to her. She cursed him as he walked away. He had never heard such filth from the mouth of a child.

"I don't understand this delay," Egan complained to Becker. "We've got them boxed in; they can't get out. So let's take them and have some fun with them."

" 'Taking them,' as you put it, will not be as easy as you seem to envision. And I knew something about this Ted Bernard troubled me. He is not who he professes to be."

"Who is he, Master?"

"I don't know. But he has gone over to the other side; took Ava with him. She killed a nurse at the hospital last evening."

"But when he showed up here, I came straight to you, didn't I. I mean, you—"

"Yes, yes," Becker waved him silent. "Stop sniveling and groveling. I accept the responsibility for his treasonous behavior. I just wish I could place the man; I know I've seen him before. Ah, well. It's of little importance."

Egan met the man's yellow eyes. "Barnard?"

Becker laughed. "Not hardly, Egan. I would recognize even his ghost; and our Supreme Master would warn us if he were walking. Put the matter out of your mind."

"When do we make our move?"

"I will inform you."

Becker was gone. No trace of him remained, only the slight tainted odor of sulphur.

Mike drove the parish roads, reviewing the damage done by the storm. It was extensive. Bridges were washed out; trees blocked the roads; roadbeds were damaged, undercut by the flash-flooding. But only a few power lines were down, and those were being repaired by men wearing coveralls with Becker Utility on the back.

"Cute," Mike muttered. "The guy almost made it. Looks like I'm the only fly in the ointment."

That was true. To a degree.

No doubt about it, Mike mused. We are cut off.

Groups of teenagers were gathered in loose bands every few miles. All were armed. At least one in each group held a handy-talkie. And they appeared restless.

Mike tucked that in the back of his mind and kept it there for future reference. Young people with all morals trained out of them; young people who appeared restless; young people with guns.

"Makes for a potentially bad situation," he muttered.

He turned around and drove back toward town. "Better get everybody ready," he said aloud. "I think it's about to get rough."

A highway patrol car flashed him over about two miles from town. Tina had told him about Trooper

Duval and what he looked like. This was Duval. Mike watched the highway cop, accompanied by a local man, a deputy from the sheriff department's substation in Butler, walk toward his car. Tina had finally told them all of the full horror of the rape. Now a coldness washed over Mike, rage building almost to the maximum. He no longer tried to fight it back. Looking at the arrogant strut of the man, the rage could no longer be contained.

"You Duval?" Mike called, his right hand on the butt of the .41 mag.

"That's right. What's it to you?"

Mike stepped from the Jag, the .41 in his hand. With one fluid, practiced motion, he jacked the hammer back, leveled the powerful handgun, butt resting in the palm of his left hand, centered the sights on Duval's crotch, and pulled the trigger.

The pistol roared and bucked in his hand.

Duval's feet were knocked out from under him from the force of the expanding slug. He was wailing and screaming in agony as he hit the blacktop, smashing his mouth and nose on the asphalt. He thrashed on the highway, his ruined crotch gushing blood.

The entire procedure had taken less than two seconds to accomplish. Mike centered the muzzle on the deputy's stomach.

"Freeze!"

"Son of a bitch!" the man hollered. "Man! I ain't movin'!" A dark stain appeared at the crotch of the man's trousers.

"Unbuckle your harness and kick it to me," Mike told him.

Gun belt and hostler hit the blacktop. The frightened man kicked it to Mike.

"Get down on your hands and knees," Mike told the man.

The man dropped like a stone, both hands on the

blacktop.

Mike shifted the muzzle of the .41 and shot Duval in the center of the chest. The rapist thrashed on the road and then lay still.

"Oh, my God!" the deputy hollered.

"You calling on God?" Mike laughed over the ringing in his ears. "You're a vacillating bastard, aren't you?"

"Yes, sir! Whatever that means, I am."

Gas escaped from the almost dead Duval.

"Your name?"

"Tommy Wilson, sir. Man, don't shoot me. I'm beggin' you. Please!"

"What church you attend, Tommy?"

"The Church of Friendship, Fellowship, and Faith. But I can change! Man—you just say the word and I'll join any church you name."

"You know who I am?"

"Yes, sir. Everybody—I'm—I mean. Yes, sir," he said weakly.

"You know why I shot Duval?"

"I reckon so, sir. He tole me he got some brown on his pecker from Tina Ford last night." Sweat dripped from the man's face.

"And I'll bet you thought that was funny, didn't you, Wilson?"

The deputy, sensing his time on this earth was very swiftly closing the gap between living reality and lifeless eternity, began crying. "Yes, sir," he blubbered. "I laughed some."

Mike cursed him until he was breathless. "You are one sorry son of a bitch. You know that?"

"Yes, sir. I reckon so. But if you'll give me just half a chance, I'll do my best to make it all up."

Mike hesitated. He lowered the muzzle of the .41 mag. "How? How would you do that?"

The deputy raised his head. His tears ceased their falling. His eyes gave him away. Mike was going to let him live until the slyness appeared in the man's eyes.

"You're a lying bastard, Wilson."

"I reckon I am, Colonel. All praise the Prince of Darkness!" he shouted.

"You're not fit to live."

"Maybe not. But most folks git a judge and jury to make that decision, Colonel."

Mike jacked the hammer back on the .41. "Then I shall take this opportunity to shorten the process of our often cumbersome method of jurisprudence."

He shot the man between the eyes.

EIGHTEEN

Cars and trucks were parked in front of Mike's house. He recognized most of them. He glanced at his watch: eleven-forty-five. He walked up the steps and stood for a moment looking first up the street, then down. They were still there.

He pushed open the door and stepped into his house, almost colliding with a woman.

"Colonel Folsom," Father Grillet said, rising from the couch. "This is my wife, Nickie."

Nickie Grillet was most certainly not the stereotyped preacher's wife. She was beautiful, in a pouting way, an almost tangible air of sensuality lingering about her. She was very shapely, with full breasts, good hips and long legs, light brown hair, worn long. Her frankly sexual eyes appraised Mike.

"Colonel," she said, extending a small hand.

Mike took it; cool to the touch. "Mrs. Grillet."

"Nickie," she corrected.

"Mike."

She smiled up at him. Mike got the distinct impression this lady never had and never would get enough cock.

"You people better all sit down," he said. "I've something to tell you." He looked around the room, his eyes finding Rana. "Is this all that's coming?"

"All but Ed Coder and Marge," she said. "They'll be here any minute. What's the matter, Mike?"

He quickly and bluntly, without embellishment, told them what had happened on the parish road. First the armed teenagers, then the shooting incident.

"You killed Duval and Wilson?" Jack cried. "Oh, my God, Mike! They'll be coming to get you. Put you in jail!"

He still had not gotten it through his head that law and order and justice were only words now. They applied only to the outside world, but were meaningless here in Butler.

"Your parents named you correctly when they named you Michael," Ted said. The news of the killings seemed to have no effect on him; he was as unruffled as ever.

Mike glanced at him. "How's that?"

"God's warrior."

Mike shrugged that off.

"Honey," Rana said, "what did you do with the bodies?"

"Left them in the road," Mike said, with about as much emotion as discussing the making of a peanut butter sandwich.

Father Grillet bowed his head and prayed silently.

"I'm glad you did it," Tina said. "I hope Duval died horribly."

Mike's smile was grim. "I first shot him in the crotch."

"Good," she said.

"My God!" Jack said. He seemed to be in mild shock. Ann Geraci looked as if she'd aged ten years in

242

hree days. She sat on a couch and stared dully into
pace. Mike wondered what was happening in her
nind.

Ten seconds later he found out.

Ann rose very primly from the couch and walked almost childlike to the front door. She looked around and
smiled sweetly. "I think I'd better go home now, Jack.
My parents will be worried about me."

"What?" her husband said dumbly.

Louis Weaver whispered. "Her parents died five
years ago, Mike."

"Come on, now, Jackie," Ann insisted. "You be a
good boy and take me on home. It's getting late and we
really shouldn't have done that bad thing tonight." She
giggled, a note of madness in the childlike laughter.

"What—bad thing, honey?" Jack asked. "Ann,
what are you talking about?"

"It felt good after a while, Jackie; but you really
shouldn't have put that big old thing in me. It was—
ugly. And it was bad and sinful." A wistful look came
into her eyes. No one in the room spoke or moved. "I
wonder if maybe I should go talk with Father Lewis?"

Nickie Grillet looked frightened.

Dave and Dee Dee held hands, seeking comfort in
their touch.

Ann said, "Jackie, I just don't know what I'll do if
you made me pregnant."

"Honey," Jack said almost desperately, "you had a
hysterectomy ten years ago!"

"Oh, poo on you, Jackie Geraci!" she stamped one
foot. She giggled. "It's not that far; I think I'll just
walk home."

Mike started for her. Her face darkened with fury.
She hissed at him. "Don't you touch me, Mike Fol-
som! Don't you dare. I know what you and that Bonnie
Roberts do all the time. You're nasty! She's nasty! You

243

leave me alone!''

"She's flipped out," Tina said.

"Bonkers," Lisa added.

Rana walked toward the woman. Ann bolted, jerking open the door and running onto the porch. She was screaming. She jumped into the yard, pausing only long enough to look wildly around her. Then she ran toward the Trans-Am parked just up the street.

"Help me!" she yelled. "They're after me."

A man jumped out of the car, grabbed the woman, and threw her into the back seat. The Trans-Am roared off. Ten seconds later, another car took its place near the curb. Watching.

"She's gone," Jack said, his voice dull. "She must have heard the music too. It's so pretty. But I don't know who those men were. Do you know, Mikey?" He looked at Mike; his voice was childlike.

"Music, Jack? What music. You didn't know those men?"

"What, Mike? I can't hear you."

"You want me to go after her, Jack?"

"Afterward? After what, Mikey?" Jack looked at him. "Tell you what, Mikey—we'll go exploring later. Right now I have to go home. My mother is singing to me. It's so pretty, Mikey." He took Mike's hand. "Come go with me, Mikey."

Mike jerked his hand away. A .38 snub-nosed appeared from under Jack's shirt. His hand was steady holding the gun, the muzzle pointed at Mike's stomach.

"I'll be going now, Mikey. We'll go to the movies tomorrow afternoon. *The Thing* is playing. It's a good one. See you later, Mikey."

Mike planned to jump the druggist when he turned to leave; but the man backed off the porch, the gun in his hand never wavering. He ran down the steps and across the yard to his car. Then he was gone.

Ed Coder and his wife, Marge, were pulling up just as Jack was roaring off. Neither of them was familiar to Mike; but Coder had a firm handshake and the set of his jaw was reassuring to Mike. Marge looked like the type of woman that could cope with a bad situation. And, he thought, we are definitely in a bad situation.

"What's with Jack?" Ed asked.

Before Mike could reply, Tina sat straight up on the couch, her hands clasped to her ears. "Make it stop!" she screamed.

"The music! The music!"

Mike could hear nothing.

Suddenly all the people in the room except for Mike and Ted were holding their hands over their ears; some were rolling on the floor, writhing in agony.

Lisa appeared at Mike's side. She took his hands and pressed them to her breasts. Mike could feel the hard nipples against his palm. The girl wore no bra. "Fuck me, Mike!" the girl breathed, her breath hot on his face. "That's a way to make it stop. Fuck me."

He tried to pull away, but her strength seemed equal to his.

"Don't my titties feel good, Mike." Her face was flushed and she was panting in sexual heat. "Look— I'll give you head, Mike. Cum in my mouth. I'll—"

He tore his hands free and backhanded the teenager. The force of his blow knocked her spinning. "Grab her, Rana!" he yelled.

Ted ran around the room, physically jerking people to their feet. "Sing!" he shouted. "It's Satan's forces; they've gathered, sending waves of thought through the Prince. That's what happened to Jack." He slapped Dave twice, jarring the man back to reality. "All of you, gather in a group, hold hands, and sing. 'Faith of Our Father.' 'Onward Christian Soldiers.' 'Peace in the Valley.' Anything Christian. But hurry.''

Mike could hear nothing out of the ordinary. It wouldn't have surprised him to see Governor Jimmy Davis come strolling in, guitar in hand, to lead the singing. He concluded that he would rather see a full company of Combat Rangers.

Hurriedly, they gathered in a group and joined hands. Embarrassed, they looked at Rana. She began singing, in a soft, sweet soprano voice. ''Beyond the Sunset.'' Ted looked at Mike curiously as he stood alone by the front porch door, watching the street. He did not join in the singing.

It seemed that no one knew the words to the song. After a moment, the strains of ''He Lives'' rang from the house. Mike stepped out on the porch.

The men in the cars backed up hurriedly, away from the house, but still close enough to watch.

They backed away from the singing, Mike noted. I'll keep that in mind.

He looked back into the house, at the adults and the young people holding hands, singing religious songs, forcefully, if not well.

Why don't I feel this—force, this invisible coercion they say is coming at them? Is it real or imagined? he wondered.

He could find no answer to his questions.

He counted the people. Fourteen adults. Three teenagers. One ten-year-old girl.

Against . . . ?

Fifteen or sixteen hundred worshipers of Satan.

Fantastic odds, Folsom, he sourly reflected.

The singing stopped. ''Colonel?'' Ted spoke from behind him.

Mike turned.

''You didn't feel that force?''

Mike shook his head. ''No, did you?''

Ted's expression was a curious one, a facial shading Mike had never before witnessed on any man. He evaded Mike's question by saying, "You are chosen." He spoke the words softly.

"You can't know that for certain," Mike countered.

Ted turned and walked back into the house without replying.

Rana came to Mike's side and slipped a hand into his. "What are we going to do, Mike?"

He looked at her. "Fight," he said.

Jack Geraci stood by his wife's side. They were in the basement of the Blake mansion. They were both naked. Ann had been raped repeatedly; Jack had been beaten. But only Jack was really aware of his surroundings.

Ann was lost in a shadowy world of never-never land. She knew she had been assaulted, was in pain; knew men and women had used her body, physically and sexually torturing her; but she did not know why.

"They will do," Becker told the servants guarding the man and wife. "Prepare them for wrapping with the Old One. But we need at least two more. Younger, stronger. Tell Egan to send us two girls."

The servant left. His feet shuffled on the concrete and then on the steps. He walked zombielike.

"Did you enjoy watching your wife being entertained by my people, Mr. Geraci?" Becker asked Jack.

Jack did not reply. He had been humiliated as a man, beaten, and forced to watch his wife raped in every conceivable way. But he had somehow found the strength to stand the pain without screaming. He would not give his abusers that pleasure.

"I'll make a bargain with you, Mr. Geraci," Becker said. "If you will renounce your God, I'll let you live and restore your wife's sanity."

Jack shivered in the coolness of the stinking room. He could see the hideous shape of the Old One sleeping on a huge bed. He wondered if he was looking at Satan.

"No," Becker read his thoughts. "But very close, Jack. Very close."

"I won't renounce God," Jack said.

Becker shrugged. "It's of no matter. I wouldn't have kept my part of the bargain anyway."

Jack spat on the floor.

Becker smiled. "We'll see how brave you are as the Old One turns in his wrappings and embraces you, prior to eating your face."

Sweat broke out on Jack's body.

Becker howled his laughter.

"You have a plan?" Ted asked Mike. He had joined the ex-soldier on the porch of the Folsom home. "I noticed you sending the men out to get more supplies."

"Fight," Mike said simply. "I'm a soldier, Ted. That's what I'm trained to do."

"Fourteen against at least fourteen or fifteen hundred?" Ted smiled. "You are a very confident man, Colonel Folsom."

"I'm just waiting for a sign from the Five Star General," Mike said sarcastically, pointing upward with one finger.

"You still don't believe you've been chosen?"

"Come on, Ted! It doesn't make any sense that *He* would choose *me*. I don't attend church on any regular basis; I've whored around all over the world; I haven't just killed in battle—I've assassinated men and women. No, I don't believe I've been chosen."

Father Grillet joined them. The small, slender man sat on the steps and looked out into the empty street, his fists under his chin. He looked more like a lost orphan than a priest. Mike wondered how the mismatched pair ever got together as man and wife.

"What are they waiting for?" Grillet asked.

"Night," Mike said.

"How do you know that?" the priest asked.

"I just know."

Ted smiled. "And still you doubt."

"That's just common sense," Mike retorted. "And it might not be this night—or any night, for that matter."

"All right," the government man said, the smile still on his lips, "what are *you* going to do this night?"

"I might decide to attack."

"Oh? Attack whom?"

"Anyone who isn't a part of this group."

"I killed in Vietnam," Ted said. "Certainly you have killed many times. The rest haven't. How do you know they are even capable of killing?"

"They'll either kill or be killed. It's just that damn simple."

"Including the women?" Grillet asked, looking up at Mike. "And me?"

"Including the women, Father," Mike said. "And you."

"I've never fired a gun in my life!"

"It won't take you long to learn, I can assure you of that," Mike said flatly.

"Suppose I refuse to learn?"

"Tina?" Mike called into the house. "Come out a minute, will you, honey?"

The girl appeared at the door. "Yes, sir?"

"This might embarrass you, dear, but I'm trying to make a point with Father Grillet. Tell the good Father what will happen to his wife if Becker's people should take her."

Tina blinked; her face flushed. "I never talked that

way to a priest.''

"It might save some lives, honey," Mike urged her.

Father Grillet looked up at the pretty girl, just scarcely out of childhood.

She met his gaze. "First they'll strip her, then kind of pass her around, so everybody can feel her and—well, stick their fingers in her. Then they'll beat her, just for the pleasure of it, hearing her scream. That way she won't make any trouble for them; she'll do anything just to make the pain stop. Then she'll suck off two or three of them.''

Grillet paled, a mental picture of his wife being forced to do that vivid in his mind's eye.

Just inside the house, by the window, Nickie was listening. Just hearing the girl talk about it got her so worked up she came.

"Then they'll take turns with her," Tina continued. "Raping her. The—normal way, to begin with; then they'll take her like a dog, from behind. I had two in me at once last night.'

Grillet nodded and sighed. "I get your point, child." He looked at Mike. "You have a gun for me?"

"A .38 revolver and a shotgun will probably be best for you. Yeah, I took a .38 off of Wilson. Ted, will you take the Father out back, down by the creek, and check him out with the weapons? As a matter of fact, Ted, take the whole group and check them out. Let those bastards in town hear some gunfire."

Ted nodded. "Right away, Colonel. Come on, Father."

Grillet put his hand on Tina's still-bruised cheek. "I'm very sorry for what those men did to you, Tina."

"It's done, sir," she said. "It can't be undone. I just don't want it to happen again."

"With God's help, guiding Colonel Folsom's hand, it won't happen again, Tina."

"I believe that, Father."

The faith of a child, Mike thought, who has been very rudely initiated into a harsh adult world.

And with God guiding my hand, Mike thought sourly, it won't happen again.

He touched the butt of the .41 in leather at his side. Thanks a lot, Grillet.

The awful wailing of the girl bounced off the stone walls of the basement. Her screaming intensified as her clothing was stripped from her and she was led to the Old One.

"I don't wanna do this!" she squalled.

"Consider yourself serving your Master," Becker said with a smile. "It's an honor to fuck the Old One. Very—ah—fulfilling experience."

She screamed as she was lowered onto the Old One's huge erection and howled as he penetrated her. She was bent forward until her face was pressed against his lipless mouth. She was thus tied, her body tight against his heavily oiled skin.

The Old One grunted with pleasure as he hunched in and out of the young girl—his final sexual pleasure for months.

Jack fought the hands that dragged him to the grotesqueness; but it was a futile struggle. He screamed in pain as the Old One, the young girl still impaled upon his organ, was lifted with a chain winch and Jack placed beneath him, the massive weight of the Old One breaking ribs as his weight settled on the man. Jack lay on layer after layer of thick cloth.

It would take many long, slow, painfully excruciating hours before death would take him.

Ann was placed on the Old One's right side. Another screaming young girl was secured to his right.

"Wrap them," Becker instructed.

And as the last mummylike wrappings were secured, the faint sounds of Ann singing could be heard through the thick cloth bindings.

"Mary had a little lamb,
Little lamb.
Little
La—"

NINETEEN

It was if they were all in an alien world, ostracized by the planet's inhabitants. No one had bothered them as they practiced during the late afternoon hours, as they fired several hundred rounds of ammunition at tin cans and bottles near the line of trees by the creek bank.

They were watched from all sides, by armed men and women, but no one bothered them.

After watching them practice, Mike concluded that most of them might be able to hit a man at ten feet with a pistol. All the men were adequate shots with rifle and shotgun. Father Grillet was much less than adequate; but he was trying and had avoided shooting himself in the foot. Among the women, only Rana, Elaine, and Lisa knew anything at all about weapons. Of all the adults, except Mike, Rana was the best shot.

Mike was moody as he sat on the porch, watching the sun change to blood red as if signaling what lay in the night that would follow its descent in the west.

Ted joined him on the porch, sensing his mood.

"Oh, ye of little faith."

Mike looked up. "You surprise me, Ted. I wasn't aware you could read minds or that you were a preacher."

"I'm not a preacher," he said, avoiding the first question. "But I am a religious man." He laughed softly.

"That's funny to you?"

"It's a private joke, Colonel. Don't take offense."

"Just who the hell are you!" Mike's tone was sharp; he was irritated by Ted's mysterious manner.

"A man who has a mission, that's all."

"Bullshit."

Ted shrugged.

"You're weird, Ted, you know that?"

Ted clasped him on the shoulder. "You're a good man, Colonel Folsom, whether you believe that or not. Now tell me the rest of your thoughts."

"So you do have the ability to read minds?"

"No. Just trained to pick up vibes, that's all."

"Sure," Mike said dryly. "All right. Before I go head-hunting—if I decide to go—what about the people of Butler who have accepted neither world of the beyond?"

Unlike him, Ted hesitated for a few seconds. "I—really don't know, Colonel. Our God is a forgiving God; but also a very vindictive one. Look at it this way. It was their choice. You can't accept responsibility for what happens to them."

"And what will happen to them?"

The men looked at one another. Ted said, "They will probably be treated badly. Satan's religion is a very vulgar, savage one. You mentioned the young people of this community, armed, restless. Yes. They will turn savage."

"Against those of neither faith." It was not phrased

254

as a question.

"Yes."

"And there is nothing I—we—can do?"

"Regretfully, no."

The sun edged closer to the edge of the horizon. Shadows began springing up, dark pockets amid the reddening light. Both men could sense the evil rising from the town.

"That doesn't seem very fair to me," Mike said.

"It was their choice, Colonel. The opportunity to accept God as their Father and Savior was always present, always available to them. They chose to ignore Him. So shall it be their punishment."

"I get the impression you are very well-schooled in the Bible."

"Yes, I am, very much so. My father was a minister. I got my knowledge—at first, shall we say—by a process of osmosis."

"And you really rejected God to serve Satan? I find that hard to believe."

"Yes, I did. Twice. Some people are unbelievably hardheaded."

"What's that line about the path to heaven? How does it go?"

"The path or road to heaven is lined with many pitfalls. Yes. I happened to stumble into more than my share, I would say."

"You said you were in Vietnam."

"Yes. I was an LRRP."

"Damn good outfit."

"Very."

"I wonder why our paths didn't cross. I worked very closely with Long Range Recon."

That smile, hidden, secretive. "Oh, we did meet once, Colonel. Back in '68. You were—a Captain? No! A Major, I believe."

"I don't recall it."

"It was an ugly situation. There wasn't much time for handshaking on Black Virgin Mountain."

"Now I remember the event. The young sergeant who said there just couldn't be a just God; not if he could allow all this waste to occur."

"Correct. You have excellent recall."

"And you went back to worshipping Satan after that?"

"Yes. For a year."

A yowl of sudden pain ripped the dusk.

"It's begun," Mike said.

"Yes," Ted replied quietly.

"I didn't trust you at first," Mike admitted.

"You still don't," was the reply.

Mike looked at the younger man. For the first time, he noticed the small tattoo on Ted's left forearm. He looked closer. It was the face of a—hell! Mike didn't know what it was, only that it was ugly. "What the hell is that thing on your arm?"

"The face of the devil." Ted turned and walked back into the house.

The young had turned on one of their own, a young girl who had refused to service several young men at once. They had stripped her, then tied her face down on the ground, her pubic area directly over a huge fire ant mound. The young people sat and squatted and crouched a safe distance away from the suffering, screaming girl. Their faces were, for the most part, impassive as the aggressive biting ants, by the hundreds and thousands, injected their poison into the flesh of the girl.

The girl began jerking as she went into an allergic reaction. She screamed once more, stiffened, and died.

"Shit!" Curt Babin said. "Ain't no fun in watchin' this."

"It was your idea," he was reminded.

"Well, screw you, too!" Curt said. "You got a better idea?"

"Yeah," Cindy said. She lifted a flat, blue-steel .32 automatic and shot the young man between the eyes. He slammed to the ground, the hole leaking blood and gray matter.

"Now what?" a young man asked.

Cindy smiled maliciously. "Let's carry him into town and dump him in the street in front of the Folsom house."

They kicked that idea around for a while, then finally agreed to do it. But nobody wanted to touch the body.

"Aw, fuck it!" Robert Weaver said.

That seemed to sum up the general mood of the crowd of young people.

The bottles of wine, the grass, the dope—uppers and downers—were brought out.

Something to do, man.

Dusk drifted into evening, but no one came near the Folsom house. No cars or trucks or motorcycles drove the street in front of the home. And no one complained of hearing that strange thought-thrusting that had provoked the singing earlier that afternoon.

"I don't understand any of this," David said. "We're trapped in here like ducks in a bucket, yet it's almost as if they're saving us—but for what is the thing that nags at me."

"The best for last," Mike said, a tight smile on his lips. He had changed into dark clothing and put a pair of dark blue jogging shoes on his feet, a stocking cap on his head.

Ted looked at Mike. "Strange time to go jogging, Colonel."

"Head-hunting," Mike said.

The room fell silent. Rana asked, "What do you mean, Mike?"

"I mean we can't just sit here and do nothing. They are saving us for last because we're organized, armed, and ready for them. Now I have been wondering what's preventing them from coming up here, setting the house on fire, and shooting us as we try to escape. I don't know why they don't do that; I would if I were in their shoes."

Ted looked at him, that faint strange smile once more on his lips.

Mike ignored the silent message. "But I'm restless, so I think I'll just take a little fight to them."

"Mike—" Rana opened her mouth.

"He'll be all right," Ted told her. He had noticed Mike whittling on several long slender pieces of wood on and off all afternoon. He had sharpened a point on the stakes. Ted wore an amused look on his face as he picked up one of the stakes and held it out to Mike. "Be a shame to let all this work go to waste, Colonel."

Mike took the stake, very much aware that Ted was silently laughing at him. He shoved the stake into his belt.

Mike touched the haft of the stake. "You trying to tell me something with that smirk on your face?"

"Some things are best learned by experience, Colonel."

Ted had been right. Mike still didn't fully trust the man. There was something about him that troubled Mike, some little elusive quality that he could not pin down.

"Good hunting," Ted said.

Rana walked to the kitchen with him. They stood in

the darkness, not touching. "Why are you doing this?" she asked.

"I really don't know," he admitted. "To learn something, I think."

"What?"

"I don't know that either, honey."

She kissed him on the mouth and walked back into the den. Mike stepped out onto the darkened porch.

Neither of them saw the basement door open or the eyes that peered out through a faint mist.

Mike squatted down in the shadows of the big house and mentally went over his equipment: his .41 mag in leather at his side; one of his dad's big hunting knives in a sheath on his other side; a bandoleer of shotgun shells looped bandit style across his chest; extra cartridges for the .41 in loops around his waist. He was ready.

But for what? the thought nagged at him.

He did not tell Rana, but he knew he had received some sort of order to go out into the night. But to do what? To kill? Or had he received any order at all? Was it just a product of a tense imagination?

He didn't know.

But there was one way to find out.

He looked carefully around him; he picked up the dark shapes of those watching from the rear. It was almost as if they wanted him to see them.

He had left the house through the darkened kitchen and back porch; he was certain he had not been seen. He moved to the edge of the lots separating his home from the next house, then belly-crawled through the tall grass to the edge of his nearest neighbor's lawn: the Benson home. Correction, he reminded himself; the Bensons had moved away years ago, his mother had written. Mike didn't know who lived in the house.

He slipped up to the rear of the home, wondering if the people had a dog. No barking greeted him. Staying close to the house, he came to a lighted window and cautiously peeped in.

A man and a woman sat having a late supper. Two young people, a boy and a girl, in their mid-teens, sat at the table with them. Mike watched. Supper finished, the girl rose from the table and walked to the man's side. They had the same shade of hair and facial features. His daughter, Mike guessed.

The man caressed the girl's crotch and she kissed him on the mouth. Lots of tongue action.

Daddy-dear, Mike thought, viewing the scene through disgusted eyes. Let's get close, Daddy. Like maybe incest.

She sat down in his lap and the man fondled the girl's breasts through her shirt. The older woman laughed and said something Mike couldn't catch. He wasn't at all sure he wanted to hear it. The woman rose from the table and walked to the young man, kneeling between his legs. She unzipped his jeans and took out his half-erect penis, popping it into her mouth.

Dessert, Mike grimaced.

Sick.

He clicked the shotgun off safety, backed away from the window and raised the muzzle.

TWENTY

The Evil Old One was resting, his breathing slow and low. The wrapping had been completed and the huge mummylike object lay in a specially-built crate. Only a faint moaning sound could be heard through the thick wrappings. A low cry. Already the sickly-sweet odor of death was seeping through the layers of cloth.

"Secure the lid," Becker said.

The lid was closed, locked. The satin-lined, coffinlike thick oak box was silent—as death.

"Get out," Becker told the servants.

He walked to the resting place of his Master on earth and his friend for centuries. Together they had seen and caused more evil than could be written in a hundred volumes of filth. Becker put one hand on the temporary home of the Master of the Living Dead. "Rest well, old friend," he said.

He walked to the single candle illuminating the dank room and blew out the flame. He did not need light to see, for he was a servant of the Prince of Darkness. He walked from the resting place of Evil, gently closing the door behind him.

"Now, Colonel Folsom," he hissed, his yellowish eyes burning with a fever from the pits of hell. "Now, I deal with you."

Mike couldn't pull the trigger. As badly as the scene disgusted him, as badly as he wanted to blow them all to hell, as sick and depraved as the sexual scenario before him was, he had no right to kill them for it. He lowered the shotgun and once more turned his unwilling voyeuristic gaze to the kitchen.

It had turned into a full-blown orgy of incest.

Mike walked away from the scene, slightly sick and shaken by what he had just witnessed, many emotions boiling inside him. He walked slowly back to the house, making no effort at concealment.

He didn't know what else to do.

Ted's eyes met his as he walked into the den. "You couldn't do it, could you?"

"No," Mike said quietly.

"I knew you wouldn't kill without a sign."

"Sign?"

Ted pointed upward with his index finger.

Mike's eyes followed the gesture. "I killed Duval and Wilson," he reminded the man.

"That was different; they deserved to die. Besides, they were going to kill you."

"How do you know that?"

"I know."

"Sometimes you irritate me, Ted—you know that?"

The man smiled. "It's my electric personality."

"It's your damned mouth!" Mike said, softening the words with a smile.

"Now, now, Colonel," Ted said. "Ladies present, you know." He laughed at Mike's expression and said, "It really is my electricity, Colonel. Really. You just

262

haven't put it all together yet. But you will; you're a smart man."

Mike shook his head and walked out of the den, heading for the stairs. "You all know what watch to take; I'm going to bed."

"Lennie," Becker called. "Come here."

Lennie shuffled to the desk. He stood patiently in front of his Master.

"I want you to do something for me, Lennie. I have decided that Colonel Mike Folsom shall live after all."

"Yes, Master."

"You know that Jimmy Grayson is walking among us and that he is as you?"

"Yes, Master. I talked to him not too long ago."

"Marvelous. I'm quite certain the conversation simply sparkled with wit and originality. Find Jimmy. Go to the Folsom house and lure Folsom outside. One of you shall make him as you are. Do you understand?"

"Yes, Master. And the blonde woman?"

"Rana is mine! Touch her and you will find yourself in the very depths of hell before the next breath can leave your lungs. Is that clear?"

Lennie drew back in fear at the rage coming from Becker's mouth and the yellow fire that seemed to leap from his eyes. "Yes, Master." he said.

"Lennie? If you fail, don't return here."

"But—where could I go, Master?"

And Lennie, with his infected blood and brain that was as much animal as human, covered his eyes as Becker's thought sank into his mind.

He would be doomed to walk the earth forever, never knowing peace of any kind.

Lennie bowed slightly and backed out of the study, his heart thudding heavily in his chest.

The vapor that met him on the porch of the huge mansion soon became the shape of a man, finally solidifying into Jimmy Grayson. Together, the undead walked to a car and drove away.

"Don't let him bluff you, Lennie," Jimmy said. "Becker made you as you are, just as he made me. I'm out now, and I intend to stay out."

"Can you fuck the way you are?"

"I can do anything any human can do," the undead said. "And many things they can't do. I can be in Shreveport in one second."

"No!"

"Oh, yes. And so will you as soon as you learn some things about the way you are. Alex, Monroe, New Orleans, anywhere in the state. But you won't be able to leave the state."

"Why?"

"I don't know. What difference does it make? There is blood and pussy enough for a million years. But long before then it will be over for everything."

"You mean . . . ?"

"The Masters of both sides and of all things will tire of the game eventually. Sooner than most think. Then we will all be gone."

"How do you know these things?" Lennie asked, picking his nose.

"Because as I was going Home, being escorted there by one of the Keepers of the Book, Becker drank from me. That prevented me from entering heaven. I didn't think it was very fair; but what could I do about it? I was sent back."

"But it couldn't have been a very long trip? Not really long enough for you to learn all you say you know."

"You have a lot to learn about the world beyond this life, Lennie. A second is a year, a year only a moment.

It all depends on what plane you're on."

"You go there on a plane?"

Grayson sighed. "Lennie—drop it. Look, what are we supposed to do this night with Folsom?"

Lennie pouted for a moment. Maybe he wasn't as smart as lots of folks, but he wasn't no dummy, neither, he thought. "Make Folsom like us," he said.

"I never said you were a dummy, Lennie."

Lennie almost lost the car. "How . . . ?"

"I'm not trying to insult you, Lennie. It's just that you wouldn't understand. Believe me. You will someday, I promise. I told you, I can do lots of things humans can't. Colonel Folsom, huh? Well, that won't be easy."

"Piece of cake," Lennie boasted.

"No, Lennie, it will not be a piece of cake. It isn't even going to be possible. I wonder why Becker didn't realize that? Folsom doesn't know it yet, but he's got a lot of animal in him. As much or more than us. I understand that now where I didn't before. And don't ever underestimate the power and fury of God; if He wanted to, He could shaft Satan every time."

"Why don't He do it, then?" Lennie was in doubt about that.

"I don't know, Lennie. It's a game They play, I think. And I really don't care who wins it."

"How can you say that! You're—you're one of us."

"No, I'm not, Lennie. And that's something you'd better understand, as well. We're nothing, Lennie. We're caught between heaven and hell. This is it for us, Lennie. Forever." The last word was spoken very grimly.

Lennie hissed like a snake. His eyes turned wild with fear. "But Mr. Becker said—"

Jimmy cut him off with a curt slash of one hand. "Fuck Becker! Becker's a con artist. He's had to be to stay the right hand of the Evil One for centuries. Lennie—listen to me. Few things can destroy us, very few things. And forget all that bullshit about silver bullets and stakes driven through the heart. We are as immortal as the evil that spawned us. I didn't like it, at first. Then I learned to accept what I could not change."

"I—do feel kind of different, Jimmy. It's like—like I'm dead, but not really. I don't know how to explain it. That sounds stupid, don't it?"

"No, not to me. You'll soon get over that, though, as you learn more about who and what you are. And you don't have to obey Becker, either."

"But he said—"

"That's right, Lennie, *he said*. Fuck Becker. Lennie, think about it. What can he do to you? Kill you? That's a joke. How can he kill you when you're neither alive nor dead? Becker put those thoughts into your mind, that's all. Let the devil take Becker and Folsom. We are what we are, and we can't change. So let's have some fun doing it."

"You—sound as though you're—speaking for, working for—the other side." Lennie could not bring himself to say the word God.

"I'm not working for any side except my own, Lennie. I owe no allegiance to anyone. I don't belong to either side. Neither do you. But understand this—you can choose the side of the Dark One, if you want to. But once you do, that's it; there is no turning back. And that's the only side you can choose; we're barred from heaven. Look, I've found it a lot more fun to play the field alone. It's all up to you, Lennie."

Lennie thought about it for a moment, with only the hiss of the tires on the blacktop. He looked at Jimmy Grayson. "Fuck Becker!" he said.

"That's the way, boy! Tell you the truth, I'm glad you're one of us. There's a few more around the state;

266

but they're real creeps, believe me. If they're not moaning around trying to get into heaven, they're using their powers the wrong way. They've forgotten how to have fun. Bonnie's around; I been trying to get the pants off her for years. But she runs every time I get around her."

"How can you fuck Bonnie? She's dead!"

"For a fact. But she hasn't been called home yet— not on a permanent basis."

"Why?"

"She's waiting for her kid. She's looking for a chance to grab the kid and slip back across the mist. But you can't take living life through the mist and across the river; can't be done; isn't allowed. So she's got a long wait. Besides," Jimmy's grin was of the blackest evil, "every time she gets too close to her kid over at the institute, I make an appearance; scares her off. Now that's fun. Anyway, Bonnie thinks if she gives me some pussy, it'll jeopardize her chances of getting Home."

"Would it?"

"Beats the shit out of me. Besides, who cares? Anyway, it's more fun with humans. Tell you what, Lennie, you swing both ways, don't you?"

"Yeah."

"But you like pussy?"

"Oh, man, yeah!"

"Then you haven't lived—wrong choice of words— until you've made it with a woman that's so scared she'll do anything you ask. I like to get 'em in their sleep; you'll learn how you use your voice to keep them asleep. Then when you've got it about halfway in, you bring them to consciousness; they look up, and you're grinning at them, teeth and all. Talk about a gas! And just as you cum—together—you make them as us. Sometimes they don't realize what they've become for months, even years. Then, when the moon is right, or a certain dog's howling triggers the blood-emotion, they start walking the night—looking. Man, that's fun, Lennie. I'm gettin' a hard on just thinking about it.''

"Let's do it!"

"I got someone in mind, too."

"Who?"

He told him, and Lennie howled animallike laughter. He laughed so hard and so long, he had to pull the car off the blacktop. Sitting in the car, close to what had once been a living human and was now neither life nor death, Lennie fondled Jimmy's growing penis.

"You don't mind if I suck you?" Lennie asked.

Jimmy giggled in the dim light from the dash. "Only if you don't bite me."

TWENTY-ONE

She had no business being the wife of a man of God, Nickie concluded. Had known that for a long time. Her passions ran too hot and too wild and too strong. And she had to keep them in check for the most part. Missionary position only. Once a week. Set your watch by Father Dan. Just once she'd like for him to go down on her; really eat her.

No way.

And why, she asked herself this night, with her lewd thoughts and wild passions, had she been spared by Becker's people? She didn't know.

She'd had several little bump and run affairs over the years, but they were dangerous. And in her own very peculiar way, she really cared for Daniel. Wouldn't hurt him for the world and wouldn't endanger his position with the church. But just once she'd like for him to walk up behind her, cock in hand, KY-Jelly in the other, and see how much he could get it up her ass. He was built right for it; but she didn't even dare suggest it to him.

She remembered that cowboy in that little motel outside of Longview, Texas, the night her car broke down and she'd had to spend the night.

What a night. She got wet just thinking about it. She'd snorted some coke, smoked some really dynamite grass, and blew her mind right up against the wall with Methedrine. Then they had fucked and sucked all night long. When that cowboy—illiterate bastard that he was—finally got that king-sized dong of his up—and it was a full ten inches—it never got soft.

She had to sit on cushions for two days after she got home. Told her husband she had hemorrhoids.

She grew restless on the pallet beside her husband and quietly slipped from his side. Father Grillet was sleeping soundly. As a matter of fact, she thought, looking around her to the den, *everybody* was sleeping very soundly. Nickie wore only a thin, almost sheer nightgown. She could see down the hall, through the archway, past the den, the dark shape of David Babin, sitting in a chair on the porch, his head slumped. He was asleep. She walked to the kitchen. Sam Marshall, who was supposed to be guarding the rear of the house, was asleep, his head on the table.

I'm so well-guarded, she thought.

Then she saw a shape standing on the back porch. She hissed in fright. Then, suddenly, she was not afraid. Only curious. She stepped closer, taking a fresh look at the man. He smiled and beckoned to her to come to him. She shook her head. He shrugged.

He doesn't look evil, Nickie thought, unaware that thought had been sent to her.

She made up her mind. She tiptoed past Sam, not knowing that two sticks of dynamite would not have awakened him. She quietly pushed open the screen door and stepped out onto the walkway. The man gestured for her to follow him. She hesitated for only a second. She could always scream if anything went wrong.

Behind the storage shed, she stopped when the man stopped. The night wind had picked up, blowing hot, whipping and holding her gown to her, pressing against her breasts and cunt.

"What do you want and who are you?" she whispered, her voice carrying just above the rushing hot winds.

"Names aren't important," the man said. "But you may call me Jimmy. What is important is what you want—and need."

"I don't know what you mean. Maybe I ought to yell."

"Why would you want to do that? I have what you want. Weren't you lying beside your husband, thinking about that cowboy in Longview who fucked you up the ass?"

She was not afraid at the man's power to read her mind, just more curious now than ever. "How did you know about that?"

"I know many things. I know you're not happy with your husband's performance in bed. I know you have a dildo you use often. I know you fantasize daily—always about sex."

"You're—one of Them?" she questioned, the wind whipping her hair about her face.

"No," the man said. "No, I am not. And that is the truth. I am neither one of them, or one of you."

She believed him. She did not know why she believed him, but she did. "What do you want from me?"

He laughed and she understood.

"I'm not a whore!" she flushed in the night.

"And I don't intend to pay you. No, I never thought you a whore. Tell me, Nickie, have you ever fucked standing up?"

"No."

"Yes, you have. In Monroe, one evening. That

271

singer with the gospel group. He fucked you standing up against the wall in his dressing room."

"If you knew, why ask?"

"To see if you would lie. You lied. Not an admirable trait for a priest's wife."

"I don't have to stand here and be insulted, either," she said, throwing back her head, then brushing wind-blown silken hair out of her eyes.

Jimmy could see her nipples straining against the thin fabric of her gown.

"Like what you see?" she asked, her tongue wetting her lips. The words seemed to pop from her mouth without her brain taking any part in the formation of the question.

And that confused her.

He took her small hand in his and pressed it to his groin, to his thickening hardness. "Like what you feel?" he countered.

"This is insane!" she hissed. "Crazy." But she made no effort to remove her hand.

"It's a crazy place," Jimmy said with a grin. "And believe me, I do know it well."

Her fingers unzipped his trousers.

Jimmy Grayson, Becker thought, watching the proceedings with his third eye, is going to present a problem. Lennie would be no loss; the man was little more than a fool. But if either Jimmy or Lennie believed they would be at all difficult to kill, they did not fully understand the forces that moved darkly about them. All things died—in time. All things could be destroyed. Including the Old One. It was just a matter of the hunter knowing the correct method, that's all.

And Becker knew Colonel Folsom did not know the procedure. Yet.

But he could, and would, if the opportunity presented itself, screw things up royally.

He watched as Grayson buried his erection into the woman, her gown bunched up around her shapely hips. Grayson had certainly changed since his denial into the Kingdom of Peace and Light. Had a terrible rage in him over that alleged injustice. But oddly enough, he blamed both Masters.

Becker closed his third eye and concentrated on problems more pressing.

That first night the townspeople of Butler were not at all concerned with Colonel Folsom and his little band of so-called Christians. There was so much more to do, so many ways to have fun—now that all restrictions were off them.

Like . . .

Taking that prissy, snooty English teacher from out at the school, stripping him naked, pouring gasoline on him, and setting him on fire. But that really wasn't as much fun as they thought it would be. It had all ended too soon. They would have to think of something that would take a bit longer.

Like . . .

Slowly hanging that old bitch from the hardware store, the one that looked down her nose at everybody in town. That had been fun, and it had taken her about an hour to die. But there must be something better.

Like . . .

Yes! They had it. Crucifixion!

At the mansion, Becker sighed. He had been wondering how long it would take the people to arrive at that method. No matter how far they had drifted from that accursed Book, the people always seemed to come back to the Bible for ideas.

He knew that to interfere would only cause trouble. The people, even though they worshiped the Dark One, had to have an outlet for their long-controlled emotions; some freedoms were allowed them.

Again he sighed. Oh, well, a couple of more days and nights would make no difference in the overall outcome of matters.

Becker didn't know it; but he was very wrong in that assumption.

Nickie had felt the second man approach her from the rear; had experienced a moment or two of panic, and then realized what he was going to do and relaxed. She felt the jell-like substance being applied to her anus and relaxed her muscles.

This promises to be a fun evening, she thought. Two guys at once.

What was the matter with her? The question was forced out of her brain in a moment of clarity. Then it was gone, erased from her memory.

When Lennie got it all in, and the men had settled into a workable rhythm, Nickie started cumming. It was like nothing she had ever experienced in her life. And it was all she could do to keep from screaming.

She felt a slight pinprick of pain on the right side of her neck, and then a few seconds later, another pinprick of pain on the left side of her neck. But she was too engrossed in sexual self-gratification to think much more than a mosquito had nailed her.

And she did not know that eyes were watching her sexual antics from a depression in the vacant lot next to the shed.

Nickie's juices wet her thighs as the semen from the men poured into and then out of her.

They relaxed, softened, and withdrew. And then

they were gone.

Nickie stood in confusion in the moonlight. She could not understand what had happened. Had she been-screwed or was it all a dream? Yes, she thought, dipping her fingers into the fur between her legs, she had been well-screwed. But where did the men go?

So she had not been dreaming. Her asshole was sticky. No dream there, either.

She put her fingers to the side of her neck. They came away sticky with dark blood. The other side was the same.

"One damn big mosquito," she said.

"No mosquito, sweetie," the voice whispered from the darkness.

Nickie whirled, opened her mouth to scream, and a hand clamped over it, stopping the wail of terror before it could push past her lips.

She looked into the crazed eyes of Chief Ford.

One of them.

"I got to take you to see a man," he whispered, thick wet lips pulling back into a grin, exposing stained yellow teeth. "And I don't think you're gonna like it very much."

For the first time since Stinky had met Mr. Becker, ten years back, the man wore a worried look in his eyes and on his face. Becker looked into the chief's eyes.

"Yes, Ford," Becker said, announcing the inner thoughts of the chief. "I am a bit worried. But it is nothing that should concern you—yet."

"I sure wish I could read a mind," Stinky said, a wistful note in his voice.

"No doubt," Becker's reply was dry. "But what you can do now is to take this woman," he pointed to Nickie, "and get her cleaned up. She reeks of sex. And

275

then bring her back to me here!''

"Yes, sir.''

Stinky prodded the weeping and frightened woman from the elegant study. He pushed her down the carpeted hall to a bathroom and jerked the soiled gown from her. Stinky dropped the lid to the commode and sat down. "Take a shower and then do them things a woman does to git her pussy clean.''

"I most certainly will not! Not so long as you're sitting there grinning at me.''

He rose from the seat and slapped her. Her head banged against the tile of the stall. Lights popped painfully in her head.

"You're perverted!'' she cried.

"You jist got screwed up the bung-hole and you're callin' me perverted? That's funny, bitch!'' He turned on the water, drenching her. She hopped around in the stall until the water warmed. "Wash your ass, lady. And be quick about it.''

To her immense embarrassment, Stinky stood in the bathroom and watched her douche. Red-faced, she finished, rose and faced him, naked. He tossed her a terrycloth robe from a hook on the back of the bathroom door.

"Put it on and let's go.''

"You're a filthy man, Chief Ford!''

He laughed at her. "Your turn's comin','' he said, shoving her out into the hall.

"You're a very attractive woman, Mrs. Grillet,'' Becker said, his eyes appraising her charms, which were more than considerable.

Nickie didn't know what to say, or even if she should reply. She remained silent.

Becker smiled. "I have entered your mind many times over the years, Nickie. You are a most unhappy woman.''

276

She nodded her head in silent agreement. Both sides of her neck hurt, and her head felt funny.

"Good, we agree on something. That's a start. I have a proposition for you, Nickie. Interested in hearing it?"

"Will it get me away from this horrible man?" She cut her eyes to Stinky.

Becker laughed. "Yes. If that is your wish." He picked up a tiny silver bell from his desk and rang it. A servant shuffled in. The man's eyes were dead-looking. Nickie didn't know it yet, but so was the man. "Bring us something to eat and drink, Arnold." The servant shuffled out. "Please sit down, Nickie. Make yourself comfortable."

Nickie sat apprehensively on the edge of a chair.

Becker nodded his approval. "Much better, Nickie. We can chat like civilized men and women." He looked at Stinky. "More or less," he added acidly.

"The people back at the house will be worried about me," Nickie said.

"They're sleeping," Becker said. "Like the dead," he laughed.

"You're the devil!" she said.

Becker roared with laughter. "Oh, no, my dear. No, you're wrong—quite mistaken. I am a servant of the Prince, that's all."

He was still chuckling as the servant brought in a tray of tea and scones.

"What's this icky-lookin' stuff?" Stinky asked, gazing at the silver tray.

"Leavened cakes," Becker said, his dislike for the man evident in his tone. "What would you prefer, grits and ham hocks?"

"No, sir," Stinky said, realizing he was on very shaky ground.

"Fine. Then eat them, or don't eat them; but by all

means, shut your mouth.''

"Yes, sir.''

Nickie nibbled daintily on one of the small cakes. "They're very good,'' she said. Her head still felt funny.

"Thank you,'' Becker beamed. "Now then, there are a few things you need to know about yourself.''

As he spoke the damning words, Nickie's world began to spin in a cloud of sulphuric gas; she was hurtled about in a dark void filled with demons and imps and howling beasts.

Then she felt herself falling.

"Colonel Folsom,'' Father Grillet cried. He stood at the foot of the stairs. "Colonel Folsom! It's Nickie— she's gone!''

Mike was coming down the stairs, taking them two at a time. "All right, Dan, calm yourself. When did you discover her gone?''

"Just a moment ago. I—felt something pulling me out of a very deep sleep. A voice, I think. I looked in the bathroom, then searched the bottom part of the house. She's gone. Colonel, everybody was sleeping, and I mean everybody!''

"All right, Dan. I was sleeping very soundly myself. Too soundly, I think, for it to be normal. I believe we may have been put to sleep.'' He looked at Ted. "You seem to know pretty much what's going on—any ideas?''

The man shrugged. "Obviously, she left of her own volition; otherwise one of us would have heard something.''

"You didn't hear anything?''

"I was not present,'' Ted said. But he offered no further explanation as to where he had been. "But, yes, I believe your sleep was induced from the outside."

"Why would she leave?" Father Grillet protested, a shrillness to his voice. "She knows it's not safe out. My Lord, she wouldn't just take a walk in the middle of the night."

"I'm perfectly all right, Dan," Nickie spoke from the back porch.

TWENTY-TWO

The kitchen jammed with people all relieved to see Nickie. Mike cut his eyes to Ted; the man was sitting at the table, sipping at a cup of coffee. He neither appeared relieved nor surprised to see the woman. He lifted his eyes to Mike. Mike could read nothing in the man's gaze. It was blank—neutral.

"My Lord, Nickie!" Father Grillet said. "Where have you been? Look at you. Your gown is filthy!"

"Sitting down by the creek," she calmly replied. "I fell asleep and rolled down the bank. I'm all right; I just feel like an idiot."

Grillet touched his wife's neck. "You've hurt yourself."

"It's nothing, Dan. A little iodine and a hot bath and I'll be fine. I'm sorry to have caused you all such concern."

"Don't leave the house again, Nickie," Mike told her. "You might have been grabbed by one of Them, or one of us could have shot you by mistake."

"I know, Colonel," she smiled up at him. He noticed there was no expression in her eyes. None. "I won't. And once again, I'm sorry."

Mike nodded and looked at Ted. The man's expression was unreadable.

Odd, Mike thought.

Most went back to their beds and pallets. Mike relieved the sentry on the front porch and sent him to bed. He automatically checked the street. The cars were still there. The Trans-Am had returned. Mike could not see the men in the cars.

What are they waiting for? he silently questioned. They've got us pinned, hemmed in. Why don't they try to take us?

Why don't you take the fight to them? the thought leaped into his mind. No—it was more than a thought. A voice.

You're going to have to do better than that! Mike thrust his feelings.

No reply.

"All right," he muttered to himself. So it was merely my own wishes surfacing, not a message from God.

He leaned back in the chair. He looked up into the sky. Then he sat rock-still in the chair. One by one, stars began falling from the sky. He counted six of them.

Six. Why did that trigger something in him? And was this a sign from the heavens? He could not recall ever seeing six falling stars in succession.

Six.

He looked to his right, toward town. For some reason only the street lights on the right side were burning. Odd, he thought. He counted those he could see—until the street curved, eliminating the view of lights—six.

Then the lights abruptly went out, plunging the street into darkness. They came back on, blinking. A signal? From whom? For whom?

What's going on?

Six falling stars, six blinking street lights. What next?

And why does six seem to ring a bell with me?

Suddenly he recalled the calendar in the kitchen—that first day of his return, when he had noticed the date. It was still May, but the calendar had been on the month of June. The first day of June was circled.

The sixth month.

Six falling stars. Six blinking street lamps. The sixth month.

What was the date? Mike punched the date indicator to his watch.

The message glowed on his wrist. June the first.

Six, six, six.

The Mark of the Beast.

Yes, that one word thought, command, comprehension jumped into his brain, glaring at him under full, harsh light.

Yes. Yes. YES!

"All right," Mike said aloud, rising to his feet. "I finally hear you."

He turned. The eyes of Ted Bernard were fixed on him, unblinking eyes set in a stone face.

"What does six, six, six mean to you?" Mike asked.

"The Mark of the Beast," came the soft reply.

"And it's in the Bible, isn't it?"

"Revelation. Chapter Thirteen, verse eighteen."

"I see," Mike said quietly, his voice soft in the night.

"Yes," Ted smiled. "I believe you do."

Mike silently padded up to the Trans-Am, coming up behind the automobile. Two men were in the front seat. The back seat was empty. The windows were down. He put the muzzle of the shotgun against the neck of the man on the passenger side.

"How badly do you want to live?" Mike asked him.

The driver's hands were on the wheel; he kept them there, tensed.

"My death would be inconsequential," the man said, no fear in his voice. "Kill me, another takes my place. My Master has so decreed."

"And my Master has told me He is at war with your Master."

"As it has always been, Colonel Folsom," the man replied. "And so shall it always be."

Mike pulled the trigger. The man's head separated from his torso. He shifted the now-bloody muzzle and blew out the driver's throat.

The Datsun's headlights sprang on, the powerful little car lunging toward the source of the booming shots. Mike dropped to one knee and pumped the shotgun. The reports were enormous in the stillness of predawn. Slugs sparked off metal; the windshield shattered; the Datsun slewed to one side as screaming filled the early morning. The sports car left the street and slammed into the curb, jumping it, barreling into a house.

It was quiet for only a moment.

The lights in the house with the Datsun in its den came on. A man, a woman, and two teenagers came running out, guns in their hands. They were shouting and screaming foulness at Mike.

From the porch of the Folsom house, an automatic weapon began chugging its staccato message of death. The family in the street went down like kingpins hit by the ball of a master bowler. The woman continued to flop and squall in the street. Mike shot her in the head.

The early morning was again still and quiet. No other lights shone in the dark houses along the street. Mike walked back to his house.

"That's an interesting-looking weapon for a government agent to have," he said, looking at the Russian-made AK-47 assault rifle. "Haven't seen one of those in a while."

"I have two of them," Ted said. "And a rather large amount of ammunition. Would you like to have one?"

Mike looked at him. When he spoke, his voice was laced with sarcasm. "Do tell me again what government agency you work for?"

Ted laughed, holding out the AK-47, along with a harness filled with pouches of clips. "You take this one, Colonel. I know it works."

"Can we birth them?" Becker asked the white-coated doctor.

The men stood in the Womb-Room of the hospital. They were dressed in sterile clothing, masks protecting their mouths and noses. The unborn Servants of Satan floated peacefully in their man-made sacs, curled in the fetal position. The low hum of the constant flow of information being fed to the unborn was the only sound in the room other than the bubbling in the glass and the stainless steel holding tanks. The young doctor had himself been birthed in this manner. Thirty years past.

"No, Mr. Becker. Not yet. We need another seventy-two hours, at least. They are not ready."

Old evil eyes met young evil eyes. "I'll try to buy you that time."

"Try, sir?"

"All is not going as planned, I'm afraid."

"This Colonel Folsom?"

"Yes. He has been chosen."

"Shit!"

"At least that."

"We need this birthing to complete the Master's

285

ideal six, six, six," the doctor reminded the Devil's Agent. "Only then will the Many-Headed Beast be allowed to again surface. And it has been thousands of years."

"I do not have to be reminded of that, Doctor Perry." Becker's reply was acid-tongued. "I have said I will try; that is all I can do."

The doctor bowed his head. "I did not mean to—"

"I know." Becker waved him silent. "We are so close to winning this time, so close to having the first University of the Master. I can almost taste victory on my tongue."

"It will be ours," Doctor Perry said confidently.

"His," Becker corrected. "His. Don't ever forget it."

The bodies lay in the street and slumped stinking in the cars. Bloody piles of death. The morning sun had risen bubbling in the east, searing away the slight coolness of night. Summer blasted its way into Butler.

A reminder of hell's fury.

But still a lot cooler.

Mike sat on the porch and watched and listened to the sounds of doors slamming and cars and trucks roaring into mechanical life. Every few minutes a vehicle would race from the driveway of a home, burning rubber as it thundered down the street; never up the street, running from the Folsom home, never toward it.

By eight o'clock that morning, the street, as far as Mike could see, was deserted.

Rana came to him and touched his arm. "Where have they gone, Mike?"

"I don't know; but I can tell you why they've gone. They're running from us."

"No," she disagreed. "Not from us, honey, from

you." Her eyes glanced over his weapons: the AK-47 propped up against the porch railing, the .41 mag belted at his side, the heavy knife on his belt, the ammo harness hanging by the AK. "Did you enjoy killing those people, Mike?"

"Not particularly."

"Did it bother you?"

"No."

"Has it ever?"

"The first time or two."

"Then you got used to it?"

"That is correct."

"Does everybody get used to it?"

"No, baby," he said. "Most people do not get used to it."

"Will I?"

"I don't know. Hopefully you won't ever have to find out. But I know this. It will be over in seventy-two hours."

"Why seventy-two hours, Mike?"

"I don't know. I just know it will be over in that time period."

"And will we win?"

"I don't know, Rana."

"You mean He didn't tell you?"

"I'm not sure He has told me anything. I can but hope He has."

"Mike—if it means anything to you at this time—I love you."

He put his eyes on her. "It means everything in this world, honey."

She smiled. "Then kiss me, Warrior!"

TWENTY-THREE

"Why do I get this feeling you know more than you're telling?" Mike asked.

Ted smiled. "Each of us knows something the other doesn't, Colonel."

"Very shifty reply. But it doesn't answer my question."

"Maybe it's because you're—we're—cut off here and you can't use what contacts you have to check out my story?"

"I guess that's part of it. But I've never seen a man quite like you, Ted. And that's a compliment, of sorts."

"Thanks, *Comanchero*," Ted replied, looking straight ahead into the still-littered street.

Mike cut his eyes at the man. "I thought I left that nickname in Vietnam?"

"Obviously not, Colonel."

Mike had earned the nickname because of his fierceness in battle and because some of his men has whacked off a few ears of dead Cong.

"*Commanchero?*" Rana said, joining them on the

porch. "Wasn't a *Commanchero* a—bandit—kind of savage guerrilla fighter in the southwest?"

"Correct," Ted said.

"That's a strange kind of compliment to offer a man," she said, sitting down.

Mike turned to her. "You don't understand guerrilla warfare, Rana. Few do. There are no rules in that type of warfare; it's the bloodiest, most savage type of fighting. Only the best of men—the strongest mentally—are picked to fight, and many of those break under the strain. Writers struggle to put the horror on paper; but even those who have been through it can't do it justice. It is something that is almost indescribable."

Conversation ceased at the sounds of a pickup truck roaring up the road. A sack was hurled from the back of the truck. It landed on the hot street with a sickening thud. A thickness oozed from the canvas bag.

"What in the world—" Rana started to say.

Mike put out a cautioning hand, pushing her back in the chair. "Don't go out there, Rana. I know what's in the bag."

Ted sat calmly in his chair, saying nothing.

Mike left the porch, walking into the brilliant glare of mid-morning sun. He knelt down by the bag and cut it open. He felt his stomach roll over in a quick series of flipflops.

The bag contained a dismembered human body. The body of a young girl. Judging from the torso's still budding breasts—the nipples had been cut off—Mike thought the girl might be anywhere between twelve and fourteen, certainly no older.

"Bring me a blanket, Ted," he called up to the porch. "And find a shovel. We'll bury what's left out by the creek."

Father Grillet walked to the scene and looked down at the pieces of human flesh. The open, pain-filled and

290

horror-filled eyes of the head stared back at him. The young priest lost his breakfast. He composed himself and said, "That's—was—Emily Geeson."

Mike closed the bag and waited for Ted to bring the blanket. This had cleared away any lingering doubts in his mind. He had seen the horrible look on the girl's face and in her eyes. She had been tortured and probably dismembered while still alive.

"You—have a strange look on your face, Colonel Folsom," the priest said.

"I'm glad you can't read my thoughts, Father," was Mike's reply.

Emily was buried in a shallow grave by the creek, under the shading arms of a huge oak tree.

"I heard her sing once at a school function," Marge Coder said. She was crying openly, tears running down her cheeks. "She had such a pure, sweet voice."

"She's singing in heaven, now," Elaine said.

"I know a bunch of people in this town who'll soon be singing in hell," Mike said, pushing the words past tight lips.

"Mike—" Rana put out a hand to stop him.

He brushed past her without looking at her. He walked to the house and began buckling on combat gear.

"Are you going to warn the townspeople he's coming?" Burke Rider asked.

"They already know," Becker replied.

"But they're still partying and screwing and getting drunk," the banker protested. "Why can't you intervene and stop Folsom?"

Becker's smile was grim. "It's all in the rules of the

game, Burke." He shifted his yellow eyes to Attorney Wallace. "What about the young people?"

"About a hundred and fifty of them still gathered in small groups. Waiting."

Becker drummed his fingertips on the desk top. He had not anticipated this unpredictable action on the part of the young people. Had he ever been a natural parent he would have known to expect anything from young people. For once, Becker did not know what the young people were going to do; he did not know because they did not know. He lifted his gaze back to Wallace.

"Will there be any problems with the estates of those at the Folsom house?"

"In the event of their deaths?"

"Of course!" Becker snapped at him. "What did you think I meant—a church revival with dinner on the grounds?"

The lawyer remained cool under the verbal barrage. "No trouble, sir."

"Ford? Get those two old workmen from the Drew Ranch. Don't harm them. Just let Rana see one of them and tell her what will happen to them both if she can't convince Colonel Folsom to back off and pull out." But his words had a hollow ring; he knew Folsom would not only not pull back—he could not.

"Yes, sir." Stinky left the room. The ranch hands and their families had already been seized, held at the Church of Friendship, Fellowship, and Faith. The women were, at that moment, being raped.

"If something happens to me," Mike told Ted, "you're in charge. The rest of these men are pilgrims; cherries when it comes to fighting. They're good men. But they need a leader."

"Nothing will happen to you," Ted said.

"You got that from the Top Sergeant, huh?" Mike smiled.

Ted did not return the smile.

Mike kissed Rana. He did not say goodbye. He did not like goodbyes. He just smiled and patted her on her shapely butt, laughing at her embarrassment.

He backed the Jag out of the garage and slowly drove down the street, his mind busy. He believed he had finally put it all together, and wondered why the people of the town had not done so.

Friendship, Fellowship, and Faith.

F. The sixth letter of the alphabet.

FFF. Six, six, six.

The Mark of the Beast. Spawn of the Devil. Child of Satan.

How simple it all was.

On impulse, Mike switched on the radio. He had been listening to a radio station on the way into town—was it only a few days back? So much had happened. But the station was not broadcasting for some reason. He searched the dial, both AM and FM. Nothing.

Blocked, the thought came to him. Everything is being blocked. How?

He could not find an answer for that.

Then he saw the cross, starkly outlined against the blue backdrop of the June sky. An elderly man hung from the wooden tower. He had been crucified. Mike got out of the car and walked across the vacant lot. He stood at the base of the cross and looked up. The man was very near the end of his painful ordeal. He opened his eyes and looked down at Mike.

"Why did they do this to you?" Mike asked. "And who did it?"

"Took me out of the—nursing home—last night," the old man said. "Kids—young people. Took about a dozen of—us. Mostly women—some of them—senile. You'll see—boy—scattered all over—this—evil town. Evil—people in this—town. I—"

He closed his eyes and died.

Mike felt the iron grip of rage overtake him. Looking around, he heard someone moaning in pain. He followed the sound to a ditch, some thirty or so yards from the cross. An old woman. She had been tortured, her eyes jabbed out. She was babbling incomprehensibly. Mike could see knife wounds in her chest and stomach.

The bastards had tortured her and left her to die alone.

He took the .41 from leather and cocked it, hesitating for a few seconds. Tears filled his eyes. He blinked them away. The old woman screamed out in pain, blood leaking from her mouth, blood that bubbled with pink froth. Lung wound, Mike thought. He shot her between the eyes.

He pulled the Jag over to the curb at the edge of Butler's square. The town had once been the Parish Seat—for a short time—and the town had grown around the old court house, seventy-five percent of the businesses located on the square. A group of young men sat on the curb of the street, in front of the drugstore, drinking whiskey and chasing it with Coke. They were all armed, rifles and shotguns leaning against the store front, pistols belted at their side.

But they made no hostile moves toward Mike. They would not even look in his direction.

Mike slipped the Jag in gear and drove slowly past them. He wondered what had happened to Jack and Ann. He pushed them from his mind. Looking in his rear-view, he saw one of them make a profane gesture at the Jag. The others laughed. But none of them made ny move for a weapon.

Voices struggled within his head.

Go back and destroy them.

"How do I justify that? What do I know for sure they have done?"

"You killed those men outside your house, did you not?"

"Yes. But I knew what they represented. Knew what they were. And one of them told me who he worshiped."

Then go back and ask the young men.

"And then . . . ?"

The battling voices fell silent.

Mike stopped, turned around, and drove back to the drugstore.

The young men had vanished.

The street was empty, deserted. Mike got out of the Jag, walking to the curb; the AK was held at combat ready, off safety, on full auto. He nudged an empty whiskey bottle with the toe of his boot. It rolled slowly to the edge of the curb, teetered there for a few seconds, then dropped, breaking from the impact. The sound was very loud in the empty street.

Mike heard footsteps coming up from his left. He smelled perfume before he turned around.

"What's the matter, Colonel?" the woman asked. "Having trouble deciding how to fight us?"

The woman was pretty, in a dark, mysterious way; her eyes were deep and unfathomable. Mike said nothing. He just stared at her.

"I love Satan, Colonel. Worship the Prince. Are you going to kill me?"

Mike gripped the AK tighter.

"I also like to fuck," she smiled. "And I'd like you to fuck me."

"I think I'll pass. Thanks anyway."

She put her slim hands under full breasts and lifted them. Mike could see the nipples lunging at him through the thin blouse. "You like, Colonel?"

"I'd be a liar if I said no."

"You don't know what you're missing, Colonel. And I mean that. Everything is open and free. Tell me—didn't you get a sudden charge when Lisa fondled your cock yesterday?"

How could she have known about that? Was there a pipeline in the house? If so, who?

Mike looked at the woman, choosing not to reply.

She licked her lips. "I give great head, Colonel."

"Congratulations."

She hunched her hips and smiled at him. Her teeth were very white against the tan of her face and the deep red of her lipstick. But it was her eyes that finally gave her away. They shifted ever so slightly, to Mike's right, narrowing almost imperceptibly.

Mike spun, the AK rising. He squeezed the trigger and the men behind him screamed as the slugs tore into flesh and bone, scattering the pair, flinging them to the sidewalk. They flopped and howled in pain.

Mike whirled as something bright reflected off the store window. The woman had a knife in her hand. Mike shot her in the stomach and she fell back against the window, shattering the glass. She screamed and thrashed in the perfume display. She howled pain and profanities at Mike as she lay jerking in the bloody broken glass.

Mike went into a crouch, peripheral vision catching a running figure across the street. He squeezed the trigger and a man stumbled and fell facedown. He lay still under the sun.

A bullet showered bits of brick against his cheek, bloodying his face. A man with a rifle leaned out of a second story window. The AK bucked in Mike's hands. The gunman did a slow roll out of the window, screaming until he hit the street below. His head burst open, splattering gray matter and fluid on the concrete.

Mike ran for the Jag, expecting at any moment to catch a slug in the back. None came at him. He tossed the AK onto the seat and cranked up, fishtailing down the street. A bullet spider-webbed the windshield, blocking most of his vision. Blood ran down the side of his face from the cut inflicted by the flying bits of brick. Mike spun the wheel, jumping the curb, driving into a furniture store show window.

He abandoned the Jag, leaving it as he grabbed his gear. He hid in the darkness of the store; his blood was hot, the adrenaline surging in him.

He felt good.

He did not know it, but he was smiling.

"He's boxed in!" a man's excited voice yelled from the outside. "Come on, now we got him."

"You think," Mike muttered. He shifted positions, edging closer to the shattered window. A man recklessly exposed himself just outside the showroom's perch, his figure dark against the outside light. Mike shot him in the chest and the man fell backward, arms and legs flung out. He lay on the sidewalk, hunching his hips grotesquely. He screamed once, then was still.

Looking out, Mike could see several pairs of shoes and boots in the space between the car body and the street. He leveled the AK and squeezed the trigger. Screams of pain filled the hot morning as the slugs shattered ankles and shins and feet. Men howled and flopped helplessly on the street.

Mike lunged for the back of the store, toward the exit, then changed his mind at the last second and dashed for the stairs that led upward. He took them two at a time. He passed two offices, then came to a closed, locked, and barred door. He removed the bar and kicked open the door. A long hall greeted him, the air thick with the sweet smell of death hanging in the gloom. Apartments were located above the furniture store. He cautiously opened one door, the stench hitting him in the face, wrinkling his nose. He knew what he would find before the door opened.

A middle-aged man and woman lay sprawled in naked, tortured death. Both the man and the woman had been sexually mutilated.

Mike closed the door.

He walked down the dark hall to the next apartment. He opened the door.

A maddened creature out of a psychopath's nightmare came howling and leaping at him, foam dripping from the fanged mouth.

TWENTY-FOUR

"Rana!" The voice came from behind the house directly across the street. "Chief Ford here. I got something maybe you ought to see. Do I have your guarantee you ain't gonna shoot me?"

Rana stood just inside the open door of the home. She held the snub-nosed .38 that Stinky had dropped on the floor of the home as he bolted in fear. Rana cautiously peered out at the empty street. "You make any funny moves, Stinky," she yelled, "and I'll shoot you dead. And you know I can shoot."

"Yeah," Stinky muttered under his breath. "I know you can shoot, you cunt." He yelled, "Okay, Rana, no funny moves. I jist want you to see one of your ranchhands, that's all. Old Walt."

Rana looked at Dave. "They've taken Walt. Oh, damn!"

The faint sounds of automatic rifle fire rolled from the downtown area.

"All right, Stinky!" she yelled. "What do you want?"

A man was shoved out from the corner of the house.

His hands were bound behind his back. "Git on out there where she can see you!" Stinky growled. "You try to run, you old bastard, and I'll knock a leg out from under you."

The man limped to the sidewalk.

"That's far enough," Stinky said.

The man stopped.

"Have they hurt you, Walt?" Rana yelled.

"Not yet, we ain't!" Stinky shouted. "But if you and Folsom don't git out, and git out now, he's gonna be more than hurt. And I guarantee you, it'll take him a long time to die."

Before Rana could reply, Walt yelled, "Miss Rana —they've got Alice and the grandkids. They've raped Dottie and Margret—made us watch them doing it."

"Shut up!" Stinky screamed. "Shut your fuckin' mouth, you old goat."

"They're gonna torture us, Miss Rana. They said they was gonna nail Roy to a cross."

"Shut up, goddamn you!" Stinky raged, helpless to expose his position.

"When we left they was rippin' the clothes off my wife, Miss Rana. She was screaming as they raped her. They was hurtin' her!"

Stinky shot the man twice in the back, low in the left side, the second slug several inches higher. The bullets tore out the front, after ruining a kidney and lung, tearing apart Walt's stomach.

Walt fell to the sidewalk, screaming in agony.

Stinky fired at the Folsom house, the slug burying itself into the jam of the open door, forcing Rana back.

"Oh, God, Miss Rana!" Walt screamed. "Oh, God, it hurts—help me."

"Yeah," Stinky yelled. "Go on and help him, you cunt." He fired again, the slug whining through the open door.

300

Rana heard an ugly splatting sound. She turned around. The slug had struck Paula Marshall in the face, blowing away part of her jaw. One eye had been knocked out from the impact. She slumped to the floor, horrible bubbling sounds coming from her ruined mouth.

"Please, Miss Rana!" Walt shouted. "It's awful. Shoot me, for God's sake; somebody shoot me!" Ted lifted his AK and shot the man in the head, stilling the cries for help.

"You son of a bitch!" Stinky yelled.

Paula jerked in agony on the floor, cawing, choking sounds rolling from her throat.

Rana put her head against the wall and wept out of frustration and anger and helplessness.

It was a large German Shepherd, and it had gone mad from the heat and the stench of the dead in the closed room, and from being without water for days.

Mike reacted instinctively, the muzzle of the AK already raised in anticipation of trouble. He pulled the trigger and sent the maddened animal flying backward; its head and chest ripped apart from the impact of the slugs.

Mike fought valiantly to keep his stomach from betraying him as he looked at the second pair of naked, tortured people. Whoever had done this had deliberately left the couple alive; Mike could see where they had clawed at the carpet and furniture in an attempt to get away from the dog.

The dog had eaten of his masters.

"He's up there!" a voice shouted. "Gunfire up 'bove Bennett's store."

"All right, boys," Mike said, knowing he was going to have to shoot his way out of this. "You love Satan so much—prepare to meet him.''

He put a fresh clip in the AK, jerked back the curtains, and held the trigger back.

The screams of the men on the street seemed puny when compared to the now-echoing roar of the AK-47. A dozen men lay in various stages of death. Like the inexperienced almost always do, they had been in a tight knot when they rushed the store, instead of being spread out.

Mike slammed home a fresh clip and ran out of the stinking apartment of torture and death and down the steps to the furniture store. No one shot at him, yelled at his approach, or met him. He darted down the street, inspecting several pickup trucks beforé finding one with the keys in the ignition. He cranked it and drove back to the home of his youth, now a sanctuary for a pitiful few who chose not to accept the teachings of Satan.

He met Stinky on his way back to the house.

Mike hastily buckled his seat belt, pulling it tight just as Stinky tried to block the road with his patrol car. Mike rammed him, the pickup knocking the car spinning. The patrol car lifted up on two wheels and slowly rolled over. Mike could hear Stinky screaming inside the car.

The pickup was gone, the front end caved in, steam gushing from the smashed radiator. Mike slowly got out of the truck, .41 mag in hand. He walked up to the patrol car, looking down at the bloody face of the man he had gone through all twelve grades with, had played sports with, had called friend.

Stinky's face was bloody; his front teeth, top and bottom, were missing, knocked out by the impact with the steering wheel.

''Always buckle up for safety,'' Mike said.

Stinky spat at him. He hissed, ''Figured the boys would have got you by now, bastard.''

Mike smiled. "You figured wrong, Stinky."

"You still ain't got a chance, hotshot."

"My chances are oh-so-much better than yours, Stinky," Mike replied.

He lifted the .41 and shot the Chief of Police between the eyes.

A badly shaken member of Egan's church had made his stuttering report to Becker and been curtly dismissed by the Devil's agent.

"Damn him!" Burke Rider said. "Is the man now infallible?"

"No," Becker said calmly. "He's mortal. But he has—ah—certain protections afforded him that most mortals don't."

"He's going to ruin everything!" Doctor Luden said.

Becker waved him silent and stilled the suddenly erupting babble of voices before they became an intolerable cacophony of confusion. "Egan," he said, "tell your people to ring the Folsom home and burn them out."

He will not permit it, the voice lashed into Becker's head.

"Wait!" Becker held up his hand, waving Egan back into his seat.

The room began to stink of sulphur.

The humans shifted uneasily in their seats.

Only Becker could hear the voice. *The man is a Warrior, Therefore it must be warfare as God's Warrior knows it.*

Becker inwardly fumed.

See that it is conducted as I have ordered. Tempt him. Harass him. Send waves after him. I don't believe it is possible to kill him. But—perhaps. And remember, John. It is only a game; We've played it before. The Old One is the only matter of paramount importance.

303

Attorney Wallace leaned forward, his eyes bright with interest. "Was that—"

"Yes," Becker said. "Forget about burning the Folsom house. Forget about everything except physical and mental temptation, harassment, and methods conventional to Folsom's type of warfare."

"But he's been in every type of war!" Burke protested.

But Becker was not listening. He was mentally tasting the unpalatable flavor of defeat that lay heavy on his tongue. So close, he silently mused. We were so close. When he looked up, he said, "Order a large truck sent to the mansion. A large bob truck. I want four of the most trusted men of your church with the truck. Four of the strongest. Make certain the truck has a Tommy-lift and a winch on the front."

"I don't understand," Egan said.

"You don't have to understand," Becker said. "Just do what I tell you to do. Now get out! All of you!

Mike walked up the street to his home. He was not afraid of being exposed out in the open. He saw the body of the old man in the street and called out to his house. Rana came onto the porch.

"Walt Harris," she said. Then she told him what had transpired, ending with, "Paula is dead. Half her face was shot off."

"What do we do?" Dave asked, joining Rana on the porch.

Mike looked at the man and shook his head. "Bury her," he said shortly.

Paula was wrapped in a blanket and buried beside Emily, under the huge old oak tree by the creek. Sam

Marshall looked and acted as if he was in deep shock. Back at the house after the short service, Rana found a sleeping pill in her purse and gave it to him. He was knocked out in less than ten minutes.

Mike sat in the den, letting exhaustion flow over him, dulling him, enjoying just being quiet and still—for however long it would last.

It did not last long.

David sat down on the couch and asked, "Mike, Rana said you told her this would all be over in seventy-two hours. If that's true, why can't we just barricade ourselves in the house and wait it out?"

"You people can," Mike replied, his voice husky from fatigue. "I can't."

"Why?"

"Because I have a job to do." He told them about his radio search.

Shocked, disbelieving faces stared at him.

"Go to your cars," he told them. "Try it."

They were back in five minutes.

Ed said, "I don't understand any of this."

Mike glanced at Ted, but the man's face was void of expression; any explaining would be up to Mike. "I—think, people, we're in some kind of box. Call it a time warp, if you will. Yes—I believe that might be it. I don't think we exist to the outside world."

"People," Mike sighed, "I don't understand much more of this than you do. But I—think—believe—that for the next two and a half days, we're out of time and out of touch with the outside."

"Why, Mike?" Louis asked.

"I don't know, Louie. But I believe it's some sort of game They play."

"Game?" Rana questioned. "A game that who plays?"

"God and Satan," Mike replied. "I don't know who

makes the rules, or how often it's played, or really whether God wants to even take part in it; I'm betting He is an unwilling participant, only taking part because if He didn't, Satan would have all the cards. That's just my opinion, people, and don't ask me where I got my information; my reply would be as crazy as my hypothesis.''

Ted was smiling.

Dee Dee said, ''I don't believe God would do something this awful to His people on earth. I mean—I just *can't* believe it.''

''You're forgetting,'' Father Grillet said, ''that Satan rules the earth.''

''You mean,'' Elaine said, one arm around the tiny waist of her daughter, ''that out of this entire community, we're the only ones with enough faith to sustain our belief in God Almighty?'' she looked at Mike.

''No,'' Father Grillet answered quickly. ''No, I don't believe that. I—have certain knowledge of these matters. Knowledge that lay persons do not. And don't ask me to explain further. Call all of what is occurring a—test, if you will. We're—you're—just making higher grades, that's all.''

Mike looked at the man curiously. ''Well, Father, I had certainly not lived a very exemplary type of life.''

''Perhaps not a pristine lifestyle, Colonel,'' Grillet said, a smile on his lips. ''But consider this—all of you. Mike, have you ever or are you now contemplating losing your faith or verbally or mentally renouncing or denying your God?''

''Of course not, Father Dan.''

''Have you ever or are you now sponsoring a needy child through any type of mission: CCF, Holy Land Christian Mission International; any of the others?''

Mike shuffled his feet. ''Well, yes, Father, Four kids as a matter of fact. Been doing that for years; seen a uple of them grow up."

"With your help?"

"If—that's the way you want to put it." Mike was
mbarrassed.

"Well," Grillet smiled, "it might interest you to
now that most people don't do things like that. Most
ould prefer to spend their money on pleasures, not
aring that kids are starving to death around the world.
ou obviously care; and I know that most in this room
eel the way you do."

"Heaven, my friends," the small priest said, "is
oing to be sparsely populated. I know that for a fact."

Nickie stirred restlessly beside him.

"Whatever," Mike said. "Look, I'm going to have
o get some rest pretty quick; I'm knocked out on my
eet. But before I do, let's get those bodies out of the
treet. We're going to have a health problem if we
on't."

As Mike worked with Louie Weaver and Ed Coder,
ody-bagging with tarps the bloating and stiffening
orpses, he saw Rana step out on the porch, a rifle in
er hands. He watched her chamber a round and stand
ooking at him. He nodded; she returned the nod. He
ent to his work, a handkerchief covering his mouth
nd nose.

The next thing he knew, a slug whistled over his head
nd he hit the street, Louie and Ed close behind. A pis-
ol discharged to his left, the slug banging harmlessly
nto the ground. He cut his eyes to the space between
wo houses across the street. A man was on his knees,
oth hands clutching a bloody stomach. The man
creamed once, then toppled face-down to the ground.
He lay kicking and howling his way to death. He
unched once, as if making love to a nonexistent
woman, then lapsed into unconsciousness.

Mike got up from the street, brushing dirt off his

shirt front and trousers. He walked toward Rana, th
knowledge strong in him that he had pegged her righ
as a woman to stand by a man. He smiled at her
"That's one I owe you, honey."

Her face was very pale. "I wondered when he'
show up around here," she said. She propped the rifl
against the porch railing and held out her hands. The
were shaking.

"I don't follow you." Mike stepped closer to th
porch. "You know him?"

"Very well," she said. "That's my ex-husband."
Then she bent over and vomited on the ground.

TWENTY-FIVE

Mike slept the afternoon through and most of the night, awakening at four the following morning. As he lay in bed, the soft warmth of Rana beside him, he knew with a sudden clarity that the timetable had been speeded up—rushed ahead. It would all be over within twenty-four hours.

He did not question his source of knowledge; just knew it to be correct. He shook Rana awake.

"Hey, old woman," He smiled at her sleepy open eyes. "Get your butt outta bed and fix my breakfast. Your man's gotta go to work."

She reached up, pulling his head down to hers. She kissed him. "Who says?"

Mike pointed upward.

"Suppose He'd mind if I brushed my teeth first?"

"Ask Him."

"You seem to have a pipeline, baby," she grinned. "You ask Him."

"What's the procedure on Blessed Water, Father?"

Mike asked.

"I bless it," Grillet said simply. "And I anticipated this move. It's on the coffee table in the den."

Mike nodded his thanks. It was just breaking dawn over Butler. "Rana, would you get me about a dozen small bottles; cough medicine size or smaller. Fill the bottles with Blessed Water and cap them tightly." He pointed to a rucksack. "Pack them carefully in that. Very carefully," he added.

Mike was conscious of Nickie looking at him. "You'll be gone all day?" she asked.

"Probably. At least until it's over."

She smiled. "It certainly should be over by then." She added, "One way or the other."

The look Grillet gave his wife was almost savage. Strange, Mike thought. Very strange.

Ted said, "You want some backup, Colonel?"

"No. This is something I have to do by myself. I think you know that." Ted nodded; Mike glanced at Louis. "Mind if I take your pickup?"

"It's yours, Mike. And God bless you."

The sun suddenly broke through the mist, the light pouring into the picture window of the den.

"I believe He just did that, Mike," Father Grillet said.

Only Ted noticed Nickie shrinking away from the direct sunlight of God. Grillet did not have to notice; he already knew the secrets of the Folsom house.

Ted looked at Mike. "I put together the contents of that box." He pointed to a small crate near the door. "All you have to do is insert the timers. I believe you know how to do that," he said dryly.

"You been carrying that stuff around with you for long?"

"Not too long, but I sensed things were coming to a head around here. *Plastique,* as the French call it. It's

310

ood, pliable."

Mike nodded. "And when did you sense things were oming to a head?' "

"The day I saw you at Odey's Drive-In."

"That seems a long time ago."

Both Grillet and Ted smiled, the priest saying, 'Time, Colonel Folsom, as you will see, is a relative natter."

Odd remark, Mike thought, then pushed it from him. Rana walked him to the porch.

"I won't ask you when you're coming back," she said. "I'll just say I'll be here when you do get back. Maybe then you'll be able to explain to all of us what has happened, and why."

"I'll be back." Mike looked at her.

They stood on the porch, two adults, very much in love with each other, and now feeling, for the first time, uncomfortable.

"I put two sandwiches in the rucksack," Rana said. She smiled. "And that cough medicine bottle with the darker liquid in it is brandy. I don't think Father Dan blessed that."

"If he'd seen it, he'd have drunk it."

She laughed, then sobered. "Father Dan has changed. There is something—odd about him."

"I know; I picked up on that, too."

Rana came close and fitted her body to his. She put her face against his chest. "I promised myself I wouldn't cry."

He felt tears wet his shirt. He stroked the softness of her hair, then lifted her tear-stained face to his, kissing her gently on salty lips. "I'll be back," he repeated.

"How do you know that for sure?" she sobbed.

"Because I love you."

* * *

Mike drew first blood. He had just passed Stinky's overturned patrol car, with Stinky inside, doing his best to live up to his nickname, when Mike spotted several teenagers standing beside motorcycles. They were parked at the end of the street and had begun blocking the street with trash barrels. They were armed with high-powered rifles. Mike pulled over to the side of the street and got out of the pickup, the open door affording him only scant protection from bullets. He called to them.

"You punks part of the group that nailed an old man to a cross?"

"Yeah," came the arrogant reply. "It was a real high listenin' to that old fart holler when we drove the spikes in him."

Mike clicked the AK off safety and onto full automatic. "And your plans at this time?"

"To do the same to you, Pops. And then we'll take turns with the cunts at the house. Everybody else seems to be afraid of you—for some reason. But none of us is."

"By none of us," Mike called, "I assume you mean your peer group?"

"Huh?"

"The young people." Mike simplified the simple sentence.

"That's right, General. Some of us got together and put people all over town, just waitin' for you—that is, if you get past us, which you ain't gonna do. And when you're out of the way, then we'll get rid of Egan and Becker and Morris, and run the whole show—our way."

"Moonshine Morris?"

"Yeah. Fat old bastard. Your time's up, General."

"Yeah," another young man piped up. "I wanna fuck that cunt of yours right up the asshole. I bet she'll

312

squall when I shove the meat to her."

Mike shot them, just dropped the muzzle of the AK, stepped from behind the door, and pulled the trigger, holding it back. He knocked the tight group spinning, chunks of meat and bone flashing crimson and white from the impacting slugs of the assault rifle. He got back in his truck and drove past them; he could tell two of them were still alive. One with his chest ripped open called out for Mike to stop and help him. He did not say please. Mike could not work up one ounce of compassion for the young punk. He spat out the window and kept on truckin'.

He drove straight to the hospital institute grounds, not even slowing when he reached the gates. Using his .41 mag left-handed, he put a slug between a guard's eyes and barreled on through.

A bullet tore through the windshield of the truck. Mike spun the wheel hard and ran over a uniformed guard with a rifle in his hands. The guard crunched under the tires of the pickup. He lay screaming on the concrete driveway. Mike glanced in his rear-view. The force of the rolling tires had driven the rifle into the man's chest, the broken stock sticking out of the cavity. Mike drove to the side of the hospital institute and jumped out of the pickup, grabbing the box of C-4 and the rucksack. He ran with his heavy load to a door marked BASEMENT. He filled his pockets with plastique and timers, stashed the crate and the rucksack behind some heavy shrubs, and unslung his AK, stepping into the semidarkness and cool air of the corridor.

He leaned against the wall, catching his breath.

Outside, he could hear shouts and heavy footsteps on the sidewalk.

"Where'd the son of a bitch go?"

Mike quietly locked the basement door.

"You guys look in the parking lot over there. Rest of

313

you fan out on the grounds; check the doctor's parking area. He can't get away. Remember, Becker said fifty thousand dollars to the man who kills Folsom."

Shit! Mike thought. The VC had that much money on my head in Nam. Come on, Becker—you can do better than that.

Someone tried the basement door. "Hey! Is this door supposed to be locked?"

"Yeah. Is it?"

"Yeah. I just wondered."

"Thank you," Mike whispered, looking upward. He visibly paled as the widely-spaced corridor lights blinked off and then on as if in reply.

Cold sweat broke out between Mike's shoulder blades as the lights continued to blink. He counted the blinks. Six. Pause. Six. Pause. Six.

"Yes, Sir," Mike said, his voice shaky. "I read You loud and clear, Sir."

He walked down the corridor until he came to a heavy metal door, no window in it. It was clearly marked: ABSOLUTELY NO ADMITTANCE. RED CARD PERSONNEL ONLY. INSERT RED CARD IN LOCK FOR PRINT AND PICTURE ID VERIFICATION.

Mike stood in front of the door, studying it, trying to make up his mind. He looked at the lights in the long hallway. They blinked in rapid succession.

"Affirmative, Sir," he said. Stepping back, he took the .41 mag from leather and jacked the hammer back.

TWENTY-SIX

A slug slammed through an office window of the Church of Friendship, Fellowship, and Faith, narrowly missing the head of Judge Morris. The fat man leaped out of his chair and waddled to the window, his several chins flapping with each step.

"Goddamn!" he said, his eyes bulging at the sight unfolding on the green lawn. He pointed out the window. "Look at them kids, Egan! They all got guns. They're—attacking us."

Egan ran to the window. "Holy shit!" he said.

The far lawn was filled with young people—all running teenagers, all armed, all coming toward the church. Egan looked at Morris, the judge saying, "I told you you was going too far with them kids' minds. They've snapped under the pressure. You should have known better."

Egan looked at the fat man. "That's why you wanted this meeting, isn't it, you prick? You set all this up to get me out of the way."

"Me?" Morris squalled. "You stupid queer bastard! Why would I do something like that? And I didn't

315

call this meeting. Your secretary called my secretary over to Bay View, yesterday."

It was a terrible clarity that fell on the men—they had been suckered.

Egan was the first to panic. He clutched at Morris' shirt front, finding it damp with frightened sweat. "Let's get out of here; you don't know kids like I know them. They can be savages!"

Both men ran for the door, jamming each other up in their haste. Egan fought his way through, running past the outer office. He ran right into the muzzle of a shotgun.

"Back up, Egan," the boy said. Carl Drew, Jr. Thirteen years old. His eyes were savage, menacing; too old, too wise, too worldly. The shotgun was steady in his hands. "Now it's our turn to run the show."

"Young man," Egan said, in his most authoritarian tone, "I must insist you put that weapon down and come to your senses. You are speaking to the director of this church and I speak for the Master."

Carl laughed at the man. He pulled the trigger. Egan's head disintegrated, bone and brain splattering all over the wall. One eyeball hung from a wall lamp, staring, fat, round, unblinking, and wet.

The boy shifted the shotgun toward Moonshine Morris. "You 'member me, you fat bastard?"

"I cain't say as I do!" Morris squealed, his voice trembling. "But I'm certain we can work somethang out, son. Why don't we go somewhere and talk about it?"

The boy's grin was evil, maddened. "I was six years old when you got to me, you lard-ass. You played with my pecker and then conned me into sucking you off. You 'member now?"

"Yes, yes! And I'm sorry I done that!" Morris screamed.

316

"You fucked me up so bad, I still don't know who or what I am!" Carl screamed. He stuck the muzzle of the shotgun into Morris' mouth. "Suck it!" he howled at him.

Morris sucked. He was still sucking when the boy pulled the trigger. Judge Moonshine Morris' head blew apart, pieces of his dentures joining the splat of gray matter on the wall behind him. The boy turned just as a guard stepped into the hall. He shot Carl, Jr. in the stomach and managed to drop two other boys before he was gunned down.

A young man of twenty, wearing Egan's dark worship robes, appeared in the hall. "All praise the Prince!" he shouted. "All praise the Dark One! This we do in his name!"

Mike holstered the .41 and kicked the bullet-shattered hinges loose. The door fell open. He stepped inside, the AK at combat ready. A nurse screamed her hate at him, her mouth resembling a hissing snake ready to strike. She reached into a drawer, coming up with a pistol in her hand. Mike shot her in the stomach and she stumbled backward, landing on her butt, legs spread wide as crimson stained her belly.

Mike was conscious of a misty shape beside him. "It's all right, Mike," the woman said. "It's me, Bonnie. Go right through that door in front of you, Mike. Destroy everything you see. In God's name, Mike—do it."

A small boy ran into the room; Bonnie grabbed him. He broke free of her grasp. He seemed confused.

Mike shot the lock off the door. Semigloom greeted him. He looked back at Bonnie; she was holding out her hands to the boy.

"Kill him, Mike!" Bonnie screamed at him. "Kill

317

him so he may have a chance to live!''

"Bonnie—I can't!''

"Do it, Mike!'' she screamed.

The lights blinked off and on.

Mike swung the muzzle of the AK and stitched the little boy across the chest. He was flung bloody to the floor. Mike felt sick to his stomach; he wanted to puke.

"The baby that was taken from you?'' he asked the misty shape.

She scooped up the child in her arms. "Yes,'' she said, smiling at Mike. "Now we both have a chance to go Home. Goodbye, Mike. Thank you.'' She ran from the room, blood from the child's wounds trailing red behind her.

Mike stepped into the dimly-lighted room, fumbling for the light switch. The room filled with harsh light. He stood in awe and silent shock at the row after row of clear holding tanks; the bubbling liquid suspended an unborn child.

"Hideous,'' he muttered. "Godless.''

He heard shouts in the corridor.

"I'll help you, son,'' a man's voice said. "But you must hurry; we don't have much time.''

Tears welled up in Mike's eyes. He blinked them away. He could hardly speak for the lump in his throat. "Dad? Is that you, dad?''

"Yes. Your mother is back at the house. She must help Father Grillet combat Nickie. Ted is on his way to the mansion. You must go there when you finish here. Destroy the Devil's Children! They are beyond saving. Bonnie's child has at least a chance because of her love and the forgiveness of God—remember that at the end, son. Now, son, in His name—do it!''

"Fire!'' someone yelled. "The corridor's blocked from this side.''

"Why aren't the sprinklers working?'' an excited

voice asked.

"Did you do that, dad?" Mike asked.

"Yes, in a way. Goodbye, son. You're a brave and good man, and your mother and I are very proud of you. We love you and we'll see you someday."

The voice was gone. Mike had never seen any shape of the man. He turned to the bubbling tanks just as a door in the rear opened and several white-coated men ran in. Mike left them piled in bloody heaps at the door. He looked again at the tanks containing the unborn. He lifted the muzzle of the AK and began spraying the tanks.

"What's the matter with this fuckin' truck?" the driver shouted. He beat the palm of his hand against the steering wheel, venting his frustration. "The damn thing won't start."

"What'd you do to it?" his partner asked. "Hell, it was runnin' just a minute ago."

"I didn't do anything to it. It just quit runnin'." He glanced at his watch. "Becker is gonna be pissed off about this."

In the back of the heavy enclosed bob truck, a man began screaming; then another man joined in the frightened wailing. "Get it away from me!" he screamed. "Oh, my God—get it away."

"Run!" the driver shouted. "Get out and run." He pushed his partner out the door. He turned, looking through the rear cab glass. He paled, his eyes widening in shock.

Some—thing, some creature was in the back of the truck. One of the men had been flung against the side of the truck, his neck broken. The other man was on his knees, praying for mercy.

The driver jumped out of the cab and went running

and screaming down the road. The truck, Becker, Egan, and the whole fucking bunch of them could just forget they ever saw him.

He got part of it right: no one would ever see him again.

The misty shape took a more human form as it sailed effortlessly after the running driver. Its feet never touched the ground. The tattoo on its arm was very plain in the morning sunlight.

The glass tanks shattered and the room was filled not only with the sounds of babies crying, but with their howling fury and outrage. Some managed to wriggle out of the shattered tanks and crawl toward Mike, dragging the umbilical cord as they came. They screamed insanely as they came toward him.

Mike took a closer look. These babies had teeth. Very sharp teeth. Fangs.

They snapped and snarled at his leather-protected ankles.

He kicked one in the head and felt and heard the skull pop under the toe of his boot.

He ejected the near-empty clip and rammed home a fresh clip. His stomach doing flipflips, Mike killed the creatures closest to him and then systematically put several rounds into each of the remaining tanks. He ran back to the corridor. Fire blazed at the far end; his end was free of fire and smoke. He ran back to the room of screaming demonlike naked babies, set the timers on the C-4, placed them around the room—his mind automatically seeking and finding the stress points of the room—and ran back to the corridor, racing for the door that would take him out into God's sunlight.

A man appeared at the door, on the outside. Mike blew him away with one long hard burst, in the process, knocking the door askew. He grabbed up the crate and rucksack, and, pausing just long enough to get his bearings, headed for the rear of the building. The doctor's parking area should be back there. He hoped one had left the keys in his car.

A bullet knocked him spinning to the sidewalk. He lunged on hands and knees to the safety of the building, his left hip numb. He inspected the hip, expecting to see blood. He had to laugh. Folsom had lucked out again—in a way. The bullet had struck the handle of his dad's knife and ricocheted away. He got to his feet just as the building seemed to expand; a roaring followed. Fire belched out of the first floor windows.

A screaming woman, her hair on fire, jumped out of a window and went running and wailing off across the lawn, her clothing on fire. Mike ripped open the crate and activated half a dozen soft balls of plastique. He set the timers for thirty seconds and began limping around the building, tossing the explosives into shattered windows. He made it to the parking lot before the roaring began.

He looked back as he knelt beside a car. The top of the building exploded in a mighty belch of fire and smoke, the fire leaping a hundred feet or more into the air. Mike didn't know what had caused such an eruption—probably the fire had reached a chemical storage area—but he did know Becker's hellhole of a hospital and institute were finished.

He found a car with the keys in the ignition and calmly, slowly, drove off the grounds. He wondered if the smoke could be seen outside the area controlled by—by the devil? He mentally stumbled over that. He concluded the smoke could not be seen.

But by God's will, or Satan's?

He didn't know.

He wondered how it was all going to end.

Bette Babin lay sleeping on the pallet upstairs. The ten-year-old was deep in the slumber of the still-pure child. She did not hear the door open; did not see the woman pad silently to the pallet and kneel down beside her. The red mouth of the woman opened with a sigh. The teeth were very white, very even. Except for two. The tongue was blood-red and glistening. A slick film of saliva coated the lips. The woman bent her head and kissed the sleeping child on the mouth, murmuring words she had never before heard, words that were thousands of years old, just at that moment springing into her head.

The child fell tumbling deeper into sleep.

Mercifully so.

The woman's lips moved wetly to the neck of the child; the mouth opened further, lips pulling past fanged teeth. She gently nuzzled the girl's neck, seeking and finding the source of her evil life.

She drank deeply.

Bette stirred as a nightmare of hideous proportions entered her young mind. Her hands turned momentarily into talons. Then she relaxed as the fangs left her vein.

The Force was upon them. The adults fought it back with an effort. Tina was physically held down by her mother as words of filth and disgust poured from her mouth. Ed Coder had to sit on Ava to keep the girl's hand from caressing his thickening penis.

"Sing!" Ed shouted. "Sing!"

And the frightened group sang songs of praise to the Lord God.

"You must not do this, child," Father Grillet told

Lisa. "You must not; it's wrong."

"I got to, Dan," the teenager said. She moved toward him, stepping out of her jeans. She was naked.

The priest blinked his eyes as his throat turned desert dry. He looked frantically for a way out of the bedroom. He would have to pass the naked girl; would have to touch her flesh. And he didn't want to do that. It might spoil everything. His time and mission was clear; and it did not include this poor, temporarily possessed child.

But his human form betrayed him, and her eyes found the unwilling deception. "You're getting a hard-on, Dan," she said. "I can see it sticking out. Let me feel it, Dan; let me fuck you."

"Fight it!" he yelled at her. "Fight it, child; you have to for all of us!"

She dipped her fingers into the soft wet fur between her legs. "I've got to have it, Dan! Please love me."

He slapped her. His open palm rocked her head; bloodying her mouth. Her eyes lost the glaze of momentary possession. "Put your clothes on, child," he told her. "God forgives both of us."

She fell into his arms, weeping uncontrollably. The door opened. Rana stood looking at them, eyes wide in shocked disbelief.

"It's all right," Grillet said. "It was close for her— very close. But God helped her."

"Before you helped yourself," Rana said, her tone almost tongue-in-cheek.

"I was somewhat aroused," the priest admitted.

Screaming echoed through the house, a chilling, terror-filled wailing.

"It's time to get out of here," Jimmy told Lennie. "It's all coming unraveled for Becker." He laughed

323

softly. "He deserves it. Son of a bitch."

"But I like it here."

"There are many other places. Places that have never witnessed beings such as we have become. You talk about fun, man—we'll really have some fun."

"Where will we go?"

"Oh, I don't know. Another small town, I think. Maybe Tallulah."

"Where the hell is Tallulah?"

"Come on. I'll show you. We'll have some fun there."

Dee Dee ran screaming down the hall. "She had fangs for teeth!" she shrieked. "Oh, my God—her teeth were fanged. And there was blood all over her mouth."

"Who?" Rana grabbed the near-hysterical woman.

"Nickie!" she screamed. She pointed to a closed door. "She's in there."

It is time, the voice only Grillet could hear spoke.

"Yes," the priest replied. "I know."

"Who are you talking to?" Marge asked him.

The priest looked at her and shook his head. He walked slowly down the stairs. He went to a piece of luggage and removed a small leather pouch, taking out a container of water. On his knees, the slightly-built priest bowed his head and spoke to God. His voice was low. He looked up at the sounds of a woman's taunting laughter coming from upstairs. A grimness fell over his features, clouding his eyes. He rose to his feet and prepared to go Home.

Again.

What had his father said? Ted was at the mansion; his mother was helping Grillet combat Nickie? Was that it? It was too confusing. Mike couldn't remember it clearly; maybe he wasn't supposed to remember it?

He drove back into town, looking for the young people who were supposedly spotted about the small town, waiting to kill him. But he could find none of them. He turned around and drove back to the mansion.

So this is how it ends. Becker sat at his desk and watched Mike drive arrogantly up the drive. What a perfectly ridiculous, totally ignoble conclusion to twelve hundred years of serving the Master.

Bah! he thought.

The hospital-institute was gone. Destroyed in the flames he himself worshiped. The perfect birthing and the reincarnation of the numbered Beast would not occur.

At this time, the words jumped smoking into his brain.

Yes, Becker silently replied.

The young people had revolted; Egan and that fat fool Morris were dead. Lennie and Jimmy were gone. Ford was dead, his soul smoking in hell for his incompetent behavior.

He lifted his eyes and looked at Burke and Wallace. The banker and lawyer were sweating and frightened. Becker did not know where Doctor Luden had gone; the man had raced screaming from the house an hour before. Got in his silly sports car and roared away. Put deep ruts in the manicured lawn. Unforgivable.

And who was Ted Bernard?

He pushed that question from his mind as his third eye focused on Colonel Folsom getting out of his car and walking slowly up the steps to the mansion door. He rang for a servant; he was surprised to see Arnold enter the study.

"Where is Samuel?" Becker asked.

"Gone, Master. All gone. I am the only one left. I asked to remain, to serve you."

"Thank you. But by whose orders did they leave?"

"The Dark One."

"The Prince?"

"Yes, Master."

Becker nodded and leaned back in his leather chair. So it was indeed over. The Prince had given up. For now. But what of the Old One?

You for my friend! the words came silently to him.

That is how you wish it? Becker asked with a mind thrust.

Yes.

So be it.

Becker felt the presence of the Prince and the soul of the Old One leave the mansion.

He lifted his eyes to his sole remaining servant. "Please show Colonel Folsom in, Arnold—before he starts shooting locks off of doors."

"Yes, Master." Arnold shuffled out of the room.

"One lousy, beat-up, ex-soldier." Becker's grin was rueful. "I have possessed the bodies and minds of kings and counts and princes; I have sexually taken queens and countesses and princesses; I have ruled empires. And one ex-soldier brings me to my knees and back to the pits. Incredible!"

"What about us?" Burke cried, sweat pouring from his face.

Becker's eyes were amused. "The both of you do recall the motion picture *Gone With The Wind*?" Burke and Wallace nodded.

"Take your cue from the parting words of Rhett Butler."

The men sat open-mouthed and staring.

Becker lifted his eyes as Mike stepped into the study. "I wish I could say it was a pleasure to see you, Colonel

Folsom," he said. "Do come in and sit down; I'll have Arnold bring some refreshments in."

"I brought my own," Mike said. He lifted the muzzle of the AK and squeezed the trigger.

TWENTY-SEVEN

"Lord, you have to help me with this!" Father Grillet said.

"You come in this room and you'll die!" Nickie shouted through the closed door.

"We both will, Nicole," Father Grillet said, his brain suddenly filled with flashing light-bursts of realization. "I took the path of righteousness; but you failed again to follow me."

"What's he talking about?" Ed whispered.

"Only God knows," his wife said.

Grillet unscrewed the cap from the bottle; the cap bounced off the carpet. He opened the door and splashed the Blessed Water on the creature that once was his wife.

She screamed and howled like the animal she had again become as the Blessed Water seared her flesh; huge chunks of meat fell from her arms and legs. Part of her face dropped off in a sizzling mass. She propelled herself off the bed, flinging her smoking body against Grillet.

He managed to pour the remainder of the water on

Nickie's head; by then she had pushed him out of the room, into the hall, against the banister. The wood broke under their combined weight. Priest and undead hurtled to the ground floor. The sound of Grillet's neck breaking was loud in the huge old house.

His flesh slowly burned and melted into hers. From the back porch, a pistol shot shattered the stillness. David walked into the room, his face sweaty and pale.

"Sam Marshall," he said. "He took a pistol and blew his brains out."

The banker and the lawyer lay dead on the floor, their blood soaking into the expensive Persian rug. Becker looked down at the still-smoking holes in his chest and yawned.

"How unnecessary," he said. "You have ruined a fine shirt that was hand-sewn for me in London."

Mike lowered the AK and looked at the man with a half dozen holes in his chest. He shook his head in disbelief.

Mike heard shuffling footsteps behind him. Becker said, "Don't attempt it, Arnold. It would be futile, I assure you." He lifted his hand. "You are free, Arnold. I am releasing you. Go home."

Smoke drifted around Mike's boots. He looked around. An ugly mass lay smoldering on the floor. He turned to Becker. "What happened to him?"

"I sent him home."

"To hell?"

Becker smiled. "Perhaps. Perhaps to serve yet another Master. I am not the only representative of the Prince here on earth, you know."

Mike slowly uncapped a bottle of Blessed Water.

"Ah, yes," Becker said. "Your holy voodoo."

330

"You're taking this rather well, Becker—considering the short time left you."

Becker lifted his shoulders. "Win some, lose some. I'll be back, Colonel; rest assured of that. Probably not in this form; but—then again, who knows? But for you, God's Warrior—it is not over. There will be some vestiges of Darkness remaining. Believe that, sir."

"Care to explain that?"

"Heavens, no! You must think me daft."

Mike stepped closer. He could read only amusement on the man's face; no trace of fear.

"The Old One?"

"Why should I make it easy for you?"

Mike lifted the bottle of Blessed Water. "I can do this quickly, or a drop at a time."

"A point well taken, Colonel. I'm told it is quite painful. Very well. The Old One's physical body is in the basement; but his soul is gone."

"So I won't be able to kill him?"

"His physical body, not his soul." Becker smiled, an evil glint to his eyes.

"Why are you smiling?"

"Because his physical presence is still very much alive. And he is quite awesome, Colonel."

"I don't understand what has happened, Becker. Any of it."

"Diogenes would have been so delighted to have made your acquaintance," Becker said acidly. "The poor bastard went to his grave, his mission unfulfilled."

"Will I ever understand any of it?"

"Probably not. This conversation is becoming quite dreary, Colonel. Do proceed, won't you?"

Mike tossed the Blessed Water on him. An almost unbearable stench filled the room as hundreds of years of evil died, the souls the creature had condemned to the pits yowling and shrieking and burning. The foulness drove Mike back. When he looked again at the chair, Becker was gone, the chair holding only smoking, stinking rags.

Shaking his head, muttering under his breath, Mike roamed the huge, lushly appointed mansion. The home contained treasures from around the world, the furnishings and accoutrements worth millions of dollars. He prowled the top floor, finding nothing evil, nothing to fear. He searched the bottom floor with the same results. Then he found the door that led to the basement. With his hand on the brass knob, Mike looked heavenward and asked the question man had been asking for thousands of years.

"Why me, Lord?"

But the mansion remained mute.

Mike pushed the door open and stepped into darkness.

"I feel fucking weird, man," a teenager said. About a hundred of them sat in the main auditorium of the Church of Friendship, Fellowship, and Faith.

A young girl, her shirt open, breasts bared, walked to the stage of the auditorium and stood for a moment, looking at the upside down cross. Slowly she reached out and turned the cross upright. She buttoned her shirt as tears ran down her face.

She did not know they were all moving toward self-destruction—only moments away.

"I wish you hadn't done that, bitch," the young man wearing the robes of Satan said.

"I felt it the right thing to do. I'm sorry for all we've done. I want to go home. I want to return to the Lord."

Jeers and howls and profanity greeted her words.

The young man in the dark robes turned to the room of jeering young people. "By all means, followers of the Prince; send this cunt home."

They came in a rush for her.

She was raped, beaten, and tortured. She was still screaming as they nailed her to a flat board, driving spikes in her feet, her hands, and her sides. They left her naked in the hot sun.

The teenager who had said he felt fucking weird came into the huge auditorium. He carried two five gallon cans of gasoline. He opened the cans, then, smiling, held out a cigarette lighter. All gathered around. The young man began laughing; it was highly infectious, but it did not last long. Only about two seconds.

He sparked the lighter.

Mike followed the stench to the quarters of the Old One. He did not have to be told where to find the Evil One—or, at least, his physical being. He pried open the huge oak crate, and the stench made his stomach finally rebel. He vomited on the dirty, crud-infested, bone-littered floor.

Using a pocket knife, Mike cut the cloth bindings, folding back each layer, the foul odor becoming fiercer as he unraveled each layer.

He removed the final bindings and looked into the face of death and evil and utmost depravity. The dead young girl was still impaled on the erect organ of the most hideous creature Mike had ever seen. What were once human beings were pressed against the putrid, rotting hulk of the obscenity. Bending over the crate, a vial of Holy Water in his hand, Mike leaned over for a better look.

Ann rose up in the crate. Her face had been half eaten. "Hi, Mikey," she said. She threw her arms around his neck and pulled him over into the crate, kissing him on the mouth.

The Old One opened his ageless eyes.

TWENTY-EIGHT

Mike's screaming broke the grip of the crazed, now half human woman. She fell back against the Old One, releasing Mike just as the Old One reached for the ex-soldier. Spitting out foulness from his mouth, put there by the rotting tongue of Ann Geraci, Mike dumped the vial of Holy Water into the crate and jumped back as the smoke of evil flesh was charred by water blessed by a man of God.

Mike fumbled in the rucksack and rinsed out his mouth with Holy Water. He picked up his AK just as the Old One kicked out the side of the crate, lumbering and howling to his feet. The body of the young girl thudded to the floor. Ann stood beside the Old One, now part of him, grinning grotesquely at Mike.

Her face was pocked with open sores where the Old One had kissed her, making her his. She was naked, her flesh having taken on the rotting color and texture of her possessor.

She was hideous as she lunged at Mike, her mouth smoking like the pits of hell, screaming foulness at the man she had graduated from high school with.

Mike almost cut her in half with a burst from the AK. She slammed back against the bulk of the Old One, knocking him off his huge sore-encrusted feet. He roared as he fell to the floor, his foul breath profaning the close air of the basement room.

Mike emptied the clip into his grossness, then opened a bottle of Blessed Water, dumping it on the creature's head. His howlings were awful as the water ate into flesh and bone, finally penetrating the near-ageless brain. The monster's howlings changed into low moans and then whimperings. He kicked several times as his head began to dissolve. He put out one massive arm, pulling Ann to him; together, they began to melt into each other.

Mike walked up the stairs to the ground floor, passed what was left of Arnold on the carpet, and walked past the study where Becker had almost become the ruler of the most evil empire ever known to man. The ex-soldier, chosen by God, walked out onto the porch, into the sunlight.

It was glorious.

He did not believe he had ever before been so happy to see God's sunlight.

Mike drove into town, wondering, now that the evil was gone, would he have to continue killing? He hoped not; he was sick of it. He wondered what he would find in Butler.

What he found stunned him.

Men and women by the hundreds had appeared, standing as if paralyzed on the streets, frozen in time. Some stood shaking hands; others with a finger pointed, upheld, were making some forgotten point on politics, church, or the latest song on the radio.

An eerie silence hung over the town; the people were

ike statues. Motionless. Mike did not attempt to touch any of them; he just drove the streets of town, finding he same scene wherever he went.

He drove back to his house and got out of the car. Rana threw herself into his arms, alternately weeping and laughing and kissing him. Mike finally disengaged himself from her and told her, and the others who had gathered around, what had happened, briefly, and what he had found in town.

And where was Ted?

"He left shortly after you did, honey," Rana said. "He didn't return."

With Rana holding tightly to his hand, Mike walked up the steps and into the house, straight to the phone.

"It doesn't work, Mike," Rana said.

"It does now," he replied. He picked up the phone, smiling as the dial tone greeted his ear. He dialed the number of his oldest and closest friend, a general who worked directly with and out of the CIA building in Langley. In only seconds, using high priority codes and numbers still fresh in his mind, General Paul Carson was on the horn.

"Mike?" the general said, a trace of annoyance in his voice. "Code Red? Mike—if this is a joke, it isn't funny. No. Knowing you, it's not a joke. Where are you?"

"Paul, I—I think for the past three or four days— I'm not sure just how much time has passed—I—I think I've been in hell."

He looked at his watch. One o'clock. He punched his date indicator. He felt the blood rush from his head. He was only dimly conscious of the general yelling at him over the long lines. Rana took the phone from him.

Mike punched the date indicator several times. Each time it read the same:

Five-twenty-nine.

Five-twenty-nine.

Five-twenty-nine.

He had been frozen, locked in a time warp, since the day he arrived in Butler.

Time had stood still for all of them.

TWENTY-NINE

By six o'clock that evening, the community was warming with State Police, doctors, scientists, a platoon of Army Rangers from Fort Polk, Army, Navy, and Air Force security people, the Governor of Louisiana, senators, a rep from the White House—and a dozen or more stone-faced men and women Mike didn't even care to know.

General Carson had been placed in charge of it all. Not a job he wanted. He had become sick to his stomach when he viewed the remains of the Old One—and a few other sights: torture, depravity, crucifixion, to name but a few incidents of evil.

The residents of Butler were left exactly as Mike had found them: frozen. Scientists and doctors had warned all present not to touch them.

The press had not been invited in; they had been most definitely kept out. All roads, including dirt, gravel, and pig runs leading into this part of the Parish, had been sealed off by the police and the military.

Mike had just finished going over his story for the third time.

General Carson, having been flown to the area b
the fastest-type jet fighter known to exist anywhere i
the world, leaned back in his chair. "Jesus!" he said

"Come on," Mike stood up, stretching. "I have a
idea."

They stood in front of a group of men standing fro
zen in front of Bill's Barber Shop. Mike motioned Gen
eral Carson and the others back a few steps. He though
he recognized one of the men in stillness. He touche
the man on the shoulder.

The group of men instantly came to life. The ma
whom Mike had touched was saying, as if caught i
midsentence, ". . . and Bert told me, 'man, those nev
'72 Dodge Chargers is some kind of hot cars.' That'
what he said. So you can believe this, boys; I'm goin
down to Cedar Motors and tell Bonnie to get one fo
me."

"Cedar Motors has been closed for ten years, Ce
cil," Mike spoke softly.

The group of men seemed, for the first time, to no
tice Mike. Cecil grinned. "Hey, Mike! Closed? Sure
You always was one for a joke, boy. Good to see you,
Mikey. Damn if it isn't. You lookin'—well, older, son
Damn, I hate to say this, old son, but you've aged.'
The man suddenly noticed the carnage wrought by
Colonel Mike Folsom: the dead in the streets, the citi-
zens frozen in time and place, the smashed cars, the
smell of death. Cecil swallowed hard. "Mike?" he
whispered the words. "What the hell's happened here?
What kind of cars is them all around?"

General Carson asked, in a gentle voice, "Sir, would
you be so kind as to tell me the date?"

"Sure. May twenty-ninth."

General Carson paled visibly. "No, sir. I meant the

340

year.''

Cecil looked at him. ''You serious, mister?''

''Yes, I am.''

''Nineteen seventy-two. Hell, man. Where you been, lost?''

''One of us has,'' Carson replied.

THIRTY

Mike finally convinced General Carson to allow him to take Rana and Lisa and leave. They would stay in touch. Promise. Call every day. They went to New Orleans. There, he checked them into a hotel, spent several days straightening out his monetary affairs, resting, sight-seeing, buying new wardrobes for all, a new car—and marrying Rana.

The three of them pulled out for a long summer's tour of the United States and Canada. And they all tried very hard not to think of Butler.

The second week of August, the trio drove into Washington, D.C., checking into a motel in Virginia. Mike and Rana and Lisa were to have a final meeting with General Paul Carson at his home in Maryland.

"Well," Paul said, "unless you all have been living in a Tibetan cave for the past two and a half months, you know the shit really hit the fan. Excuse me, ladies. We've had our hands full with this situation. Some of the press is still hollering 'cover-up,' but for the most part, it's settling down. Old news."

"Butler?" Rana asked. "The people?"

"Very well, all things considered. We're using—since this Becker had no relatives—his money to help straighten out the lives of those who survived the—incident."

"Interesting way of phrasing it," Mike said.

Paul shrugged. "It's been—hell, Mike."

"Tell us about it," Rana said, sarcasm thick on her tongue.

Paul's eyes touched them all briefly. "You *really* want to know all of it, huh?"

The three of them nodded. Lisa had matured a great deal during the summer-long excursion. She was now approaching the beautiful stage of young womanhood and had turned to God for help in combating the memories of her time with the forces of the Dark One.

"All right," Paul said. "Well—there aren't many young people between thirteen and twenty left in Butler. Twelve and under—quite a few. They're stable, so the shrinks say. It seems that Egan had quite a stock of explosives stored out at his—church." The general slurred the latter. "When that nitwit kid ignited the fumes from those cans of gas—this is from the few survivors—everything went up with a bang. Using state birth records, we've slowly accounted for everyone in Butler.

"Doctor Maxwell Luden was found in his sports car, sitting behind the steering wheel. Dead. Not a mark on him. This is strange, people. Records show he did not have a tattoo. But he did, a hideous tattoo of the devil's face on his forearm."

Neither Rana nor Mike made mention of that. But Rana knew the doctor had no tattoo on his forearm. She said, "How did he die?"

"From the look on his face, he was literally scared to

344

death. His heart exploded. Doctor Perry, from Becker's hospital-institute, is still missing. We think he may have gotten out alive. We don't know." Paul shrugged. "Are you three going back to Butler?"

"Yes," Mike answered for them.

"Then you'll need to see for yourselves—at the cemetery, I mean."

"Tell us now," Mike pressed.

"We—ah—exhumed some graves. Jimmy Grayson. Bonnie Roberts. Your parents, Mike."

Mike stirred.

"You said, and I know, I went out there with you and saw the graves open that afternoon. But—when we went back two days later—Mike, those graves were all closed; the earth had not been disturbed. Scientific testing supports that."

"But—"

Paul held up a hand, stilling Mike's protests before they became vocal. "I know, Mike—I know! I saw it with my own eyes—the open graves. But—well, I'm not *about* to get into the area of supernatural happenings; I don't believe in that crap. So let's just leave it alone." He sighed in frustration. "You were in intelligence, Mike; you know how it can be.

"The town proper has—well, adapted—it's back to normal. A certain department of the government has a permanent office in Butler—to help the townspeople cope, so to speak. It's headed by a Mr. Norman Black. Nice fellow. Born in Canada."

"To help the people cope," Mike said with a smile. The smile was knowing, rueful, sarcastic.

Paul ignored it. "To a person, male and female, when questioned at length, hypnotized many times, mind-probed—they say it all started with the kids; all began with the young people."

"I'll go along with that," Rana said.

345

"Yeah, me, too," Lisa said.

Paul nodded. "All right, Mike, now I got to break the news to you."

Mike looked at him.

"There is *no* Office of Unexplained Phenomena, old buddy. Never has been. Ever."

"But—"

"I know what you told me; have it on tape, all of it. But I'm telling you, leveling with you, Mike. In this I'd toss security out the window. I'm telling you straight. No such office, now or ever. Okay—as far as this Ted Bernard person. I've had computers rolling on it; I tied in with everybody. This is what we found. A Theodore Barnard was an LRRP in Nam. A Theodore Barnard was a member of Egan's crap out in California some years ago. This Theodore Barnard fits your Ted Bernard to a T. Perfectly. Right down to the devil tattoo on his arm. It's—possible, I suppose."

"What's possible?"

"A perfect double."

"I'm not following you, Paul." Mike couldn't get certain words out of his mind. It all began with the kids.

"Look, Mike. Egan was heavily into drugs back there in the land of fruits and nuts, among other things just too disgusting to talk about. Theodore Barnard got fed up; wanted out; This is after his return from Nam, after his parents had him deprogrammed. He went back to Egan. Strong pull, I suppose. Anyway, he came to his senses and wanted out. Talked at length with a Father Grillet—a priest. This gets wild, Mike. Movie stuff. We have no records on any Father Grillet, and neither does any church we've contacted; and we've contacted them all—"

"Wait a minute." Mike held up his hand. "It's going too fast; you're skipping over some things I want cleared up. So back up. The people in Butler who

ere—frozen in time, so to speak. I know—so does
sa and Rana—some of them, most of them, were ac-
ve members of Egan's church—practicing devil wor-
ipers. Yet, God chose to let them live, to begin anew,
r lack of a better phrase. Right? Okay—why?''

The general could but shrug. ''You know I'm not a
ligious person, Mike—at all. My people talked with
inisters and priests at length. They came up with dif-
rent answers from each. Naturally. It's all hocus-
ocus, in my opinion. I'll loan you a copy of the report.
e for yourself.''

''Back to Ted Bernard.''

''There *is* no Ted Bernard, Mike! I'm trying to tell
ou that. Everything can be explained. All right, so I
w a—deformed man out at the mansion. He was
ead. He was not connected with the devil. He was a
adman; perhaps some relation to Becker that Becker
hose to keep hidden. That's the way we're going on
is thing, and that's the way it's going to be.''

''That's shit!'' Mike spat the words.

''Where is Becker?'' Paul asked. ''The hospital is de-
royed; no trace of any demon babies. Mass hysteria,
Mike. Read the report; that's the way it's going down.
ook—back to Barnard—Theodore talked at length
ith this mythical Father Grillet—no such person. We
elieve Barnard's mind had snapped. Interpol helped
s; gave us this. There was a Father Grillet in France
bout 1880. A Catholic priest. He became involved
ith a woman; got kicked out of the church. That much
s fact. Now legend has it—''

''What was the woman's name?'' Rana asked.

''Nicole Dubois. Anyway, Dan Grillet and this Ni-
ole got married. Vanished. No one knows where they
ent; changed their name, Interpol thinks. As I was
aying, legend has it this Nicole was seduced by a vam-
ire some years after they married; Dan Grillet tried to

347

kill her. Stake through the heart and all that nonsens[e]
He failed and she was condemned to roam forever, lo[st]
between two worlds. Good and Evil." He laughe[d]
"Make a good movie, huh, folks?

"Okay. This Theodore Barnard was killed in Cal[i]
fornia. Car crash. Positively identified by his parent[s]
Father Grillet? No trace of the man. A figment [of]
Barnard's sick mind, that's all. We think he made hi[m]
up; typed the letters and mailed them to himself. It[']s
just coincidence your priest in Butler was named Gri[l]
let."

"And the way he and his wife died?"

The general shrugged again. "You people were u[n]
der a strain, Mike. Naturally so. It's rare for a huma[n]
to catch on fire, right out of the blue, but it happen[s.]
It's documented. That's what happened to Nickie an[d]
Dan Grillet. They then fell and broke their necks. It['s]
all neat, Mike; all tied up. Most of it very explainable.[...]

"That's shit, Paul."

"Your opinion. Back to Ted Bernard/Theodor[e]
Barnard. We'll find the guy posing as a governmen[t]
agent. Bet on it. He'll turn up somewhere else; they a[l]
ways do. But Theodore Barnard, Mike. The LRRP i[n]
Nam, the man with a devil tattoo on his arm. He['s]
dead, Mike. Buried in California. He's been dead fo[r]
ten years."

THIRTY-ONE

Bette Babin stood at the window of her bedroom—a bedroom overwhelmed by a canopy bed and stuffed animals. She sometimes spoke with the animals, and they would come to life and speak with her. At night, she let them prowl in the darkness of the town. They killed yowling cats and barking dogs; not many animals left in Butler. Peaceful town.

The room was dark. Bette looked at her face in the glass. She smiled, young teeth fanged. She enjoyed doing that; could make them come and go at will. There were other children of her age in town like her. Many of them.

Now they waited. They would wait a few weeks longer, a few months, perhaps a few years. No one knew for sure. Except for the Master. The Prince. The Dark One. But they had time. The Master had promised them, speaking to and through Bette, telling her what she must do. Gather the young ones. Secretly. Spread the word of the Dark One. Quietly.

And wait.

The Dark One, the Hooded Master of all Evil would

tell them when it was time.

Bette turned from the window. Her pretty mouth was fixed in a smile. Her teeth were nice and even and very white. Perfect. Time to go down and kiss Mommy and Daddy good night. It was easy after a time; just a little kiss on the neck; a little taste. There were lots of parents like hers in Butler. Now.

Tomorrow she would talk with her little friends, at their secret little meeting place. Time to gather the little coven. To make their little plans. It was such fun.

And it was time to plan. 'Cause Colonel Mike Folsom and Rana and Lisa were returning to Butler next week. The Prince had told her so.

And they had to be dealt with.

Soon.

Yes. Perhaps a homecoming could be arranged for the colonel.

A strange homecoming.

EPILOGUE

And
where
are
your
children
this
evening?